Books by Sue Hardesty

The Truck Comes on Thursday
Book One of the Loni Wagner Crime Fiction Series

Bus Stop at the Last Chance
Book Two of the Loni Wagner Crime Fiction Series

Taking the Long Road Home
Book Three of the Loni Wagner Crime Fiction Series

Running Through Fire
Book Four of the Loni Wagner Crime Fiction Series
(forthcoming)

The Butch Cook Book
Co-Editors: Nel Ward and Lee Lynch

Bus Stop at The Last Chance

Book Two

The Loni Wagner Crime Fiction Series

Sue Hardesty

Launch Point Press
Portland, Oregon

ISBN: 978-1-63304-238-4
E-Book: 978-1-63304-209-4

SECOND EDITION
Re-edited and Revised 2019

Cover: Lorelei
Editing: Taylor West, Nel Ward

Published by:
Launch Point Press
Portland, Oregon
www.LaunchPointPress.com

Dedicated to the one I love.

Thank you, Nel, for the amazing life

you have given me all these years.

Acknowledgments

Thanks to my publisher Lori Lake of Launch Point Press for believing in me enough to publish my works. Thanks to my best bud Lee Lynch whose kind nudging inspired me to finish this book. Thanks to my dear friend Taylor West who suffered through vetting each page. Most of all, thanks to my wonderful forever spouse, Nel Ward, who decided I didn't have enough to do and insisted I write something! Here is the result. Peace.

Sue Hardesty
July 2019

CHAPTER ONE

Loni Wagner leaned against the side of her police car. She was parked in the shade of an old, tired, salt-bleeding Tamarac tree. As much as she hated the salt eating the paint off her car, she hated the heat more. Both front doors to the police car stood open, and Loni hoped the slight breeze would cut the heat for Coco. Her brown standard poodle sat straight up like a manikin on the car seat, watching anything that moved. The temperature in early October cooled down several degrees since summer, but the blistering Arizona desert sun remained relentless.

Staring up Highway 85 toward Tucson, Loni tilted her head away from Coco's hot breath panting in her ear and waited for the prison bus on its way south. After a short stop, the bus would continue on, taking drug runners back to the federales in Sonoita, Mexico.

Loni watched Lola Sanchez impatiently pace back and forth under a sign reading "Caliente Bus Stop" as she waited for the bus to drop off her brother Manny. Loni knew Lola was over-the-top furious with her because she refused a ride to the bus stop. She also told Loni to forget about their Saturday night date. Below the bus stop sign was another reading, "Last Chance Saloon."

Avoiding Lola's fiery temper, Loni mentally ridiculed the absurdity of a bus station in a saloon. Recalling last summer when a tornado took out the bus stop, Loni had to wonder why it was relocated in a bar. Her thoughts fell back to that night.

Loni had driven into town to see shiny wet streets covered with scattered debris in her headlights. A tin roof rested on the courthouse lawn, and pieces of a wood fence blocked the middle of the street. She used all four spotlights to dodge around tree limbs. So much damage. She knew it was worse than a dust storm, maybe even a small twister. That would be a first. Her lights bounced along the buildings as she approached the station. The bell tower from the Catholic Church was gone.

Like all twisters, it jumped through town, destroying some things and leaving others unscathed. The roof on the Catholic rectory next to the church was gone, but the stores on either side weren't touched. The bus stop was flattened. Several houses still stood across the train tracks, but the barn was a goner.

Loni thought about checking to see who needed help from the disaster. People milled around the church, and the priest wandered around in his no-longer-white gown thanking God he was spared. Next door to the bus stop, the Whistle Stop Café lost its awning. Back in the day the café once served railroad passengers, but those days were long gone and trains hadn't stopped at the town for years. Now it only served locals.

Smelling smoke, Loni ran toward flames shooting out of a house across the street. Shattering glass popped, and more flames shot out the front window openings. The fire station siren was blaring, but the truck was already headed for the barn. Volunteer firefighters couldn't get back in time to save the house. Loni had run around to the back and broken out the window in the door to reach the lock. The inside of the house was engulfed in flames.

Loni felt someone was following her. Down a hall, she heard barking and opened a door to a black Scotty dog jerking at a little girl's pajamas. "It's okay, fellow." Loni grabbed the girl. "Come now."

Someone in the hallway had an older boy in tow. "Anyone else in here?" Loni made sure the dog was with them when they got outside. The little girl was sobbing and reaching her hands towards the burning house.

"No." The boy held onto the girl. Whoever saved him moved on.

"What's she saying?"

"She's only calling for her old ratty cat."

The little girl cried harder, screaming, "Dotho, Dotho, Dotho."

"Where is it?"

"Probably in her bed under the covers."

Loni was terrified of the fire, but she ran back into the house. Despite flames shooting down the hall, she dodged back into the little girl's room. She found the cat under the covers but couldn't go back the way she came in. With the clawing bundle of fur stuffed up her shirt, she dived out the window as the fire burst into the room behind her. Though the terrified cat left red welts and dripping blood on her belly, Loni smiled and handed the cat to the tearful girl who returned her smile. She found neighbors to take care of the children before she moved on.

She checked with the dispatcher for any other problems. He reported, "Right now only a cow in a tree, bawling her head off. They think she's okay. But they don't know how they're going to get her down."

Loni cringed every time Lola's grass-green eyes shot fire at her when her pacing circled back around within Loni's sight. It was the same fire in her eyes when Lola cleaned up the cat scratches down her belly. Loni had complained, "Jesus. Don't know the meaning of gentle?"

"Don't." Lola had teared up. "Just . . . don't."

"Awww, you love me."

"God help me, I do. Don't you go and say anything. You hear me? Not a damn word."

Shaking the memory out of her head, Loni turned back to the hot road, wishing the bus would hurry. She was desperate to avoid Lola's red-headed temper, especially when she pulled Manny off the bus and hauled his sorry ass off the jail. Lola loved her baby brother beyond reason.

From the corner of her eye Loni watched Lola's silky green sundress swirl around her legs. Loni squirmed, but she knew better than to turn and stare. Lola's famous Irish and Mexican temper was in full force, and she appeared to be in no mood for Loni's appreciative attention. Loni took off her Western straw hat and swiped the sweat from her broad forehead onto the sleeve of her shirt. She sighed and wondered how long Bobby was willing to cover Lola's dispatch job at the station. Five more minutes, she thought. I'll worry in five more minutes.

A dot in the distant shimmering heat mirage slowly grew into a rectangle on the quiet stretch of state highway. Loni waited for the rectangle to slow down but it kept moving. Must be a truck, she decided—until the bus blew by her, hauling ass. Staring in disbelief, she didn't snap out of her trance until it almost disappeared in the distance. Loni shook herself into motion and nearly slammed the door on Coco's nose. The patrol car burned rubber as she spun it around. Following the bus, they flew by an angrier Lola fanning away her dust. Loni heard her screaming when she grabbed her mic and yelled at Bobby for backup. She repeated, "Find Clive. Tell Carl."

"Shut up a minute," Bobby bellowed back at her. "I can't call them until you shut the fuck up and tell me what's going on."

"The bus didn't stop!"

"What do you mean the bus didn't stop?"

Loni dropped the mic as she worked to keep control of the shuddering car. She grabbed it again and shouted, "Bobby! What part of 'bus didn't stop' don't you goddamn understand?"

"Okay, I got it! Where are you?"

"Headed south on 85 past the last of the houses." Loni dropped her mic again, clutched the steering wheel, and picked up speed. The bus was nowhere to be seen. She left the outskirts of town and flew by the few weathered houses on the desert flat. Bobby got back to her as she reached the small hills peppered with the withered cactus and plants from record-breaking summer heat.

"Can't find Carl yet, James is on a job and isn't answering his phone, and I only found one highway patrolman. Clive's on his way but he can't get there for a while 'cause he's patrolling up north. Tucson cop said bus was full of drug dealers they were takin' down to a Mexican prison, part of a gang out of Sonoita. They must have taken over the bus. Tucson said they'd send a helicopter. You copy?"

Loni reached for the mic again and gripped the steering wheel with her other hand. The car shimmied as she hollered, "Get me any help you can. Lola back yet?"

"Nope."

"When she gets there, tell her to try not to worry." Loni let up on the gas pedal to get more control over the car. Rounding a steep hill, she spotted a dust trail off to the southwest. Making a split decision, she slowed down and turned off onto the dirt road. With a big sigh of relief, she spotted wide tire tracks.

"Hope we're not wrong," she said to Coco. The dog cocked her head as if to say, "What's this WE shit?" Loni sped down the washboard dirt road. She coughed from the dust sifting in every minute crack in the car, and Coco sneezed. Loni sympathized between the teeth-jarring potholes. Topping a hill, she glimpsed a gray slash in the tan dust below her. Loni stopped to get the Bluetooth headset out of her cubby hole. She wrapped it around her ear, took off her sunglasses, and scanned the road. It dropped down into a large, wide wash with the sliver of gray now behind a grove of lacy-leaved mesquite trees on the wash bank. "Wow, Coco, look at that!" Loni said out loud. "Think they got stuck in the wash? Or trying to hide in the trees? Reminds me of a desert broomtail horse I had when I was a kid. It thought it was hiding behind a tree, peeking at me from one side as its big ass stuck out the other." Coco huffed as she listened to something far away.

Loni started to voice-dial Bobby when something popped into the car beside her arm. She dived out of the door onto the hot graveled earth and crawled around to the other side of her car. Coco was right beside her. She clicked the headset on. "Damn, Bobby. They're shooting at me."

"Shoot back!"

"I can't. What if I hit Lola's brother?"

"Do it anyway," Bobby hollered back at her.

"Tell you what. If I kill her brother, I'll tell her you told me to."

"But Lola's the forgiving kind, isn't she?"

"Not about her sweet baby brother. Where is she anyway?"

"On the phone still trying to get you some help."

Loni lifted her head as the windshield glass shattered. A flying shard bit her hand. She tried to aim through the open side window. "Damn it, Bobby. They shot at me again and it hurts!"

"Duck."

"How far away is the helicopter, anyway?"

"Don't think it's in the air yet."

"I can't wait that long. They're trying to keep me down so they can get behind me. I gotta move now." A bullet whizzing by popped the Bluetooth out of her ear, kicking her head sideways. Loni reached up to stop the blood running down the side of her neck, but the bleeder on the bottom of her ear wouldn't stop. She backed around the car, still holding onto her ear, and called Coco. Another bullet zinged past, shattering a side mirror, sending her flat to the ground.

Bullets hit more windows, raining glass shards on her. Loni crawled up to rocky hill beside the car to find protection. "Well, shit!" Loni cringed. She'd already demolished two cars in the past five months. Carl was going to kill her. Muttering, she snaked up the hill, wincing from sharp cactus needles and hot rocks until she wiggled herself into an outcrop of rocks big enough to hide her. At least this was the first car since Carl got elected chief of police. Maybe the other two wouldn't count. Her thoughts were interrupted by another bullet spraying pieces of rock into her face.

Whirring helicopter blades jolted Loni coming in low overhead and pass over her. "Hey." Loni started to stand and wave as the copter hovered over her car. Suddenly a missile exploded it into a fireball. Loni dropped back down in shock as the copter glided down the hill and landed beside the wash. Five men ran from the bus to the open door of the helicopter and climbed in. It lifted and banked to the south toward Mexico, disappearing in a whiff of smoke.

Loni collapsed and grabbed Coco in a tight hug. She stared in wonder at the gun still in her hand. She hadn't fired one shot at the helicopter. Or anything else. Well, shit.

Loni cringed, trying to understand what happened. Jesus Christ. Carl would never believe this one. Coco yelped and wiggled away from Loni's adrenaline-tight hold. Letting go of the squirming dog, Loni stood and forced herself out of her safe hole in the rocks. She ran in a zig-zag pattern toward the bus to the protection of the nearby trees and stopped behind the first one. Nothing moved. All she heard was Coco's panting. She signaled the trained dog to hunt for anything living. Coco returned from circling the parameters of the bus and sat, her way of reporting she found someone alive.

Hoping Manny wasn't one of the five who climbed into the copter, Loni crouched and ran, sinking into deep sand as she struggled to the back of the bus. She stopped and listened, Coco hovering close. In the silence she heard moaning from the bus. Coco's head jerked up, and she gave a low growl. Loni quietly took short steps along the side of the bus and peeked around the edge of the open door. The driver stared at her with empty eyes. She knew he was dead. Carefully stepping into the bus, she saw another cop slumped against the door to the unlocked cage behind the driver. Blood surrounded the large hole in the back of his head. Behind him a man whose face was covered with blood struggled to sit up.

"Manny?"

The man sagged in relief. "God, Loni. Never thought I'd say this, but I'm glad to see you."

"How many prisoners were on the bus with you?"

"Five."

Relieved the threat was gone, Loni grabbed a first-aid kit from under the dash and stepped over the dead cop sprawled in the doorway. She dabbed around the bleeding slash across Manny's forehead with the tail of her shirt and wrapped gauze around his head like a headband. "Let's get you out of here." She pulled him to his feet, and he leaned on her.

They climbed out of the bus. Loni left Manny in the shade, sitting against the large tire on the bus before she climbed back inside. The radio was shot into oblivion. Loni climbed back out and settled against a mesquite tree across from Manny. She unrolled more gauze and wrapped her ear to stop the dripping. "Shit, Manny. What'd you do this time?"

"Wasn't my fault," Manny propped his elbows on his knees and held his head with his hands.

"Never is," Loni bit back sarcastically. "Tell me what happened?"

"It wasn't," Manny insisted. "I was only having a few beers in this Tucson bar waiting for my girlfriend to show up, minding my own business."

"And?"

"Her husband Jacob came in and fussed at me like an old woman, walking back and forth behind me, saying, 'Who was that sonofabitch that ran off with my wife, Manny. You see who that was?'" Manny groaned. "He kept at it and repeated over and over, 'Come on, Manny. Who was that asshole who ran off with my wife?' I got off my stool to leave peaceable when he grabbed my arm and said, 'Oh, yeah. I remember now! It was you!' He slugged me and I fell into the side of Sam's bottle cabinet. Bottles poured down like a waterfall. Every one of them broke."

Manny's expression darkened. "Not a bottle left. Thought for a minute Sam was going to shoot me while Jacob pounded on me, but he threatened to shoot Jacob if he didn't stop, and then he threatened to sue me. Again. Lucky for me he threw me out instead."

"What were you doing in Tucson?"

"Can't you listen? Went down to see my girlfriend, is all. I didn't know Sam sued me for damages and had me arrested until a Tucson cop showed up at Della's door."

"She Jacob's wife?" Loni asked in a stern voice.

"So?"

"Right. So, what happened on the bus?"

"I'm not sure. I tried to sleep. You know how noisy jails are? Next thing I know I got blood all over me and I'm sitting here with a dead guard and driver."

Loni had no response. She briefly closed her eyes in exhaustion before she stiffly climbed onto her feet. Back in the bus, she hoped to find a cell phone in somebody's pocket. The dead driver had one. Loni mentally apologized to him while she fished it out. Back outside, she called the station.

Lola answered in a panicked screech. "How's Manny!" she screamed in Loni's ear.

"He's good, Lola. All he has is a small cut over an eye. Would you send—"

"Cut!" Lola interrupted again. "How big?"

"I told you, small, Lola."

"Let me talk to him," Lola demanded.

"Wait a minute."

"Now!" Lola's voice was so loud Loni had to hold the phone away from her ear.

Loni raised her voice. "Listen to me, Lola. We have two dead cops, and you need to send the coroner out here now. And get the crime scene guys from Tucson out here. And it would be good if you sent somebody out to pick us up."

Lola went silent several seconds. "Two?"

"Yes."

"Oh, god." Lola was quiet a few more seconds. "Wait a minute. Why should I send someone out to get you? What's wrong with your car? What the hell did you do this time?"

Loni rubbed the bumps from breaks on her nose. "You don't want to know."

"Please don't tell me you wrecked another one?"

"I didn't wreck it!" Loni insisted. "Somebody blew up."

The silence was deafening before Lola continued. "God, Loni. Wasn't it three last summer?"

"No, it was only two, damn it! How come everybody keeps saying that! And I didn't wreck this one."

"Okay." Lola's curiosity must have gotten the better of her. "What happened to it?"

"I told you. A helicopter blew it to smithereens. By now it's pretty well burned to the ground."

"So what'd you do? Start World War Three?" Lola sighed. "Clive's on his way. Let me talk to Manny now."

Loni handed Manny the phone. "Your sister." A siren screamed in the distance, and Loni stood and brushed the sand off her Levis. She walked up the road to wait a few yards away from the still-burning car, watching thick, inky black smoke roll high in the air from the burning tires.

A police car came flying over the hump in the road, almost hitting her burning car. Brakes squealed and dust flew as the car fishtailed. It spun in a full circle and shuttered to a stop, clinging onto the road's edge next to a deep drop-off. Loni got a clear view of Clive Monroe's huge brown eyes and face, frozen in terror as the car finally settled.

Loni doubled over laughing at Clive's expression until she heard a whirring. Her whole body tensed until she finally saw large letters spelling out TUCSON POLICE across the side of a chopper. Thank god! Fed up with the hot rocks and cactus needles in her belly, she was relieved she didn't have to leap for the rocks. "Over here!" she hollered. She finally stopped waving at the helicopter when she realized she didn't have to worry about signaling. Boiling black smoke from her car took care of that

Clive slowly climbed out of his car and rolled his eyes at her. They stood together and watched the copter put down below them next to the bus. Three cops stepped out of the copter and hustled over to the bus. Two of them stopped to talk to Manny, and the third started to pull the driver out of the doorway of the bus.

"You can't remove him," Loni shouted as she ran up. "It's a crime scene!"

Tears ran down the man's face. "He's my brother," he sobbed.

"Should I have a lawyer here?" Loni heard Manny complain.

"Manny!" Loni exploded with disgust. "Answer the questions."

"Hell, Loni. He says I was part of it. Otherwise I'd be dead, too! Tell him I'm innocent!"

Loni turned to the Tucson cop. "He's probably right. If anything, I expect the Mexicans felt sorry for him because he's too damn dumb to live anyway."

"Or maybe they wanted to leave a survivor behind to show us cops how dumb we are." Clive spoke quietly. "Be a sad joke on us." Clive stepped forward and stuck out his hand to the taller cop questioning Manny. "I'm Clive Monroe. Highway patrolman."

"Deak Drue," the bulky man said as he took Clive's hand. He turned to Loni and held out a large hand to her. "And you are?"

"Loni Wagner, Caliente detective."

Deak pointed up the hill. "Your car burning up?"

Clive jumped in. "Her fourth."

Loni protested, "My third!"

Deak's smile at Loni revealed white teeth below a long nose in a long face. He turned to the other cop. "This here's Jimmy Whit, our medic." He lost his smile when he gestured toward the brother of the dead man. "And that's my pilot, Bud Hart." He turned to Jimmy. "Take Manny up to the copter and handcuff him in there."

"Wait a minute," Loni said. "He's supposed to be in my custody now."

Deak didn't agree. "I understand what you're saying. But those two dead cops belong to us, and we need to take them home. We need to question Manny at the station, find out what happened, what he might have heard, and make sure he's not involved. You can understand that."

"Yes, I can." Loni reassured Manny. "Sorry. I'll come down as soon as they say and get you."

Manny jerked away from Jimmy's grip on his arm. "Damn, Loni. You going to let them take me? Lola's gonna kill you."

"Sorry, Manny." Loni turned to Deak. "I've got an ambulance and coroner coming. You do need to wait on that."

Deak gestured in agreement and ran his long fingers through his thinning graying hair. "We should be through with Manny in a day or two." He handed Loni a card. "I'll call you to come get him."

Loni stuffed the card in her shirt pocket. "I'll expect your call."

An ambulance with running lights and blaring siren pump braked and slid around Loni's burning car. It plummeted down the hill to skid to a stop at the edge of the wash. All six foot of Lu, the driver, jumped out of the driver's side as Doc Benjamin, local medical doctor and coroner, carefully climbed out of the passenger side. He hurried over to the bus, trailing behind Lu's long stride.

"Loni? The doc stared at the gauze wrapped around Loni's head and blood on her shirt. "How bad is it?" Above the gray fringe of hair, his balding head blistered from the sun. Reflective sunglasses hid his eyes, but Loni knew he would bulldoze anyone down to get to a person in need.

"I'm okay, Doc. I was calling for Manny, but their medic patched him up."

"You sure? That's a lot a blood."

"Only a nick in my ear." Loni lifted her shirttail. "This is Manny's."

"You sure you're not hurt?" Lu hovered. The rangy medic with long legs and arms was so tall Loni had to tilt her head back to find Lu's concerned face.

Clive punched Lu in the arm. "What's your hurry?" Clive fake coughed as he swiped at the dust stirred up by the sliding ambulance. "You just now learning how to drive that thing, Lu?"

"Heard you needed help." Lu slugged Clive back, knocking him into Loni. "Guess not."

Clive sighed. "Lu, if you were only ten feet shorter . . . "

She laughed.

"Sorry you wasted a trip, Lu." Loni nodded her head at the copter sitting across the wash. "We got a crime scene, but the Tucson police is taking the two bodies and Manny back with them on the helicopter." Loni pointed to the men around the bus door. "Doc? They're waiting on you."

"Seems to me you're hurt, Loni." Lu scrutinized her bandage.

"I'm good now. I want to get the crime scene processed before it gets even more disturbed.

"You sure?" Doc quizzed Loni.

"Tell you what, Doc. I'll stop by the clinic as soon as we're done here."

Doc turned and walked over to the bus. Clive joined him, taking photos with his cell phone.

Loni dropped onto a rock near the side of the road, fighting the cold creeping shock, ignoring the voices around her.

Finished with his inspection, Doc released the crime scene to the Tucson cops and walked back up the hill to the ambulance with Lu. Loni stood. "Okay, Deak. They're yours now."

Deak gave a great sigh as he went into the bus. "I hate this." He carefully lifted the body and carried it out of the bus over to the helicopter. Back for the second body, he rubbed Bud's back. "Let's take him home, Bud." Lips in a thin line, Bud's eyes glassed up with moisture as he followed Deak to the helicopter. After helping as best they could, Loni and Clive turned their backs to the lifting copter, ducking from the spray of sand as the copter shrank into a small speck.

Loni and Clive carefully lay out the crime scene, determining who shot whom. They found tape under a seat where someone hid a gun. Satisfied they had filmed, collected, and covered everything, they walked back to Clive's car, swiping at each other in a hopeless attempt to brush off the dust. Loni always ended up a mess by the end of the day, but Clive was always as crisp and polished by the end of his patrol as at the beginning. For the first time in Loni's memory, his patrol uniform was dirty and wilted.

Settling into Clive's car, Loni was grateful for Clive's friendly presence. She knew she had to go back and face Lola. The reprieve didn't last. He gave her a shit-eating grin and drove slowly back by the disintegrating heap of smoldering metal. "That makes four cars now. You been back home what? Five months?"

"No, it's only three. But keep it up and your car could be number four. And it's been more than a year."

Clive didn't stop laughing until he dropped her off at the clinic. Inside, Loni checked out the large, square room, a hallway, and four small exam rooms as she searched for Chelsea, the nurse practitioner running the clinic. She found her in one of the rooms with a crying teenage girl and sat down to wait.

Chelsea came out and walked up to Loni, staring at the blood on Loni's face and shirt. "What happened?"

"It's only a nick in my ear, but it must have hit a bleeder."

"What hit a bleeder?"

"A bullet," Loni said with a shrug.

"You got shot?"

"I just said. Only a nick."

"Do you have a death wish, or what? How many times did I patch you up last summer?" Chelsea's burnt-red kinky hair bounced up and down as she dragged Loni into one of the rooms. She peeled the rag off Loni's head and wiped at her ear with a disinfecting swab.

"Damn it, woman!" Loni complained. "Leave the rest of my ear."

"Still a cry baby," Chelsea tsked at her. She dressed Loni's ear with a large Band-Aid and patted her on the shoulder. "There, there. It's even skin color. Like what we put on the other children." Her voice became somber. "I heard you know something about sexual assault crimes. Is that true?"

"I've had training, yes. But if you have one to report, you need to tell Junior."

"I talked to him. Twice. He told me girls are always screaming rape when they don't get what they want, but they don't mean it." Chelsea stopped. Her face registered disgust and something else Loni couldn't read. "I'm convinced somebody is drugging Mexican girls and raping them."

"Did they go to the clinic for testing?" Loni's sex-crime training kicked in.

"The first one did. It was too late when this one talked to me."

"When did you see the first one?"

"Weren't you involved in the case about the girl who got raped last summer at a party at the assistant coach's house? The couple who died from ricin poisoning?"

"I was." Loni glowered. "She thought Billy Joe Kildare was involved. Do you know anything about Billy Joe and his friends?"

"Sorry." Chelsea's dark eyes stared at Loni.

"Could you ask her if Billy Joe's group hassled her or if she remembers any of them around before she was raped?"

Chelsea was already shaking her head. "I did and she says she doesn't remember any details."

"Sounds like the same date rape drug as last summer's rape case."

"Yep."

Loni thought for a minute, and Chelsea continued. "The rape victims are all young Latinas."

"Wonder why."

"Good question. A better one, who could do this to another person?" A tear rolled down Chelsea's cheek before she quickly wiped it away.

"Chelsea. You're assuming these guys actually think it's wrong. They don't."

"How can you say that, Loni? Think about what it does to the girls!" Chelsea wiped away more tears. "It's plain evil. How can such evil be allowed to exist?"

Loni hugged Chelsea. "You're assuming there's something out there gives a shit what happens to any of us women."

"Who does care?"

Loni rubbed her eyes. "My first year in the police academy, I had a real chip on my shoulder. My self-defense instructor finally got tired of me and said, 'You know what, kid? Don't expect your troubles to end when the sun comes up tomorrow. And don't ever, ever expect a fair world. We all come into this world in pain and go out the same way. All that matters in the end is helping each other avoid as much pain as possible in between.' " Hugging Chelsea one last time, Loni walked back to the station.

Lola was in Loni's face before she got through the door "You got blood all over you. Is it Manny's blood? How bad is Manny hurt? Where is he?"

"He's fine. I already told you it was only a small scalp wound. This is my blood." Loni pointed at her bandage with one hand and brushed at the blood streaks down her shirt with the other. She held up her shirttail. "This is Manny's. Tucson cops took him back to Tucson."

"What? Wait! Go get him back." Lola practically screamed at her.

Loni cautiously scooted past Lola's waving arms, only to be blocked by a big body reeking of cigar smoke and testosterone. Her nose jammed against a Texas Ranger star, and she stepped back and stared up into Junior Gatlin's angry eyes. He was tall and skinny, dressed like a drugstore cowboy. His skintight Levis held up with a wide leather belt were topped by a blazingly white Western shirt, ruby red snaps, and an elaborate turquoise bolo tie. His outfit was completed with flat-heeled boots, telling Loni he probably had never been on a horse. His arms were crossed, and his Texas drawl came loud and clear through thin flat lips. "That was so stupid, Loni. Manny's your prisoner."

Fanning herself, Loni tried to push around him, but he blocked her. "Let me by," she insisted as she struggled to hold on to her anger.

"Not 'til you answer Lola."

Loni had no idea why Carl hired Junior last month to replace Chui. Even if Chui was arrested for helping human traffickers, he wasn't as bad as his replacement. "Hell, Junior. You haven't been here long enough to boss me. You got no idea what's going on, so butt out!"

"Doesn't matter, Loni. You don't give away nothing."

"Nothing to give away, you stupe. They had a right to him and needed to know who was involved in the breakout. All they want to do is find out what he knew."

"Don't change nothing!" Junior barked. "In Texas we made 'em come to us so we could stay in control. Giving up control like that makes you dumb."

"You know what, Junior? I'm so sick and tired of all your talk about how Texas does it better and how dumb we are. Why'd you move here, anyway?"

Junior stared down on Loni with an arrogant twist to his mouth and declared, "Somebody has to do the missionary work."

Loni laughed until she realized Junior was serious. "Good one, Junior. You must be one fine Christian boy."

"Just because your kind don't believe in the Bible . . ." Junior left the statement hanging.

"What do you mean my kind? Heathen, Indian, queer, what?"

"What you do against what the Bible says. It's disgustin' wrong."

"I've got my own Bible saying different."

Junior shook his head so hard even his words wobbled. "King James Bible is the only true one. Everything it says is what's true."

"Those old men who wrote your Bible believed the earth was flat. Was that right?"

"You one of those Darwinites?"

"Junior!" Lola shouted. "Stop it!"

"Hell, Lola. Bible's clear on who can sleep with who."

Loni was pissed. "You must be related to Ma Ferguson?"

"Huh? Who?"

"You don't even know who Ma Ferguson is? Your own Texas history? She was one of your governors who wouldn't let any schools teach Spanish. She said if the English language was good enough for Jesus, it was good enough for her."

"And she was right!" Junior shot back at Loni.

Loni rolled her eyes. "It's true—I can't fight stupid." She finally succeeded in shoving her way past Junior. "You know what, Lola? Much as I hate to admit it, I'm sorry Chui messed up."

"Who's Chui?" Junior followed Loni back to the dispatch counter.

"Even his sorry ass was better than this idiot!" Loni was shouting now.

"Who's Chui?" Junior asked again.

"You took his job," Lola turned and called Coco. They circled around to the back of the long counter where Coco sat down next to Lola.

"What happened to him?"

"He got arrested for trafficking undocumented workers to Carl's ranch," Lola explained.

"Our Carl? Our chief of police Carl?"

Loni wanted to slap Junior silly. "Yes, our Carl. He leased his ranch out and didn't pay any attention to what went on, much to his regret. People died." Loni was sorry she brought up the whole subject.

"Letting someone take your place over like that? Never happen in Texas." Junior smirked.

Mocking Junior's Texas drawl, Loni scoffed. "Junior, may a camel piss on your ugly boots."

"You're kidding me? These are Lucchese boots, you idjit, and a whole lot better than those rough-out shit-kickers you wear!"

Lola slammed her hand on her counter and set off the ringing in her stack of colorful metal bracelets on her arm. "Damnit, can't you try to get along here? We're family."

"I'm not family to no Injin," Junior insisted.

"Or Mexican either." Loni turned to Lola. "Did he tell you what he wanted to do to those three undocumenteds we brought in last week? It was not family love."

Shaking a finger in Loni's face, Lola ordered. "Don't say it, Loni. Not another word." Junior snorted and Lola turned on him. "That goes for you, too, Junior. No more."

Before Loni could finish her argument with Lola, she heard Carl's voice yelling at her. "Loni! Get in here!"

"In a minute, Boss." She laughed at his dismayed expression. "Saved by the bell, Junior. Maybe I won't shoot you today." Loni hurried into Carl's office.

CHAPTER TWO

C arl Harper, Caliente's police chief, fixated on Loni's shirt as Loni stood in front of him. She became uncomfortably aware of the blood smeared down it. "You okay?" he asked.

"It's a nick on my ear is all." Loni frowned. "Still hurts like a son of a bitch but I'll live. Listen Carl," she blurted. "You have to do something about the rapes going on." She started to talk to him about interviewing Billy Joe and his friends, but he waved her off.

"Leave the rapes to Junior. He said he was on top of it." Carl shrugged. "Right now we got cocaine to worry about. Looks like its base is the same as last summer's source."

"Damnit, Carl! He's not doing anything about it!"

"Loni!"

Loni glared around the room, fighting her fury until the change finally registered, the unexpected fizzling her anger down to a low simmer. "Wow! When did you do all this?" She hated this office when it belonged to Chief, but Carl totally changed it over the weekend. The ornate oak desk and huge red plush desk chair were gone, replaced by a simple missionary-style desk and a soft-seat chair with arms. Also gone was the poster behind the old desk reading "Every day of my life forces me to add one more person who can kiss my ass." Even the monkey-vomit green paint was changed to a charged yellow, and colorful prints of cactus flowers hung on the walls. "I didn't know you had such good taste."

"You like?" Carl's pale blue eyes nearly disappeared in the proud grin on his sun-wrinkled craggy face. "The wife helped."

"Oh, yeah. I think this room even likes me."

"I hear your grandpa coming out of your mouth."

Loni laughed and shrugged. "Bahb's Indian heritage in me keeps you guessing."

"Must admit it's better than your grandma's Apache temper. Only had Shiichoo mad at me once." Carl smiled at the memory. "I ran over one of her Bantam hens. I had to keep running for a long time to keep her from beating me to death with it."

Loni dropped down into the only available chair but couldn't get comfortable. "Jesus, Carl. Don't want anyone to sit here long, huh."

Carl sat back and folded his arms. "Don't recall asking you to sit, either."

Loni ducked her head and rubbed her bumpy nose. She couldn't stop squirming.

"Loni. We need to talk."

"About?"

"Got a call from Jim Filbrite. Remember him?"

Startled, Loni said, "Sure. The narc head from Phoenix with the strange eyes."

Carl leaned back in his chair. "Remember the biker who got killed last week outside town?"

"The one with a load of cocaine in his saddlebags?"

"Yes. Jim says it's from the same source we found on my ranch last summer. He thinks the biker was delivering it to someone living in Caliente."

Loni was adamant. "No, no, no. We cleaned that drug mess up."

"According to Jim, we didn't." Carl held up his hand to stop Loni before she could argue with him. "There's more." Loni focused on Carl and waited. "They picked up this same cocaine from a well-known dealer in south Phoenix. "He swears he got it from his usual source who said it was from Caliente."

"Did they get the source?"

"Nope. In the wind."

Loni frowned. "Damn! Guess we didn't scotch the snake after all."

"So?"

"Only saying. Maybe cut off a few rattles but damned if the thing doesn't keep on striking."

Carl dropped his chair forward with a thump as he rubbed his eyes. "I thought we got this town cleaned up last summer, too." He reached his arm across the top of his head to pull on his ear. Loni knew the more upset he got, the harder he rubbed. When he got the ear bleeding, Loni knew she had to be very careful around him or get the hell away.

"Maybe the O'Neals will tell us something." Loni suggested.

"Going to trial for the death penalty? Doubt it." Carl sat thinking and rubbing. "We could offer them a deal."

"Think Judge Sal would go for it?"

Carl shrugged. "She does hate the death penalty."

"They did kill a cop but seeing as it was only your predecessor and him deserving it, guess it's worth a try."

Carl's face morphed into a comical attempt at fear. "Hope you never feel the same way about me."

"Haven't thought about scalping you yet."

Carl ran his fingers through his sandy colored hair, joking, "I got so little left I wouldn't even notice."

Loni grumbled and squirmed again. "I really hate this chair."

"Maybe it's time you got back to work. I'll follow through on talking to the O'Neals. Why don't you begin at the beginning and see what we missed. You're good at those flow chart thingies. Start filling one in."

"Carl, I think I agree with Jim. The drug distributor is somebody we gotta know." This time Loni held up her hand to keep Carl from interrupting. "Maybe not well, but somebody who's been around here long enough to be above suspicion, to be an accepted part of our everyday. Somebody may be showing more money than they should."

"What's this 'follow the money' thing you have?"

"It's the tell, Carl," Loni argued. "Lots of money with no visible proof of income. Maybe valuable art work in their house. A spendy car. Expensive trips. That's who we want."

"Maybe we should profile this asshole first."

"I don't know what to profile yet." Loni stood and stretched. "I think we should get State to track accounts of our good citizens."

"We can't and you know it. Not without cause."

Loni patted the top of the chair back. "Good one, Carl. This chair's a keeper." At the door, she stopped. "Oh and I need a car to get home. Don't say it. I know it's my third car."

Carl hollered, "Junior!"

"What are you doing?"

"Getting you a ride home."

"Please, Carl. Not him."

"Deal with it Loni. He's all I can spare right now."

"What am I supposed to drive?"

Carl stared her down. "Your truck until we get funding for a new one. At least when you wreck it, I won't have to pay for it."

"Yaw, Boss?" Junior appeared in the doorway. He forgot to duck, and the door jamb knocked off his tall Stetson hat. Loni reached out and caught it.

"Damnit Junior. How many times I got to tell you! Take that Texas Ranger star off. And take Loni home," Carl ordered Junior.

"Home where? Ain't she from the reservation? I gotta ride in the same car with her to hell and gone?"

"No." Carl halted Junior's diatribe. "Take her to the Wagner Airport."

With a pleased expression, Junior beamed. "You leaving town for good?"

"No, dumbass. I live there." Loni waved the hat in his face. "You want this back or not?"

"In an airport hangar?"

"'Take me home now." Loni sputtered as she stuffed Junior's hat into his gut. She stalked out of Carl's office and down the hall. "Coco, come!" Loni called and the dog caught up with her as they slammed out the station door.

"Hey!" Junior yelled as he caught up with her at his car. "You're not putting your stinking dog in my car."

"She smells better than you!" Loni snapped. She fanned away the rank cigar smoke smell drifting from him.

Junior complained the entire three miles to the airport. Loni had never been so glad to see her uncle's airport hangar looming in the distance. Countless dust and thunderstorms had rusted and dulled the tin pieces on the huge Quonset squatting on the other side of the runway. The hangar grew larger as she ignored Junior's refusal to believe she lived there. "I bet you live behind one of those houses," he said, pointing to the double row of single-story houses snuggled up against the eastern edge of the airport runway. They were built with fire engine red roofs and white stucco walls so they could be easily spotted from the air. The houses in the front row had large airplane garages attached. The row of houses in the back row had small planes parked inside carports.

Loni closed her eyes. "To the hangar, Junior."

"That one o' them aer-o-ports where people fly to work and back?"

Loni grunted without opening her eyes.

"Which house you in."

Loni opened her eyes to find Junior driving across the runway toward the houses. "Damn, Junior, get the fuck off the runway before a plane lands on us."

"Looks like the shortest way to me seeing as how the road goes all the way down there to the graveyard and back around. Shortest way is always best I say."

Loni winced and checked around as she listened for landing airplanes. "Take me to the big hangar door, Junior." Before Junior completely stopped, she opened the door and bailed out. Coco followed her, and Loni sucked in the fresh air. She turned her back on Junior and hoped he would get the crap scared out of him if he drove back across the runway.

Loni's cousin James sat on the bottom step of her stairs and blocked access to her upstairs apartment. He had his mother's curly light brown hair and round face along with an innocent geniality, but Loni couldn't completely trust him. There was always the memory of his hatred and cruelty toward her when they were growing up. His animosity toward her continued after she came back home last year. Until last summer. He almost warmed to her when she saved his ass by preventing an abduction by two Mexicans bent on killing him. When they spent several nights on stakeout waiting for coyotes to show up with their load of illegals, James finally accepted her as an equal. Their issues seemed resolved, but she would never forget the things he did to her in high school like sneaking up behind her in the hall and catcalling half-breed or Injin, or squaw, or buck. Or queer.

"Let me by, James. I gotta soak the blood in my shirt before it sets."

"No, no, cousin. Sit and tell all." James tried to pull her down beside him. "Heard you wrecked another car."

Loni struggled to pull back and keep on her feet. "Let go! I've got to clean the blood off. And my ear hurts, dammit."

James's light blue eyes finally showed some concern. "What happened?"

"Got shot at."

His jaw dropped as Loni got by him and trudged up the stairs. She slammed the door and stripped off her clothes. Her shower got rid of blood Chelsea missed. The nick on the side of her ear had stopped bleeding, but it hurt like a son of a bitch. She rummaged through her drawers and found an extra T-shirt with POLICE across the back. After she put her bloody shirt to soak, Loni peeked down the stairs at James. He hadn't moved. She stiffly walked back down and sat beside him. Coco pushed at James to be petted, and Loni took his beer bottle out of his hand to hold against her ear. "Where were you this morning, James? I could've used your help."

James grabbed his beer back and took a long swig before he answered. "I was called out on a church domestic."

Loni joked. "There's an oxymoron if I ever heard one. A domestic at a church? What happened? Caught the preacher shooting at God?"

"I wish. A couple of old farts took a chain saw to the preacher's billboard in front of the church."

"Are you talking about the one who says God prefers kind atheists over hateful Christians? Heard he got it off Twitter."

"Yeah. These two old farts said they already tithed three times over what the property was worth, and nobody was going to tell them God could love no atheist."

Loni was struck mute for a minute before she snorted. "Shit oh dear!"

"That's what I thought too."

"Lola tried to call you. How come your cell phone was off?"

"Don't you know? Churches have these big signs saying 'TURN OFF CELL PHONES!' So I did." James slugged at her arm. "Don't tell me you never saw one of those signs. Oh, right, I forgot. You're a two-spirit heathen. How does it work exactly?"

Loni groaned and took the beer bottle back for her burning ear. "Your wife's been dragging you to church too long."

"You'd feel a helluva lot better if you drank the beer instead of putting it on your ear."

"This is good."

"How come you don't drink it?"

"No reason. I don't drink alcohol." With a sigh, Loni handed the bottle back.

"Really! Afraid you'll end up frozen to death in a ditch like Ira Hayes?"

"If I end up dead in a ditch, it won't be from alcohol. More likely it would be from riding in a car with you."

James giggled as he reached for the bandage on her ear. "Let me see. Some jealous husband shoot you?"

Loni snorted in disgust and glared at James. "I don't do married women!" she insisted. "Would you listen to me? I already told you where I got shot."

James patted her on the top of the head. "Heard you did good, too. Except for letting Manny go back to Tucson."

Loni slapped her hand across James's opening mouth. "Don't you dare say it, James!"

Laughing, James pushed her off. He emptied his beer, flipped the bottle in the air, and caught it. The second time he flipped the bottle, Loni snatched it and they wrestled until Coco backed off, barking at them.

"Don't look at me, Coco," James said to the dog. "She started it."

"Did not!" Loni insisted. "He did!"

"Did not!"

Loni threw her hands in the air. "In case you haven't noticed, she's not listening."

"Just like a woman. Hear only what you want to hear."

Loni snorted. "Like you don't. Guess you also heard about my fight with Junior."

"Junior shoot you?"

"No, James, it was a busload of Mexican mafia."

James searched her face. "You shoot back this time?"

"No." Loni leaned her head against the railing on the stairs. "I didn't want to hit Manny."

"So." James reached his arm around Loni and squeezed her. "To summarize, you lost a bus. You lost five Mexican mafia. You lost Manny. You lost your car. You fought with Junior. And you pissed off Lola." Loni hung her head as James berated her. "Good job, Loni. I can see how well all that worked out for you."

Loni cringed. "You're enjoying this, aren't you?"

"I am." James hugged her harder. "You always were my favorite entertainment."

Loni slumped in resignation as she watched their cousin Daniel come out of the office. He took after his dad, big and stocky with straight black hair and brown eyes. Daniel was mostly dark German although his dark skin might have come from their Choctaw grandmother. Loni's dad was the oldest of the three Wagner brothers. Daniel's dad Herman was in the middle and James's dad Kirk was youngest.

Daniel squatted in front of Loni and inspected her. "What trouble are you into now?"

"What?" she snapped.

"Checking to see if you're going to live." Daniel stood up. "Scoot over." Settling down on the other side of Loni, he put his arm around her shoulders. "Talk to Daddy. Tell me all about it."

Loni got a stubble burn as he rubbed his face against her cheek. Fighting him off, she smelled the mix of the grease and Lava soap. "Cut it out, Daniel, or I'll shave you with my very dull, chipped knife, no soap, and cold water."

Daniel cackled like an old hen pecking at scratch. "I heard you talking about Junior. Reminds me, Matt Barlow was here yesterday and said you came out with Junior to see him the other day. Something about undocumented workers wandering in. Said a *coyote* took their money and dumped them. Matt said he was glad to see you home again. I didn't know the two of you were friends."

Loni fought off the second stubble-rub attempt. "Don't you remember? His dad and my granddad used to help each other round up cattle. They had the ranch to the north. His cattle were always coming through the fence onto our property."

"How come your fences were so bad?"

"Built back in Thirty-Three by the WPA. You'd be tired, too."

Daniel ignored Loni's comment. "So Matt said you got in a fight with Junior. Did you really pull your gun on Junior and threaten to shoot him?"

"I did. And I meant it. He was being his usual assholeness, talking about hauling the workers back out to the desert and shooting them. Said back home in Texas it was great sport, and he didn't understand my problem."

James poked her in the side. "Assholeness? Is that a word?"

"It is now."

Daniel grinned. "Matt said when you finished swearing at Junior, he got into an argument with him."

Loni shrugged, still upset with Junior. "Matt tried to warn him about that old Brahma bull, Hellsbent, but you know Junior, the stupid know-it-all. He puffed up and pointed to the Texas star on his chest and said, 'This star means I can go anywhere I want.' Matt told Junior he was in Arizona now and Texas Rangers had no jurisdiction."

Daniel giggled like a girl. "Did Junior say Arizona was a subdivision of Texas and since they owned it, he could do what he wanted anywhere?"

"Yep. He said it was a fact of history and we were a bunch of desert inverts." It was a while before the three stopped giggling. Catching her breath, Loni said, "He said no way was he walking around when there was a shortcut. That's when he opened the gate and started across the field. Hellsbent watched every step he took."

"Didn't he see the bull?"

"Sure, but Junior always insists on using the shortest way. Did you see him drive me home across the runway just now? Dumb bastard! Matt kept telling him to get out of there and how the bull was way too dangerous to even work the rodeo circuit anymore, but noooo. Junior kept on going."

"Matt really tried to warn him?"

"Hell, yes."

Daniel was awestruck. "That bull is big and ugly."

"Oh, yeah. He watched Junior coming toward him and began pawing the ground. Dirt flew everywhere. But Junior kept on marching forward. Even when Hellsbent bellowed."

"I can't believe Junior didn't run. Hellsbent's one nasty bull."

"He didn't, not until Hellsbent charged him. Junior turned tail, I can tell you. I was busy cheering for Hellsbent when Matt hollered, 'Hey, Texas! Show him your star!'"

Giggling, James leaned against Loni. "I'm so sorry I missed it."

"Made my day."

The boys pulled Loni to her feet and hugged her goodnight. "Try not to make so much noise, Daniel," Loni begged as she dragged herself up the stairs to her loft apartment. The drop in her adrenaline put her to sleep before she got her clothes off.

An hour later, Loni jerked awake. Coco stood by the door, fiercely barking. Still wearing nothing but her police T-shirt, Loni yanked on a pair of Levis. She grabbed her gun from under her pillow and raced down the stairs toward the frantic hammering on the hangar door. Madly barking, Coco almost tripped Loni before she threw open the door. On the other side was a sobbing Lola. Loni almost fell backward when Lola grabbed her. "They charged Manny with murder!" Lola bawled.

"But all they wanted to do was question him about the bus ride. He didn't kill either guard. I swear!" Loni insisted.

"Wasn't a guard. Please. You have to go to Tucson. You have to clear him."

"Who'd they say he murdered?"

"His girlfriend, Della. Somebody found her body off San Pedro Road," Lola cried. "They say he was the last one to see her."

"I'll check it out, Lola. I promise. Go home and be with your folks. They need you now."

"No. I want to stay with you. I can help.

"There's nothing we can do right now, Lola. It's late."

Lola let go of Loni. She stepped back, tears still streaming down her face. "Damn it, Loni, you can still call somebody right now."

"Who?"

"Don't you know anybody in Tucson?"

"Not good enough on a murder charge. Maybe somebody at the station does. But we still can't get anything done until the morning, Lola. You need to go home."

Lola shook her head, pulling Loni tight again. "I'm scared, Loni. I want to stay."

"And do what? Watch me sleep?"

"Or maybe make out a little?"

Loni pulled Lola's arms from around her neck and lifted Lola's chin as she wiped away a tear. "Not like this."

Lola glared at Loni and twisted away.

Loni watched Lola run to her car and speed away. An engine noise at the back of the hangar caught her attention. She worked her way around two small planes and a helicopter, searching for the source. Daniel was working on a motor, and James was watching him with a beer in his hand.

"Hey! Didn't you hear Lola pounding on the door?" Loni shouted through the noise.

Daniel cut the engine. "Nope. What'd she want?"

"Why are you working so late, Daniel? Don't you know people are trying to sleep?"

"I don't know anybody trying to sleep. Do you, James?"

"Not anymore." James smiled at her hostile frown.

Daniel burst out laughing through two layers of grease streaks as he revved up the motor on an AK1-3 Helicopter. "Have to finish this job before morning," he hollered.

Loni ducked and walked up close to James. She hollered in his ear. "You hear about Manny?"

"Nothing aside from you letting them take him back to Tucson," Ignoring her, James lifted the bottle for another long swallow.

Daniel gave the plane a final check and turned off the motor.

Loni reached out for a fingertip of grease off Daniel's face and smeared it down James's nose. "You listening now?"

"Damn it!" Leaning over, James grabbed the hem of Loni's long tee and wiped the grease off his nose. "What?"

She swiped another streak down his cheek while she snatched her shirt back. "He got arrested for murdering his girlfriend."

James pulled a kerchief out of his back pocket and wiped at his face. "Shit! I don't know how many times I told him to play in his own back yard. He never would listen." James stared at the black smear on the kerchief, walked over to Daniel, and stuck it in his back pocket. "Better you than me gets blamed."

Loni followed the two cousins back through the hangar to the office. James went into the bathroom and left the door open. He hollered out, "Think he did it?"

"Hell no! He's too much of a wuss to kill anyone."

"You're Manny's friend, James. Do you know any cops in Tucson who might help? Any who don't hate you?"

"How can you say that? Everybody loves me."

Loni snorted. "What I remember is the trouble you got them into when you and your buddies went to Mexico to play."

James smiled as he came out of the bathroom. "Daniel, you remember those tall VW Bugs?"

"You mean the ones they stuck on top of a ten-foot frame with wheels?"

"Yeah, those. One time we got so drunk we couldn't drive any farther so we piled out of the cars with our sleeping bags and went to sleep. Had no idea where we were. I woke up in the middle of the road with one of them VW bugs rolling right over the top of me. Scared the bejesus outta me." James sighed. "Those were the fun days."

Daniel smiled back at his cousin. "Drove one of them once. Forgot to leave our boat up far enough, and the tide went out, leaving the boat high and dry." Daniel giggled. "I drove that contraption over the top of the boat, hooked it up, and hauled it back down to the water. I had fun until the boat decided to leave with the tide and I had to swim like hell to catch it."

"See Daniel? I always told you procrastination pays. You should have waited for the tide to come back—"

James said, "Hell, Daniel. Swimming's not so bad. Try waking up with one of those ugly Bugs rolling over you. I swore it was a monster attack."

"Lucky it didn't pick you up and haul you to the water and drop you in a hole."

Loni punched James. "Focus here. I need help. Didn't you have an old cop friend in Tucson who hung out with you?"

"Harry Beal. He's a detective down there now. Want me to contact him for you?"

Relief washed over Loni. She said, "God, yes."

"I'll call him tonight. I got his phone number at the house somewhere." James finished his beer and reached over to grab Daniel's.

"Get your own," Daniel said, holding the bottle high in the air.

"Where do you keep it?"

"None of your business."

"It's up in my refrigerator." Loni grinned at Daniel.

"Shit, Loni. Thought I was your favorite cousin."

Loni and Daniel both laughed as they watched James leap up the stairs and through Loni's door. In seconds he hopped back down carrying two bottles. Handing one to Daniel, he tipped the other bottle up and emptied it with a loud burp. "Thanks for the beer, Loni. Mighty nice."

"You're welcome. Anytime."

James studied her with suspicion. "Wait a minute. You don't drink."

"I just said it's Daniel's."

"Oh, good. Think I'll have another." James immediately leaped up the stairs and disappeared into her apartment once more.

"You going to replace those?" Daniel shouted to his back.

James hopped down the stairs holding two bottles again. "Maybe."

Loni grinned. "Some things never change."

"Oh, yeah? And I still say you got those dimples from the milkman."

"Crap, James. I'm so tired of your milkman routine."

James quick tossed his empty bottle to her. Yelping, she barely caught it and tossed it back.

"Stop it, you two. I'm not cleaning up your messes anymore."

James tossed both empty bottles at her. Stepping away, Loni let them fall, glass shattering around her. Ignoring the boys, she stepped out of the glass and told Coco to stay. She got a broom and mop from a small storage room and threw them at James. Smirking, she called Coco, dashed up the stairs and slammed her door shut. She opened the door again and warned James. "I'm locking my door. You're going to have to get your beer somewhere else."

Glad her day was done, Loni gazed out the window skylight at Montezuma Mountain, feeling the peace soak throughout her body before she reached for her laptop.

> FROM: Loni Wagner
> TO: Sandi@gmailyahoo.com
> DATE: October 8
> SUBJECT: Staying here
>
> Sorry it's been so long. Going back to day work is as hard as it was getting used to night work. At least my new police car is refrigerated now. Or it was until it burned up today. And all because Lola's brother got in trouble. He's usually in trouble, but this time it's bad. A murder charge. Even though she's mad at me again and broke our Saturday date that took me two months to get,

I told Lola I would try and help though I can't stand Manny. Guess I want to help Lola more.

I'm finally finishing my project from July, painting the inside of my grandparents' house. At least this weekend I get to be in refrigeration instead of on a horse in 90-degree weather. It's October, for god's sake. I can't believe it's still so hot this late in the year. I'm so fed up with this heat.

Did I tell you about the new asshole Carl hired? Some big dude from Texas. Lola thinks he's cute. Some people might think he's cowboy handsome, but he's dumb as a post. If he doesn't get one of us killed first, maybe Carl will get fed up and fire him. I can only hope. Problem is Carl told me he's got a daddy high up in law enforcement in Texas who knows Carl's boss at State. Seems Junior got sent to us to get him away from of some kind of trouble at home. I'd love to know what it is. Maybe my next project will be to find out.

Take care.

Loni

An hour after Loni crawled into bed, she was still wide awake. In desperation, she got up and reached for the boot box filled with notebooks and letters from her dad's parents her Uncle Herm gave her last summer. Back in bed, she pulled out a notebook written by her Grandmother Wagner. She liked learning about her grandparents' life in the past. For some reason it made it easier to deal with her present troubles.

Wanting to hear a voice, she decided to read out loud to Coco. Shaking Coco enough to get the dog to raise her head, she said, "You listening, Coco? I'm going to read you a bedtime story." Loni wiggled into a comfortable place against Coco and began.

"Sal and I went hunting on the desert. Not for anything. Just hunting because the folks bought us a twenty-two-caliber pump gun. It was a dandy and we wasted lots of ammunition. Sal hit more than I did. The first thing I killed was a road-runner. I aimed at a quail and hit the road-runner instead. I hated to kill anything I couldn't eat. One time, Sal shot in a big hole in the bank of the arroyo. I thought it was a fox. Just two golden eyes.

I sent Sal to the house for a hoe to pull him out. Out it came, not a fox, but a great big owl. He landed on Sal's head. I can see her yet, standing on one foot, her arms shielding her face and yelling, 'Shoot it, shoot it.' I didn't shoot and it finally flew away. We didn't think it was funny until later."

Loni flipped the page and reached over, lightly pulling on Coco's ear.

"The day my baby sister Sal was born was also the day my cousin married the love of my life, Fred Finger. I wasn't quite six, but he promised he'd marry me if I'd only eat and grow big and strong. For six years I ate large amounts of food to please him. I grew strong but not so big. Well, it was quite a day for the Vicking family: a new baby, measles, a wedding and me howling my head off. I can still remember watching the buggy drive off and I'm hanging on the door crying my heart out. Though it took a while, I stopped crying because I had Sal to marvel at."

Loni slid down in bed and stretched out as best she could. Coco took up more than her share of the bed. "I guess not much changes, Coco." She was almost back to sleep when Daniel started banging on something downstairs. Loni dragged herself out of bed and dressed. She grabbed some soggy salt crackers wet out of a bowl on her table and stuffed them in her mouth as she wandered back down to the hangar floor.

CHAPTER THREE

Three hours later, Loni was still handing Daniel tools while he worked on a helicopter. Smelling him and listening to the cadence of his voice always helped her relax. It was like surrounding herself with clean, rich earth. "Where's James?"

"Couldn't get to my beer so he went home."

"Daniel? Did you know you're part Choctaw Indian?"

"Sure. Dad told me."

"Does James know he's part Indian?"

"I don't know. I think my dad gave our grandparents notes and letters to Uncle Kirk to read. Maybe James read them. Want me to ask?"

Loni thought for a minute. "Considering his attitude toward me all those years, it might be interesting to see his reaction."

"You can blame James's mother, Aunt Ethel. She didn't much like me either." Daniel climbed into the cabin and fiddled with the controls.

"Wanna go?"

"Know how to fly this thing?"

"Wanna find out?"

"Where you going?"

"Up?"

"I don't think so." Loni frowned. "Heard Charley Rankin skidded up to the gas station the other day and said, 'Give me a gallon of gas and a map of Texas. I'm takin' a long trip.' Think I'd get further going with him."

"But I'm offering a free ride. He'd make you pay for the gas."

Loni collected the tools and put them away as Daniel started the engine. She watched him get ready to taxi out the huge hangar door and yelled, "Isn't it too hot to get lift?"

Daniel gave Loni a cocky grin and shouted, "Probably not. It's October and night! Want to come along and find out?"

Loni crossed her fingers as the plane rose in the air. Daniel waved to her as he turned and disappeared into the dark night. She climbed up to the loft and tried not to worry. Daniel or Uncle Herm could have been in the plane wreck last summer instead of Rene. Loni settled for a long cold shower before attempting more sleep. She tried to cover up her worry until she heard the whopping of the returning helicopter.

The buzzing phone jarred Loni out of a sweet dream about Maria smiling down at a baby she was holding. Loni rolled over and swiped her cell phone. "This better be good."

"You want that phone number or not!" James's giggle was so infectious Loni relented. "James, you shit. I just got to sleep."

Loni could imagine his playful intention as he said, "I was hoping you were asleep. Only getting even, cuz, since you won't share."

"It's not my beer."

"You want this phone number or what?"

"Hang on." Loni jotted the phone number down in her pocket notebook. "Thanks, James. I owe you."

"As usual. When are you ever going to start repaying?"

"I could try real hard not to pour ground up Habanera chilies in your beer."

James giggled again before he hung up. Loni went back to bed and reluctantly acknowledged, like it or not, she would be involved in Manny's trouble. Almost back asleep, she heard her phone buzz again. This time she heard Bobby's voice.

"Teenager reported dead," he said. "No confirmation."

"Why me, Bobby?"

"You're the one on call. Don't you ever check the schedule?"

"Okay, okay. What's going on and where?"

"All-night party ten miles out on Miller Road."

"Why can't state police take care of it?" Loni whined.

Bobby said, "They're all out on calls, and I said it would be okay. Can't miss it, the caller said. They built a big fire close to the road."

That tells me a lot, Loni grumped to herself and marveled at another one of Bobby's difficult directions. She threw on her clothes and hurried down to the hangar floor. Coco hopped up into her 1994 Silverado pickup much more easily than Loni did. She had to haul herself up to the cab on the truck's raised chassis and oversized tires. The height also made it more unstable. The truck was built to challenge rocky hills and gullies. Gray primer patches covered almost all the original green paint by the time Maria bought it. That was before Maria died in a pool of blood in a Los Angeles back alley chasing a perp. Much to Loni's embarrassment, Maria called the truck her second most favorite "Butch." The truck was pretty much the only thing left from Loni's time as a cop in LA before her lover's death and her grandma's illness drove her home.

Loni pushed the truck as hard as she could. She dreaded what she would find ahead as she wound her way through the foothills. Another child lost. Loni rounded a sharp turn on a hill and dropped down onto a half-circle of car headlights around a large bonfire. She parked on the edge of the road and walked toward the lights. A figure silhouetted by the fire walked toward Loni. She saw he was a teenage boy. He pointed into the darkness and said, "He's down there."

Using the beam of her flashlight, Loni followed car tracks to a boy crumpled on the ground. He appeared to have been mauled by a bear, the bent position of his head exposing a broken neck. The front part of his shirt was torn away, and ribs stuck up through the lacerations. Loni thought he might have broken legs and arms, but his untouched face was peaceful. Loni gasped in surprise. The body belonged to Jimmy, Todd's younger brother. His parents were Bill and Janine Barclay. Loni saw Jimmy less than two months ago when he spoke at his brother's funeral. Todd died after somebody slipped meth into his drink while he partied at his coach's house. Somebody accidently mixed the meth with some deadly ricin. Coach and his wife showed up dead two days after the party, and Loni had worked hard to solve the source of the drugs.

Loni stared at the tire treads over Jimmy before she checked the back tires of a GMC pickup parked next to him. They matched. She walked back to the kids huddled together on the ground next to the bonfire. Flames reflected horror and anguish on their faces, and a dark-haired girl held a sobbing boy. She rubbed his back as they rocked back and forth. Others sniffed and swatted at tears. Loni needed answers. She squatted down in front of the girl. "Tell me what happened."

A tall kid with crossed arms stood apart from them and pointed at the boy in her arms. "Paddy ran right over him. I had nothing to do with it."

The girl rocking Paddy flared, "God, Billy Joe. You're such a lying asshole!"

"I didn't!" Billy Joe was belligerent.

"Who crowded Paddy off the road?"

"Shut up, Joy. Did I know Jimmy was there?"

"Did you care?"

Loni interrupted the hostile exchange. "Joy, tell me what happened."

"Billy Joe said he was going back to town to get more beer." She hesitated. "Next thing I see, he's driving my truck without asking me. I didn't even know he got in it until I heard it start." She stared at Billy Joe again. "You fuck! Why didn't you drive your own car?"

"You weren't using yours!" Billy Joe's arrogant voice rose in the dark. "It was sitting there to take."

"Billy Joe," Loni warned him. "I'll get to you."

"We were in Paddy's car. We tried to stop him. I didn't want him driving my pickup. He screwed around with us, driving in circles, then driving close and threatening to ram us. Jimmy ran out to stop him." Joy's voice quivered. "He just wanted to stop him."

"Wait a minute," Billy Joe interrupted. "I was barely off the road."

Loni squatted down in front of the two. "Paddy? Can you hear me?"

The boy sobbed.

"Is that how you remember it?"

"Noooo." Paddy stretched it out between sobs. "He pushed me off the road. I was trying to get away from him, and I didn't see Jimmy!" He ended the name in a wail.

Joy screamed at Billy Joe. "You wouldn't drive that way in your fancy red car!"

Loni stood. "Anyone else see what happened?"

The group glanced around at each other. A voice came out of the crowd. "None of us did. We were sitting around the fire."

Another voice came out from the direction of the fire. "We could see lights spinning around, but that's all."

Billy Joe tried to defend himself again, but Loni ignored him. Followed by his whiny sounds, she photographed the ground and measured the tracks. She traced where the pickup and car swerved off the road and found the tracks stopped immediately beyond Jimmy's body. Billy Joe kept trailing her, and Loni ordered him back to the fire. The ambulance pulled up. EMTs waited to pick up the boy while she took more photos.

The teenagers cried and argued. Loni paced around the parked cars until she found the Lamborghini. A fancy red car, the girl said. Loni had heard about this car a little too often, usually when somebody told her about raped girls. It belonged to Billy Joe's father. His dad was involved in drugs and used the money to get the car. They couldn't take the car because it was in his wife's name. Loni took names and phone numbers before she called the parents to come get their kids. She'd release the cars, but they needed to see what their kids were doing. Another call was to Bobby so somebody could notify Jimmy's parents.

The dark night was thick with fear and grief as the coroner and the ambulance slowly disappeared into the dark. The upset parents gathered their children. Only Dorothea seemed indifferent. She stood impassively, waiting for Billy Joe to get in his car. After an eternity, she pulled out after him as they left.

Loni made one more careful pass around the crime scene before heading for her grandparents' ranch.

CHAPTER FOUR

Loni pulled into the ranch driveway as the sun hit and reflected off the slowly spinning windmill fans and splashed light around her. She took a deep breath and shoved the night off as she climbed down from her truck. It was home, the one place she always felt at peace.

Coco bounced to the ground and followed Loni into the yard. The dog went over to Old Jack lying in a dugout hole under a Tamarack tree. "Come, Coco," Loni said. "He's too old to play with you now. We need to get the painting done."

Willie helped Loni move the furniture to one side of the living room. The sounds of Geri and the TO Boys gave Loni the rhythm for stirring Navajo White paint while a barefoot Willie danced around her in his favorite polka step. His dark bronzed skin popped against the white of his short-sleeved T-shirt. Loni wondered how much money his tattered Levis would bring at a designer's show.

"Yip, yip!" Loni hollered as she joined Willie. They circled the work table a couple of times before they danced into the kitchen and grabbed Shiichoo. The giggling white-haired woman pushed at them after a few turns and wiggled away. "I don't have time for your silliness this morning, she grumbled through her smile." She went back to the stove and furiously stirred something in a pot, muttering about burned stew and trying not to grin.

Loni skipped back and forth behind her grandma a few times pulling on her long braid. "Lovely dress, Shiichoo," Loni said as she pulled on her grandma's paint-streaked smock and dodged swats from the wooden spoon. She moved over to her granddad and chanted, "Chicken scratch, chicken scratch, we all do the chicken scratch."

Bahb laughed and bobbed his head as he tried to keep out of her way. "Way you dance looks chicken scratch. Move."

"When's the last time you went out dancing?"

"I think Sacaton. Years ago," Shiichoo said thoughtfully. "And you two won't eat unless you get your painting done sometime today!"

Willie and Loni playfully twisted around Shiichoo as they danced back to their painting. Loni cut the paint into the corners while Willie rolled the paint onto the walls and ceiling. When she wasn't watching, he swiped her with the paint roller until she was covered with off-white stripes. Bahb hummed as he carefully painted the woodwork. Loni relaxed until she jumped at the loud bong next to her from the mantel clock her father's parents brought across the country. Willie laughed and swatted her with the roller again. "Pay attention. You're getting more paint on the floor than the walls."

"Oh, yeah? You're getting more paint on me than the ceiling," Loni mock-complained, moving out of his reach.

The first half of the room was finished before noon, but the smells of cooking had made Loni's mouth water for a long time. The three painters washed up and grabbed cans of frozen tea from the freezer while Shiichoo put lunch on the table.

Loni gobbled her stew and got up to fix the strawberry shortcake dessert. She passed it around the table, serving Bahb first. His eyes lightened up. Loni used his favorite dessert to soften him up for what she needed to say. The quiet settled as everyone ate. Loni broke into the silence. "I need to talk to all of you about something. My boss likes us to talk to our families in case something happens to us, you know?" She squirmed in front of the six dark eyes. "My end of life directive says if I'm brain dead or terminally ill, I don't want any heroic action taken. In other words, don't keep me alive," she insisted. "Understand?"

The three of them stared at her.

"Come on," Loni begged. "Tell me you agree."

The three gawked at each other and turned back at her. Finally Bahb spoke. "If you want, okay."

"Good. And now I want directives from the three of you."

"What?" Bahb said.

"She wants to know how we want to die," Willie explained. He turned back to Loni. "I want same as you."

The other two nodded in agreement.

"Okay. How do you want to be buried? In the olden ways? Except for killing a horse. I refuse to do that."

Willie chuckled. "Old Buck not worth killing."

Not certain she disagreed, Loni watched the three of them as she said, "Last question. What do you want buried with? Shiichoo, you start."

"I want to be buried in the graveyard out back." She paused a minute. "All I want are my weaving sticks. Otherwise do what you want."

"Bahb?"

"Wrap me in blanket from living room wall and bury under a rock next to Shiichoo."

"Large, flat tombstone do?"

Bahb nodded in agreement.

"You won't get into trouble?" Shiichoo sounded worried.

"No. Law only says we have to be buried six feet or deeper to keep animals from smelling us and digging us up."

"That's a special image, child." Shiichoo frowned at her.

"Willie?"

"I want whole bit." Willie sat back and cross his arms crossed. "Set me with head pointed south. Bury at night. No one stays, just cover and go. Use my ollos to leave pinole and water with me. Tomahawk in my arms." He grinned at Loni and pulled on the long dark French braid hanging down her back. "You cut your hair."

"No, no," Shiichoo objected. "She will not! I want her hair left long."

"Part of old ritual."

"We're done here." Loni stood, picking up the dishes from the table and washed them in the sink. She'd do the paperwork later. She was just grateful she had gotten that much information out of them.

The sun dropped in the sky as the four of them stood back and admired their work. With a sigh and a small grin, Bahb looked over at her. "Now done."

"Not yet, Bahb. Tomorrow afternoon we do the second coat on the walls." Loni hugged him before she bounced into the kitchen to wash her face and hands. She grabbed three tamales from the fridge and dashed through the back door, calling over her shoulder, "You get to clean up." Popping her head back in, she said, "Oh, yeah. Can I bring you anything tomorrow?"

"Saddle soap," Bahb said.

"Prickly pear pads," said Shiichoo. "And Charmin toilet paper."

"Why Charmin?"

"That's the only toilet paper your silly cat won't eat."

"What?"

"Eat. That cat you drug in from the barn eats toilet paper. I'm tired of chasing half chewed rolls all over the house."

Bahb laughed. "She just grabs beginning of the roll and flies."

"Give her some grass," Loni suggested. "Humm. Funny what that rhymes with."

"Out! Out!" Her grandma picked up the broom and swept at Loni as she fell laughing out the door. Shiichoo opened the door again for the dog. "Better get, Coco! You'll be next." The dog flew out the door and pushed past Loni's giggles and bounded up into the cab of the truck.

CHAPTER FIVE

It was during the hottest part of the afternoon when Loni carefully lowered herself out of the truck cab. She walked toward the hangar office as Coco ran around to the back of the building. In between groans of sore all over, she was thinking how Shiichoo was on the mend, and Loni was glad to have family who loved her.

Daniel watched her shuffle into the office and slowly drop into one of the overstuffed chairs. "Been helping your grandparents again?"

"Yup. We're painting now. Plus I've been riding horses and sitting for hours at work behind a computer."

"I never did ask you. Why didn't you move in with your grandparents when you came home?"

"We talked it over. I knew Shiichoo would try to take care of me if I stayed at the ranch. When I patrolled highways at night, she'd have to be up and down all the time. I came home to help her, not the other way around." She added, "Even if I work days, Shiichoo would worry about me, and I like my space upstairs."

Daniel smiled. "You're right. Cleaning up after you, no one would get any rest."

"With her as a cop on the premise, she saves us from paying a salary for a security guard," Loni's uncle Herm reminded Daniel.

"So now you're giving her credit for being useful around here?"

Loni ignored Daniel's comment as she picked at a glob of paint on the tail of her shirt. The roar of propellers drowned any chance of conversation as a plane whipped into the big door to the hangar. The propeller slowly stopped spinning, and a small, slender woman in designer jeans, high-heeled boots, and a silver silk shirt climbed out of the cabin.

All three of them stared as the woman swept long blond hair out of her eyes and tucked it behind her ears. She walked into the office and glanced around with disapproval on her long narrow face. "Lordy, how do you live in this heat. It can't be healthy!" she said as she wiped the sweat off her forehead.

Herm stood, his dark German bulk towering over her. He drawled, "Shore is, lady. Why, when I came here, I couldn't walk nor talk nor turn myself over. Look at me now."

Daniel fell over with giggles.

Concerned, the woman spoke softly. "I see. Were you very ill?"

"Not really, little lady." Uncle Herm smiled. "I was born here."

The woman frowned in disgust. "Call me a taxi."

Daniel began another round of giggles, and Herm turned to Loni. "Do we have a taxi in this town?"

"Nope," Loni answered with a straight face.

Daniel struggled to talk. "Usually the cops take people where they need to go."

Ignoring Daniel's giggles, Uncle Herm turned to Loni. Daniel was still lost in more giggles. "Hell, Loni. Get up from there and help the woman."

Loni's sore body fought to stand from the worn-out springs and hole in her chair. She grimaced and held out her hand. "I'm Loni Wagner, ma'am. Caliente Police Department. Where can I take you?"

The woman glared at Loni, ignoring her outstretched hand splattered with paint. "You're kidding, right?"

Loni dropped her hand and inspected her paint-covered shirt. "Don't think so," she said as she dug her badge out of her back pocket and held it up.

"God help me," the woman sighed. "What next?"

Loni waited.

"I need to see a client," the woman explained, wiping her face on the sleeve of her silk shirt. "Although what I want is to fly the hell out of here. Is it always this hot?"

"Nope," Loni answered calmly. "It's usually hotter in the summer. This is fall weather." Behind her, Daniel fell apart again in giggles.

The woman seemed to collect herself. She straightened up and said, "I'm Janet Jace. I would appreciate a ride to the jail and directions to the hotel."

"Daniel? Did you know we had a hotel?" asked Uncle Herm.

"Sure, Dad. Don't you remember? Behind the old movie theater."

"Thought the fire last month closed it down."

"Only the kitchen," Daniel answered.

"Oh, for heaven's sake!" the woman snapped.

"Ignore them, Ms. Jace," Loni said as she turned to Daniel. "You're pathetic, Daniel. If you would stop giggling for one minute, you could put her luggage in my truck," She turned back to Janet. "I need to wash a bit and change my shirt. If you could give me a few minutes?"

Upstairs, Loni saw the streaks of paint on her face when she saw herself the mirror. My god! Loni thought. She must think I'm wearing war paint! She scrubbed as best she could where she could reach and changed into a fresh shirt and Levis.

Janet was tapping her foot when Loni hurried down the stairs. Determined to be polite, Loni opened the passenger door and signaled Coco who scrambled up like mountain climber into the seat. "You're next," she said to Janet.

"Does that dog have to go with us?"

"She does if you want to go to town," Loni answered. "She's a police dog and goes wherever I go."

Janet turned away from Daniel's offer of help, and resolutely grabbed the seatbelt to pull herself up into the cab. She pushed away Coco's long tongue and hugged the passenger side. Staring around she said, "I suppose you have a reason for parking in an airplane hangar?"

"I live up there." Loni pointed to the top of her stairs.

Janet Jace's mouth fell open. "You live in an airport hangar?"

"She surely does, Ms. Jace," Daniel answered as he closed the passenger door. He gazed at her three large suitcases in the bed of the truck. "You plan on being here a while?"

Janet rolled the window up in Daniel's face and sat back.

Loni drove out of the wide hangar door and headed for town before she finally asked, "Anything I can help you with, tell you about?"

"You truly are a police officer?"

"Yep." Loni glanced over at the disbelieving expression on Janet's face. "Hard to believe, huh?"

Janet snorted. "There must be an interesting story here somewhere."

"Maybe I'll tell you another time. You haven't told me yet why you're here."

"I heard there's no lawyer in this town. Is that true?"

"Yep. Last one ran off last year with the principal. Couldn't happen to a nicer guy."

"You didn't think much of him?"

"Hell, yes. Stu was fine. It was the principal I hated. I had him for calculus in high school and he was a leach. One of the other teachers caught him molesting a male student in a custodian closet. So what did they do to punish him? Made him principal which gave him even more power." Loni shut up before she got mad all over again.

"Why didn't you stop him? You're a police officer."

Loni glanced over with a snort. "I was in high school at the time. Probably couldn't have gotten him fired anyway. Small town politics. When you're here long enough you'll see. Plan on staying awhile?"

"I don't know yet. I have a case here, and I was wondering what it was like around here."

"You caught the Charlie Thornton case?"

Janet shook her head. "I don't know anything about that case."

"If you're here very long, I bet you catch it. A big-time murder case by a big-time citizen. Owns a big farm outside of town."

"Who'd he murder?"

"His wife, of course."

Janet sighed. "I hate domestic violence cases."

"What case did you get?"

"I'm representing a young man by the name of Ronnie Dobbs."

Taken by surprise, Loni burst out, "How'd you catch that one?"

"As I said, I wanted to check it out so I'm doing it pro bono. I understand Dobbs is very poor."

Loni snorted again. "He comes from the Dobbs Ranch in the Alter Valley. Make the old man pay or you'll get laughed out of town." She felt obliged to explain. "There's nothing that old man likes more than ripping off someone. He'll brag to everyone and embarrass the hell outta you."

As they drove, Loni entertained Janet with a running commentary about the town. They passed the Mormon Church, stucco white with a tall, cone-shaped sphere reaching into the sky. "One of several churches I'm sure would welcome you."

"But not you?" Janet guessed.

Loni glanced at Janet with an acknowledged grin. After an empty service station came into view, Loni pointed to an old abandoned movie theater with a faded yellow sign on the big double doors reading "CONDEMNED." The marquee pushed out over the sidewalk in all of its past splendor. Carved wood with chipped gilt surrounded a few plastic letters hanging precariously from their railings. "I think those letters once read *To Kill a Mockingbird*," Loni said. "Only theater in town. Closed when I was a kid. The last owner was old man Jandas, mostly deaf and blind. After he died, the city closed it down."

Janet said curtly, "My favorite movie."

"Justice freak, are you?"

"You're in law. Aren't you for justice?"

Loni snorted. "Sorry, but I don't believe there's such a thing. I think it's a word we made up to explain our crappy behavior." She turned a corner onto the main thoroughfare and avoided Janet's dirty look. "A Civil War deserter who ripped off a bank founded the town. Or so the story goes. When he got to the river, he decided it was too deep to cross and too damn hot to go any further. The river's got so many dams on it now it's dried up."

They passed several bars, the grocery store, and the bakery before they reached the lopsided courthouse squatted splat in the middle of a town block like a square peg somebody tried to pound into a round hole. Over the last century, the original building expanded to city and state police departments, a small courtroom and judge's chamber, a jail in the second story, and a half-basement for storage with mostly unsolved case files crammed into it. The police department used the north entrance, and everybody else used the south entrance to get to court.

Loni drove into the parking lot and parked nearest to the police station door. Coco dashed out of the truck and explored as Loni buzzed the dispatcher to release the door and let them in. The woman followed Loni up to the main counter. Loni was relieved to see Lola wasn't there and enjoyed watching Harris Harris's eyes bugging out of his flaming red face. She introduced Janet to the evening dispatcher.

"Your first and last names are actually the same?"

"My mom loved redundancy," he shyly stuttered with his head ducked down. "Can I help you, ma'am?"

Loni studied the room through Janet's eyes. Cheap forest green dividers stretched around the bull pen to the left of the counter in a failed attempt for privacy. The green gave off the aura, and sometimes the smell, of dying plants. Loni heard somewhere the color was supposed to be calming, but she hated the ugly institutional vomit-green paint. The garish fluorescent lights hanging by chains from the ceiling made the color reflect even worse.

The faded ragged ribbon tied to the cooler vent in the ceiling barely fluttered in the stifling air, and the moisture in the air turned everything into a wet mess. Wanted posters, yellowed with age, lined the wall above four-tier filing cabinets behind Harris. In the center of this wall the door to the property room stood open.

Janet finished making arrangements to meet her client and turned to Loni. "How about the hotel now?"

"Sure. Go back out where we came in and walk across the street. It's two buildings down on your left. Unless you want to climb back into my truck."

Janet said coolly, "No thanks, I'll walk. What about my luggage?"

"Hang on a minute, and I'll be right behind you.

"Please. I need to get out of these clothes fast."

Loni turned back to Harris. "Tell Lola about Ms. Jace, would you, Harris? Maybe she can help Manny."

"Why don't you tell her yourself?"

"She's not speaking to me," Loni ruefully admitted.

"Again? What'd you do this time?"

Loni ran her hand along the cool wood as she walked the eight-foot length of the counter, feeling the nicks and chips dug into the dark surface throughout the years. Reaching the end, she sauntered out the door after Janet, listening to the quick clicks of the woman's heels.

Settling Janet, Loni left the hotel, Janet, and her luggage behind. She drove back to the hangar and found herself bombarded with Daniel's questions about what Janet was doing in town. He chuckled when Loni told him she was there to get Ronnie Dobbs off. "So how does she plan to get Ronnie off."

Loni sank into the same hole in the couch. "Shit if I know, Daniel." He kept poking her with his finger, and she knocked it away in frustration. "Uncle Herm. Help me out here."

Her uncle said, "Looks to me whatever stupid that lawyer drank sure was effective. She got took with Ronnie's case."

"Maybe not, Uncle Herm. You forget how erratic Judge Sal is." Loni reminded him. "She could win."

"Gads!" Daniel slapped his head in horror, mocking Loni as he clutched for her. "It's Judge Sal!"

Loni pushed Daniel away and ran up the stairs. She slammed the door to her apartment, grateful for the silence and the air from the cooler. Calming down, she collapsed on the bed to catch up with some sleep. When she woke up, hours later, she was groggy from sleeping. She finally remembered she was supposed to call James's friend in Tucson. She opened her cell phone. Hope he's open to an outsider looking over his shoulder, she thought.

"Harry here. Shout back."

Loni took a few seconds to understand the slow Western drawl of his deep voice. "Hello?" she squeaked.

"Hey there, little lady. What you need?"

"How do you know I'm a little lady?"

"It's my polite-to-callers day."

"Oh." Loni nodded her head at the phone before she realized he couldn't see her. "I mean hello. You got a call from James Wagner? Told you I'd be calling you?"

"Yep. Said you were his cousin. About right?"

"Today it is. I can't guarantee what he'll say tomorrow."

"He said you were a real pain in his backside, but you promised to be nice to me."

"Seeing as I'm the one doing the asking, I'll do my best."

Harry's loud laugh bounced against Loni's ear. "James said you wanted to see what we got on Manny Sanchez. It's a done deal, you know. Caught the little son-of-a-bitch rifling around in her house. Word was she was going back to her husband and he was pissed."

"I heard it, too. My problem is Manny is brother to one of our own. The dispatcher here."

"Listen. I understand if you have to make your people happy. Come on up, and I'll show you what I can."

"Hey, thanks." Loni sighed in relief. "When can I come?"

"Depends. What do you want to see?"

"For starters, where you found her."

"For starters, huh." Loni jerked the phone away from her ear to avoid the harsh sound of his laughing. "What then?"

"I don't know yet. Seems like a good place to start is all."

"I can't meet you before next Thursday. Okay?"

"Sure."

Loni wished she could quit saying whatever he thought was so funny. "You know a bar called The Watering Hole down your way on Old 85?"

"Sure."

"Meet you there around seven a.m."

"Why so early?"

"I hate heat." The line went dead.

Still grinning, Loni closed her phone and climbed back in bed.

An hour later she was still wide awake. Sitting up she grabbed her laptop and wrote to Sandi.

FROM: Loni Wagner
TO: Sandi@gmailyahoo.com
DATE: October 12
SUBJECT: Still here

I spent some time trying to get End of Life Directives from my grandparents. I think I'm growing up. I am finally beginning to appreciate and understand how they left everybody they knew to live in a white man's world and raise somebody who came home every day from school angry and miserable. They sacrificed a lot to raise me. Maybe it's just as well I didn't know about their pain. I'm not sure I could have survived both mine and theirs during those years. I'm having a hard time with it now. They spent their lives away from friends and family to take care of me and the ranch. I'm trying now to give something back. The difference in how we all grew up in the same general area is amazing.

Please take care of you and yours.

Love, Loni

Still wide awake after her nap, Loni picked one of her Grandfather Wagner's stories to read to Coco. She was delighted to find another one of the same kind of ink drawings she found on the water tanks across the years. The story was titled, "Written in my old line shack, the warming, drying spring of 1978."

"You ready, Coco?" Loni climbed in the bed next to Coco and began reading.

"I can't remember how long it took to gather cows to bring into the farm to put on irrigated pasture. I must have been all of six so you know Krissa, the old buggy mare made me a good saddle horse. The last time I was at Winter's Well to stay, Roach Richards lived there and ran cows. The cook sure didn't use a recipe book that called for a clean dish.

"Poor old Krissa pulled the buggy to school lots of years and to Sunday school, also the literary meetings. She was later killed by lightening way back among the big sage brush. She couldn't run fast enouf to scatter her shit but she always got you there.

"I saw all of the old Winter headquarters cleared away to make room for progress. To prove it was progress, now the mortgage holders have it all. Back then we called the old mother cows mortgage lifters but waited a whole year for the calf crop.

"Due to the long dry hot summers, the grass and browse became sparse. If there had been lots of late spring rains the old cows mite carry thru. If not they had to be brot into pastures. If you left them out there and they did survive, there'd be no calf crop. Since the brahma crossbred they survive much better.

"The winning of the west was a reality for very few. For some it was a glamorous dream enchanting them as much a state of mind with a fast horse, a long rope, and a runnin' iron. Tho more was won by another kind that stood on their own.

"Being a kid and full of you know what, I admired cowboys who stood around with one leg of their levis stuffed in their boot and their hats cocked on one side of their heads. They talked of makin money pickin up wild cows from the desert. So I made a big circle one morning early and cut for sign. I brot on home two long ears, put them in the pasture at home. I had no brand at the time as I hadn't planned on doing any stealing of calves. So pa asked me the next morning where I got them and who from. So proudly I answered they didn't belong to anyone but were mine now. He told me short and to the point to take them back where I got them and said he hoped at least someday I'd understand. If you didn't earn it, it wasn't worth haven. I did I'm proud to say.

"I recollect plainly in the early twenties a land and cattle baron had a small-time one-horse operator arrested for stealing his calves. Judge Harvey listened for a while to the pros and cons. He said he'd have to dismiss the case as all that the stealee knew about stealing and rustling the stealor had taught him. He said he could tell by the method he had used."

Warmed by her grandfather's images, Loni snuggled Coco as her thoughts drifted to Lola. Still stinging from Lola's rejection, her thoughts drifted to Maria. She ached from missing her, missing the feel of soft skin intertwining over and around her so she couldn't tell where Maria began and she left off. She missed the whispers of love in the night. Loni folded up into the fetal position and cried.

CHAPTER SIX

Loni rolled on to her side and stared. The numbers on her digital alarm clock took forever to change. By one o'clock in the morning, she decided she wasn't going to sleep anyway so she might as well get up and drive to the ranch. She'd rather be there when she got out of bed to get a good hot breakfast. The dark of night lulled her on the ride over to the ranch, and she was jarred to see a man stepping out on the road. He hailed her down, and Loni jammed on the brakes. She waited for him to come to her in the headlights? Recognizing him gave her a sense of relief. "Hey, Gerald, what's wrong?"

"Ran out of gas," he said. "Want to get that light out of my face?"

"Sorry." Loni lowered the flashlight. "Want me to take you back to your pickup and call your wife?"

Gerald hung his head. "Already did that."

"She wouldn't get out of bed?"

"Nah. She brought me a gallon of gas. I guess I was still drunk."

"What happened?'

He pulled at his hat and stared way off. "I poured the gas in her car."

"What?"

"You deef? I poured it in her car."

"What happened then?"

"She thanked me and drove off."

"She didn't come back?" Loni couldn't help laughing almost hysterically. Gerald gave Loni an exasperated glare. "Would I still be here?"

"Did you call someone else?"

Gerald dropped his head again. "Dropped my cell phone the other day, and my horse stepped on it."

"How'd you call her tonight?"

"Gene Berrington came along and called for me." He leaned against the front of her SUV. "God, I'm tired." He took off his hat and rubbed his head. "Didn't want to leave my truck to go with him. It's full of tools. Then I thought, to hell with it. Nobody would want that junk anyway. So I started walking."

Trying to be serious, Loni said, "Get in. I'll take you home."

Gerald gazed out the window. "Man, it's dark out there. Hard to know where I was walking."

"I know," Loni answered. "The moon's riding with the sun. Guess you won't be planting tonight, huh?"

Gerald glanced at her sideways and sighed. "You have no idea."

Loni let it pass. "Still live up the tracks?"

"Yep."

"How's the stockyard business doing these days?"

"Good thing people still eat beef, or I'd be on the food line." Gerald squirmed. "Had to fire two men with families today, so I got drunk."

"Did it help?"

"No, but you shoulda seen my wife's face when she watched me pour the gas in her car tank. It was almost worth it."

"I'd rather seen yours when she drove away."

Loni dropped Gerald off. He opened the back door and she heard a chorus of dogs barking. He yelled "Shad'up!" as she backed out onto the road.

Gerald was right.

Loni was drained when she pulled up in front of her grandparents' house. She sneaked inside, pushed Coco upstairs, and stripped her clothes off. Falling into bed, she was asleep almost before her head hit the pillow. Shiichoo knocked on her door before the rooster crowed. Blinking awake, Loni turned on the light by her bed and lay on her back rubbing her eyes to stay awake.

"You up?"

Loni rubbed the wet out of her eyes and groaned, pretending to complain, "Damn, Shiichoo. What if I don't want to get up?"

"Watch your mouth, child. Can't help it if you get to bed three hours before it's time to get up."

Loni struggled to work her way to a sitting position. She gratefully took the cup of coffee her grandma handed her and sipped it. As the letters on the cup came into focus, she read, "To err is human; to forgive is not my policy." Loni snorted. She gave the cup to Shiichoo years ago.

"How come it never takes long to stay all night at your house?" Loni moaned. Her grandma's laughter faded away as she left Loni to wake up. Nothing had changed in the room. She felt as if she was in a time warp. Slanted walls followed the peaked roof, leaving ten feet of walking space in the forty-foot-square room. The water stains running down the slanted walls from past storms reminded her of all the times she forgot to close the skylight windows.

Tattered and yellowed posters stapled between the skylights were left over from her high school years. Her favorite was Urshel Taylor's painting called "The Real Ira Hayes." Dressed like an Indian warrior, the World War II hero stood behind four Marines as they pushed up the American flag on Iwo Jima. Grandma had asked, "That thing legal?"

"Of course!" Loni retorted.

Snorting, Shiichoo had walked out the door. "I like mine better." Loni knew she meant the copy of Joe Rosenthal's Pulitzer Prize-winning photograph hanging downstairs on the living room wall. Same five Marines, but Ira Hayes was wearing his marine uniform.

Loni reviewed what hadn't changed. Her horse Roani was still there even though he was much older and slower. But so was she. Loni smiled wryly as she remembered how crippled she got last July when she rode him to trail the rustlers. She could barely walk for a week. Her memories moved to gentle, patient Stonewall, the ranch's Brahma bull and the favorite ride for children on the ranch. She loved watching them climb on and hang onto the yellow bull's hump as he switched his tail and flapped his plate-sized ears. She heard a crowing outside in a tree close to the open skylight. Shiichoo's beloved Banties still roosted in the trees and still crapped on her truck.

Creeping downstairs to the bathroom, Loni heard her granddad chanting. Bahb's beautiful high voice sent shivers through her, and she stopped to listen. The sound of ringing came from his tapping a beat with a spoon against his coffee cup. The beat changed when he started singing a "get up in the morning" song with enough sound effects to wake the Bantam rooster. If he hadn't been already. Loni's eyes teared from his love and warmth.

The caffeine jolt moved Loni down the hall to the bathroom. She closed the door and inspected the tired room. Everything she saw was faded and peeling. Vacated blobs of red and white striped wallpaper around the wash bowl revealed the original pink paint beneath it. While she peed, she reached with closed eyes for the toilet paper which wasn't there. She opened her eyes and finally found it on a shelf behind her, stacked so high the rest toppled all over the floor when she pulled a roll out. Exasperated, she rolled her eyes toward the ceiling only to find Geronimo's stoic portrait glaring down at her. Double crap.

Rust stains streaked the washbowl, toilet bowl, and bathtub. Loni retrieved the toilet rolls and pushed aside the yellowed, cracked shower curtain. She turned the water to cold, and stepped in. The cracks she felt on the bottom of her feet might be leaking, dry-rotting everything underneath. She'd better fix it, she decided, as soon as she had time. The sour-smelling, discolored water stayed lukewarm. Loni reflected on the times she cleaned dead birds and insects out of the water tank and wondered if she should check the last time the water tank was cleaned. Or maybe not. She didn't stay in the shower long. The air was so dry there was no need for a towel. By the time she started dressing, her body was already dry.

Images of the disgusting things that had crawled into the water tank made dressing difficult. First she put her pants on backwards. She forgot about socks. She couldn't figure out why her boots wouldn't pull on. Her gun belt felt heavier than usual on her shoulder. One last check, and she knew where she'd make the next repairs.

Breakfast was on the table when Loni followed her granddad's singing into the kitchen. The new song about lost love was so sad Loni briefly froze before she quietly hung her gun holster on the hat rack at the back door. At the table, she played with her fork as she studied her granddad's brown smooth face.

"What's the song's name? I don't remember it."

"Old song I learned as a child. Something like 'I'm sad your dog ate my cat.'"

Loni eyeballed Bahb waiting for the small wry grin on his bronze face. "Come on! You didn't even have cats."

"Bobcat. I found a baby."

"You made a pet out of it?"

"Easy to pet if you don't mind bites and scratches. Hard to catch though."

Loni quipped. "That's because it thought you were going to eat it."

The small grin was back on Bahb's face. "Probably."

"Eat!" her grandma demanded. "And no talk about eating dead dogs and cats at the table."

"Which reminds me," Loni said to her grandma. "Heard Janey Henry had her baby."

"A little girl. So?

Loni joked. "Heard all she craved was road kill."

"Enough! Eat!"

Loni ducked her head and stuffed her mouth a few minutes, loving her grandma's egg and prickly pear scramble. "Bahb? You hear Old Man Wampas died?"

"Yi."

"They found him sitting against a tree, reading glasses in his hand, like he peacefully went to sleep."

"Yi. Death should be easy." Bahb ate a few bites, smiling at a memory. "He was a second world war German prisoner of war who stayed. I remember he started all his sentences with 'Dot Damn!'"

"And answered any question with 'Ya, by Gott.' Remember the time he was talking to JimBob? Wampas talked about fishing at the same time JimBob talked about working?"

Bahb added. "They both deaf as a post. Thought they talking about the same thing."

"Which reminds me." Shiichoo turned to Loni. "When you get back, bring me up a sack of saguaro cactus fruit from the barn. We're getting low on wine."

"I can't help you make wine. It's illegal!" Loni insisted.

"Okay then. I'm making cactus candy."

"Okay then." Loni reluctantly replied as she stood and took her empty plate to the sink. "So, Bahb?" Loni rinsed her plate. "You gonna let me dance with you at the wine dance?"

"What was that jab about breaking the law?"

"Didn't say I was going to drink the wine. Thought I'd enjoy a dance."

"I'll drink your share."

"It would be good time to remove last summer's evil from around you Loni," Bahb said quietly. "Your chief of police was a truly evil man."

"How did he hide it for so many years?" Shiichoo wondered in an equally hushed voice. "Never saw him around much after work."

Bahb took his plate to the sink and rinsed it. "Evil thrives in dark."

Loni thought about her granddad's remark as she followed him to the sink with her plate.

Bahb grabbed his hat off the rack. "Time to go. Be a hundred degrees out there. Hard on the horses."

Loni winced. What about me? she thought. She turned to grab her gun.

Shiichoo made a tsking sound as she watched Loni put the gun holster across her chest. "Talk about evil."

"I know."

"Wearing that makes you careless. I want you to be more careful."

"What's the fun in that?" Loni teased Shiichoo.

Shiichoo swatted Loni out the door. A pitiful brown face stared hopefully up at her. "Stay, Coco," Loni ordered before she followed her granddad and Willie into the dark. She envied their easy movements and wished for their night sight as she stumbled across the yard. Near the ancient pickup, she hit her knee on the horse trailer hitched behind it. "Shit, Bahb. Wish you'd pick up after yourself. Where'd this come from anyway?" She heard her granddad's low laugh as she felt her way up to the pickup door. The horses waiting in the trailer stomped and swished their tails. Buck softly whinnied.

Loni groaned as she climbed into the seat beside Willie. "What time did you get up, anyway?"

Bahb didn't answer as he started the ancient GMC. It coughed and shuddered. Loni tried to buy him a new pickup a few months back, but he refused. "I barely able fix this," he balked. "I not understand electronic things."

Loni had forgotten about the bailing wire needed to keep the door shut, and it bounced open. She didn't even ask how to close the window. Both the handle and glass were gone.

Bahb pulled out of the driveway, and the horse trailer jerked the pickup a few times before it settled in. They bumped along the ruts left from years of tires banging and tilting along the desert road. Loni clenched her teeth and held on tight as worn-out shocks nearly jarred her off her seat. The inside of the old pickup gave off heat from the prior day's burning sun, but the dry breeze through the open window waffled cool on her sweating face.

The pickup's bouncing headlights mesmerized Loni. Shiny leaves from the greasewood danced in the reflection. After they spent several silent miles, small shards of light from a windmill silhouette in the dawn haze joined the headlights. The black of night changed to pink dawn by the time they pulled under an ironwood tree and unloaded the horses. "I love this tank," Loni said, thinking about all the wildlife counting on it for survival. A handful spurt of water out of a spigot splashed into a small pond with every up and down evolution of the well rod attached to the slow spinning fan reaching into the sky. A road runner shot in front of the horses and spooked Loni's horse. She had to shove him around, and he huffed against the tightening of the cinch and chomped on the bit. "Don't say it!"

Willie said it anyway. "Get the cinch tight or you be riding upside down under his belly."

The windmill squawked, and the saddles creaked as they silently mounted and turned their horses north. Loni broke the quiet, complaining, "How come it's still so hot, Bahb? You forget to say your prayers?"

Bahb studied her a few seconds. "If I say prayer, it be for you. You keep slouching in the saddle that horse dump you."

Loni sat up straight as the horse crow-hopped, and she almost lost her seat. Roani limped yesterday so her granddad had saddled her a horse she didn't know, a pretty Appaloosa. Before she got on, she thought his long legs would make him fun to ride, but she couldn't get him into a rolling walk. There was no way to relax with his jaw-breaking trot. "You could of warned me about this horse. Where'd you get him, anyway?"

"It's Carl's horse. Good cutter."

"Hope so. He's not worth a shit to ride. What's its name anyway?"

"Jarhead."

"Figures."

Bahb turned his head away but not before Loni caught his slight smile. He guided his horse down a sharp incline, hoofs kicking loose rocks. Her horse skittered as she followed him to the bottom of a wash. When the sliding, side-walking horse headed for a wait-a-minute bush, she hollered, "No, you don't!" She pulled his head away from the bush during the horse's downward rush. "You are NOT piling me in that thing."

Willie's grin was bigger than Bahb's. He waited until she got the horse under control and they rode side-by-side in the wide wash. Loni nervously babbled. "Should have been named Shithead," she said to the horse. "Bahb?" Loni turned to her granddad. "How'd you end up in this country?"

"After school came down here to work. My ma from O'odham reservation. She had brother maybe help me, but I never found him. Your grandfather Ben Wagner gave me job breaking horses and a nice place for Shiichoo and your mother." He stopped talking as they climbed out and around a long drop that would make a beautiful waterfall during the next rain. Dropping back into the wash, Bahb continued. "I broke many horses for ranches around here." Loni watched him remember. "He good man, Ben Wagner. Took your ma in as his own when your dad marry her."

"How'd you end up half Navajo and half Papago?"

Willie frowned at her. "How many times I tell you how I hate the name Papago."

Loni turned to her granddad, "Do you hate it?"

"Na. Sounds better than Pima," Bahb teased Willie.

Willie grumped. "Most O'odham people don't like being called bean eater."

"Fine. Half Pima?"

Bahb shrugged. "My ma tell different story every time she drunk. I don't know which true."

"What do you think?"

"One I like best is how my pa save ma during a raid against the cavalry. They had a young Pima girl with them as they rode into Navajo country where my pa ran into their camp. Pa snuck in and grabbed my ma and he took her back to O'odham land. She fell in love on the way back to her home and wouldn't leave him." The only sound for a few minutes was the plod of the horses' hoofs scrunching against the dry white sand. The mountains were still purple with the dawn, but the rising sun was already hot on their backs. "He got kicked in the head by a bad horse. When the government came to take children to boarding schools, she ran with me."

"How old were you?"

"Maybe ten. I do not know when I was born."

"Where'd she take you then?"

Bahb turned Buck and climbed out of the wash. The chestnut horse's four white legs flashed as he crow-hopped a few steps before her granddad settled him down again. "Willie. You circle that way." Bahb pointed to his left. "Loni. You go other way. Meet me back at the tank."

"When?" Loni hollered at his back. Her granddad shrugged, and she hollered at him again. "You don't want to paint this afternoon."

He waved at her without turning around and disappeared into the giant saguaro cactus forest thickly scattering the hill.

Loni liked being alone, especially on the desert. When she was young and everything seemed too hard for her, she'd saddle Roani and ride for hours. The desert always smelled good in the early morning before the wind kicked up the dust. She took several deep breaths as she followed the south-leaning barrel cactus to maintain her circle. Carefully avoiding the jumping cactus patches in her path, she searched for cow tracks.

Two hours and three sightings later, she was retracing her trail when suddenly she jerked her horse away from her granddad's horse running straight at them. He was bucking and throwing a hind leg out behind him in his headlong rush past her. "Oh, my god!" Loni froze a few seconds. "He's been snake bit!" She turned her horse onto Bahb's trail. "Bahb!" She drove her horse into a run, rushing dangerously along the edge of a canyon in her frantic search. "Bahb!" she cried into the wind.

Loni forced herself to calm down and pay attention. She climbed down from her horse and began tracking. Buck's hoofed shoes had dug deep in his frantic running and kicking. Loni pulled her reluctant horse behind her into a thin wash as she screamed for her granddad. She intermittently stopped and listened, praying for a faint reply. Nothing answered her except for the sad "coo coo" from a mourning dove in a mesquite tree. Her panic mounted. Please don't be dead, Bahb!

An hour later Loni trailed along a stock path leading high up on the side of a black rocky hill dangerously steep and narrow. She tripped over a huge diamondback rattlesnake with its head smashed and flattened. "Bahb!" Loni cried out. "Where are you?"

"Here," came the subdued answer. Loni rushed around a huge outcropping jutting out from the side of the hill. Bahb was sitting in the shade under a ledge. A scalp wound left dried blood down the side of his face. "Rattlesnake got Buck," he said in greeting. "He fell back on me, broke my leg."

"Oh, shit!" Loni kneeled by him. "We've got to get you home!" She spun around as her eyes frantically leaped around.

"Calm down, Loni."

Stunned by his sharp tone, Loni squatted back and took a deep breath. "I'm okay."

"Good. Find two sticks." Bahb's tone went back to normal.

Finding them and binding them to his leg was easy. Getting him on the tall horse wasn't. "What I wouldn't give for a squatty desert broomtail right now." Loni grunted. She pushed her granddad onto the saddle until he settled in. "What do you think? You want your foot in the stirrup? Maybe tie your leg to the fender?"

Grunting, he shook his head. "We just get."

Loni climbed on behind Bahb as Jarhead flattened his ears in displeasure. He turned his head back to stare at her. She kept her legs out of Bahb's way, and they began a slow trek back to the tank. Loni knew he had to be in pain from the jostling of the horse, but his quiet voice didn't reflect his misery. "You find any mother cows?"

"No. I ran across Willie though. Said he found old Bossy. She had two heifers with her. They looked good."

"Yi. Bossy's youngins, Rain, and Jiggers."

Loni tried to keep him from thinking about his leg. "Let me guess. Rain was born on a rainy day. How come Jiggers?"

"That's Willie's name. Bossy had a hard time, calf badly twisted in birthing. When Russell sees the calf born he said, 'By Jiggers. It lives!' Willie thought it was funny."

"You find anything?"

"Yi, up on north canyon. They were also good, lovin' last thunderhead brought up six-week grass."

They didn't stumble into the tank area until late morning. Willie was waiting, but Buck was still missing. Willie loaded the two horses as Loni carefully placed her granddad in the bed of the pickup and continued her mindless chatter. "Damn, Bahb. Don't you think you went too far to get out of painting this afternoon?" He gave her a wry, pained smile.

Willie stayed in the back to hold Bahb as she carefully drove them home, hurting for Bahb. She fought the jerking of the horse trailer banging against the hitch of the pickup every time they hit a pothole. The springs squawked as they bounced along in the ruts of the dusty tracks. By the time they pulled up into the yard, Loni was soaked in sweat from worry and fear.

"Shiichoo!" Loni hollered as she bailed from the pickup. She quickly unloaded the two horses and handed the reins to Shiichoo as she hurried around to unhitch the trailer from the pickup. "Bahb broke his leg and I've got to get him to the clinic."

"Watch out for Buck," Bahb warned Shiichoo as she fussed around him. "If he shows up, he'll be in bad shape."

In the clinic waiting room, Loni worried about Bahb and silently thanked the old pickup for making it to the clinic. Even wide open, it didn't go over forty miles an hour. Her own truck could have made it faster, but he couldn't climb into her tall cab.

Loni relaxed as her granddad rolled out of the emergency room. His Levis were in his lap. One leg was covered with a fluorescent purple cast, and the other skinny leg was partly covered with his boot. She listened to her granddad complain about the cutting of his good boot off his foot as Willie loaded Bahb into his old pickup. Loni hurried back into the clinic office to call her grandma. "Shiichoo? We're on our way home now. Wait 'til you see his beautiful purple cast!"

A crowd of people surrounded Shiichoo as the pickup pulled into the ranch house's driveway. Bahb bellyached as Russell opened the door and picked up him like a baby. Shiichoo fluttered around them like one of her old bantam hens. Everybody else on the ranch followed them into the house. Russell's three children hid shyly behind his wife's skirt. Loni left Russell and her grandma to deal with Bahb's fussy complaints while she called Carl. "Bahb broke his leg."

"Oh, god! Is he alright?"

"He's fine now. Got a ranch full of people to wait on him. But I need help finding his horse. Buck's got a rattlesnake bite and still has a saddle on."

"You want me to come help you?"

"Yeah, I would. It'll be light enough for several more hours. I need to find that horse. I'll even saddle up your old cutting horse for you."

Carl laughed. "I'm not riding that bone-breaking nag."

"Fine. You can have Tubby."

"Shiichoo got any tamales?"

"All you want."

"Okay, I'll be there as fast as I can."

The horses were loaded in the trailer when Carl drove in. "Shiichoo's tamales are waiting for you."

Carl's trot said it all as he hurried into the house. Loni sat with the motor running. Carl came back out with a fist full of tamales.

"Bahb looks good." he said as he jumped into the moving pickup. "What the . . .?" Carl tried to slam the door shut again.

Willie leaned across him. "Door lock's broken. Tie the baling wire like this."

Carl warned Loni off the tamales he put on the dash so he could wire the door shut. "I forgot about this part of ranching." Carl groaned. He unwrapped the husk of a tamale. "You know what actually won the West, don't you? Baling wire, that's what. Back in the day it fixed anything." Carl stuffed his mouth full and talked around the food. "And a good tamale." He was already unwrapping a second one before he swallowed the one in his mouth. "Damn, these are good!" Carl stuffed a third one in his mouth before he was ready to talk again. "You got a plan?"

"I think so. He was running south toward the ranch."

"Sure. He'd try to get home if he could."

"We can unload at the tank. I'll ride up toward the place where Buck and I crossed trails and try to find his tracks. You go west a few miles and turn south. Willie, you go east. That way we'll make sure to cross his tracks if he kept on south toward the ranch."

"Sounds good. How about you shoot once if you find his tracks and twice if you find him. We'll do the same."

Loni sighed. "Bahb needs us to bring Buck home."

"How come you pronounce your granddad's name so it sounds like baaab?"

"It means grandfather in Pima."

"Damn. And after all these years I thought his name was Bob."

Loni smiled. "He won't tell anyone his real name. Left over from the early days. He always says the less people know his name the less they can hurt him."

"What does he sign on papers?"

"He doesn't. Uncle Herm always signs any papers dealing with the ranch."

"What about his driver's license?"

"What driver's license?"

"Come on," Carl said in disbelief. "So what is his real name?"

"Estalote Bisupanni."

"Wow. You're right. Bahb's much better." Carl laughed. "I love Bahb's old ways. They make total sense to me."

"You know, Carl? You never told me why you didn't stay on the ranch."

"Lots of reasons. I went into the military right out of high school, and they trained me in military police work, mainly at crime scenes. I really liked it. And the wife wanted to live in town. After my dad died and I had to come home to help my mom, I hired cowboys to take care of the ranch while I tried to fix things around the ranch and figure out what to do."

Loni glanced over and saw Carl pulling on his ear as he talked. "My mom faded fast without my dad and followed him within two months. There was nothing I could do." He sat a few minutes in silence. "I took the detective job even though I hated Chief. About that time, the O'Neal's came along and gave me a long-term lease with an option to buy. At fifty thousand dollars a year, it was too good to pass up."

Loni whistled. "Wow! That's more than two year's profit if you're lucky."

Carl grinned at Loni. "Tell me about it. I thought I'd won the lottery."

"But you never suspected them of drug deals?"

"No. I researched the company they represented, and it was legit. They did sell exotic plants and castor bean seedlings. It wasn't all they sold." Carl rubbed his face in embarrassment. "I also had no idea they were going to brutally murder my boss. I admit Chief was pretty worthless, but nobody deserved what he got."

"I'm not so sure." Loni argued. "He was one sick pedophile son-of-a-bitch."

"That he was."

"You know, Carl, I liked Jenny. She seemed to care about her students."

"The kids said she was a great art teacher. I'll give her that. But to kill Chief the way she did?" Carl adamantly declared in disbelief.

"I don't know, Carl. If somebody raped me continually for years, blamed my father for the deed and put him in prison, 'caused my mother's suicide because she believed her husband raped me, and turned my brother into a crackhead, I'd have killed him, too."

"I don't care what her reason was. Murder is murder."

Loni didn't answer. She concentrated on maneuvering the trailer around the water tank. They unloaded the horses, and Loni trotted off north. Nearly a half-hour later she found Buck's track and fired one shot. She turned back south to follow three hoof prints. After another hour, the trail led her on down into a deep wash where she found him shaking under a tree. She fired her gun twice and slowly led him back to the road where Carl and Willie appeared with the pickup and horse trailer. "I heard your first shot. I knew you'd find him so I rode on back to get the trailer."

"Smart. Thanks."

They didn't get to the ranch until dark. Tori Watts, the veterinarian, was waiting for them.

Loni parked inside the hangar, turned off the motor, and climbed down with Coco behind her. She waited for Coco in the settling dark. The silence was ominous. There was no banging, no yelling for something, no sound anywhere. The moon was still chasing the sun early in the morning eastern sky, and she missed its soothing night glow. A coyote yipping in the distance shooed Coco back to her. Loni climbed the stairs, hearing Coco's huffs as she shot up ahead of her.

A bowl of Shiichoo's menudo her grandmother sent home with her filled Loni's stomach. She settled on the bed with Coco and disappeared into another of Grandmother Wagner's stories.

"You ready, Coco?"

The dog wuffed.

"We lost my brothers in the war. Papa followed in 1930. A molting sidewinder struck Chips high up his hind leg and he went crazy, falling backwards onto papa. We think he died instantly."

Loni stopped reading a few seconds. "Wow. I'm so glad Bahb's accident wasn't worse."

"I think papa was still grieving and got careless. Chips made it home but we were never able to work him again because the muscles in his leg rotted and left him limping badly. Mama followed papa in 1935 from pneumonia but I think it was from a broken heart. She missed papa so.

"I remember Papa telling me about the first automobile he ever saw, how his older brother Axal grabbed his sister and ran into the house pulling her under the bed with him and later his dad said how he wished Axal had stayed afraid. But Papa said he stood his ground. Told me how he thought it was a marvel but it'd never replace the horse. O' course it did. Still, I will never forget the wonderful horses we had over the years such as Blind Babe, my mother's favorite horse.

"I was always in Papa's shadow. Wherever he was I was mighty close at hand. One moonlight night we were sitting beneath the arbor. I didn't hear one sound and out of the shadows came a tall man, his curly hair in disarray and eyes big and frightened. He said, 'Vic, I need a horse real bad. I will turn it loose when I get to the hills.' They were life-long friends. My dad never asked one question. Papa said, 'You'd better take Babe. She's fast and will come back.' They forgot about me, but I tagged along and watched him leave. Papa said, 'Mary. This is something we don't talk about to anyone.' I didn't though I was about to burst when mama missed her mare.

"In about a week Babe came back. She was gaunt and thinner. She must have gotten to cold water after the hard ride because her eyes filmed and she was blind. We kept her for years and mama drove her in a cart. She drove by reverse signals. To go was to pick up the reins; to stop was when you threw them down. Nothing frightened her.

"Several years after that incident we had a visitor. It was the same friend who rode Babe that night. Papa and he talked of many things, of cattle and horses, local gossip.

"Vic said, 'I guess I better tell you. I haven't got the trouble now. I was cleared as it was self-defense. I gave myself up. Better let a man kill you than kill him, but you never forget his eyes as he is dying.' He had gotten to San Diego and came back. It was a knife fight over his wife. I hung on the back of my dad's chair and cried I was so sorry for him. Papa noticed I was there and sent me to bed.

"I was such a spoiled brat but I am proud I never told about Babe, even to my brother and he was my pal. I made up my mind I'd never kill anyone. So far I haven't though there have been occasions that seemed suitable. Why do big brown eyes leave such lasting impressions? And pale, certain shade of blue killer eyes send chills down my back."

Dropping the notebook back into the box beside the bed, Loni snuggled next to Coco, grateful for the warmth, and fell into a deep sleep. Coco's low growl startled her when the phone buzzed. "What?" she snarled into it.

"Hey Loni, you there?"

"We've got to quit meeting like this, Bobby."

He tittered a few seconds before he got serious. "Domestic at Hamilton Ranch. Three miles up Highway 88. You can —"

"I know where it is, Bobby. How come you didn't call James? Isn't he on duty tonight?"

"James had to go to Phoenix a few days. Anyway, some woman's holding a gun on her husband. You're the only one trained around here with hostage cases."

"Have I ever told you how much I hate domestics?"

"I think I heard you say it a time or two."

"Who's the woman?"

"Caller didn't say."

"Who called it in?"

"Wouldn't say. Man's voice, though. Sounded pretty scared."

Loni spun away from the hangar and turned north as fast as her truck could go. She hung onto Coco, longing for a police car that was safe over sixty-five miles per hour. She pulled into a circular driveway as quiet as possible and stopped behind a dark green pickup. An empty gun rack hung in the back window. She slid out of her truck and left the door open. Signaling Coco into attack readiness, she headed toward the old farmhouse. So far everything was quiet, not even a barking dog. What farm doesn't have a dog?

As Loni entered the shadows along the house, she heard a gunshot followed by the sound of breaking glass. She ducked and signaled Coco to stay behind her. Pulling her gun, she peeked inside a window. Chelsea Taylor was waving a forty-four-caliber Magnum toward a man rolled into a ball on the floor. He tried to squeeze behind a beige recliner, and Chelsea yelled over and over, "Are you happy now? Are you happy now?"

The man was so doubled up on the floor Loni couldn't understand what he was saying.

"You took everything!" Chelsea screamed at him. "Are you happy now?"

Loni peered through a small yellow triangle in the stained-glass door and gave a hard knock, hoping to refocus Chelsea. "Police! Put the gun down!"

Chelsea waved the gun and gave the man a kick. "Cops are here! Are you happy now?" The man muttered. "You called." Chelsea kicked him again. "You answer the goddamned door and explain to James what a bastard you really are." She waved the revolver at the door, pointing it straight at Loni.

"Shit!" Loni stepped sideways and ducked, waiting for another gunshot. She reached back to the door and knocked again. "Hello, the house," she shouted. "Can I come in?"

"Oh, hell, why not?" Chelsea sputtered and jerked the door wide open. She slammed it so hard against the wall the doorknob broke through the sheetrock. "Welcome to hell," she greeted Loni as she lowered the gun. "It's where all the losers live." She followed with a strange keening sound. Turning her back, she walked to the dining room table, lay the gun down, and slumped in a chair. Chelsea was barefoot and wore faded baby-doll pajamas with frayed lace around the neck and short sleeves. "He took my children," she hiccupped before a sob. "Took them to my miserable bitch of a mother-in-law."

Loni leaned over the man and recognized Brad Taylor. "Are you hurt?" He shook his head, and Loni helped him to his feet. She didn't see any blood. Loni picked up Chelsea's gun and unloaded it. She held the bullets in her hand as she waited for the sobs to lessen. "Hey," Loni asked Brad. "Does she have anyone she can stay with?"

"I'm not going anywhere! This is my home," Chelsea injected.

"Why don't you call your bitch girlfriend," Brad sneered, sketching angry quotes in the air around the word girlfriend. "She's welcome to you."

Oh, shit, Loni thought as she turned to Brad. "Where do you live?"

"Over Sunnyslope way. I came as soon as I heard about her girlfriend."

Chelsea sobbed as she repeated, "Are you happy now?"

"Listen, slut." Brad moved toward her.

Loni stepped in front of him. She'd forgotten how thick he was. Not tall, but bulky. A dark, two-day beard covered his angry face. She could smell the fear sweat coating him. "You better go on home now. It's late, and you got a ways to go." Loni laid a hand on his chest, holding him back.

"No, by god." He knocked her arm away. "I came after their things, and I'm not leaving without them."

Suddenly Coco was between them, snarling.

"Yes, you are." Loni settled her hand on the butt of her gun.

His eyes jerked back and forth between the gun and the dog as he backed through the door. Coco followed. "Wait a damn minute," Brad insisted. "Where's James?" He stumbled off the stoop and caught the handrail to stop his fall. When he straightened back up, his face was dark with fury. "Who the hell are you?" he snarled. "I didn't ask for you!"

Good, Loni thought, signaling Coco to back off as she moved into his space and eased him toward his pickup. Too dark now to read her name tag. If he didn't see her dimples. Don't smile. "How did you manage to call the police?"

"She dialed nine-one-one and tossed her cell at me. She said, 'Why don't you get James here. Maybe he'll shoot me for you.' So I did." He held up the cell phone in his hand.

Loni reached out. "I'll return it for you." Brad reluctantly handed the phone to her, and she pocketed it. "Do you have any weapons with you?" She opened his pickup door for him.

"No," he said. "What the hell is that?" He frowned at Coco.

"Your worst nightmare," she said, "if you threaten me again." Coco stood like a statue, her golden wolf-like eyes following his every move. Loni flashed the light beam under and behind the seat and in the cubbyhole. "Don't come back here tonight," she warned. She watched the pickup pull out into the road and head north before she returned inside the house.

The early American furnishings weren't to her taste, but the earth tones reflected comfort. Chelsea sat at the table, her head still buried in her arms. Loni sat down beside her. "Chelsea, what's going on?"

Chelsea wiped away her tears. "He said his lawyer told him he had a legal right to the kids because of my immoral behavior." Her voice was hoarse from crying.

"Who's got custody?"

"I do. He's an abusive sonofabitch." She lowered her head again, wiping more tears on the hem of the red checkered table cloth, leaving dark splotches. "I took it until he hit the kids. We're divorced over a year now." She swallowed a sob. "How can he walk in and take them?"

"He can't," Loni explained. "Same-sex relationships are legal. Lesbians can even get married now. His lawyer is either totally ignorant, or your ex bamboozled you."

She scrutinized Loni with faint hope in her eyes. "What does that mean?"

"It means you can live with your girlfriend and your kids in the same house, and there's nothing anyone can do about it."

"My restraining order is still good?"

"You have a restraining order on him?"

"He keeps threatening us. Shooting guns over the house. Swearing at me on the street. Following the kids, telling them I'm a dyke. I had to protect them."

"You're sure they're at his mother's?"

Chelsea snorted. "He doesn't want to care for them. Too cheap to pay."

"Who's your girlfriend?"

"Lu Staford. She's a paramedic."

"Sure. I know her. How long have you been with Lu?"

"Eight weeks yesterday."

"Your first girlfriend?"

Chelsea lifted her chin. "Is it a problem?"

"Is it serious?

"It is with me."

"Can Lu come over tonight?" Loni said softly.

"No. She's on call the next three nights."

"Have you talked to her about this?

"No. I was afraid she'd go after my ex and get in trouble."

"I know Lu. You might be right."

"Can I call her?"

"Sure." Loni placed a hand on her arm to get her attention. "But right now you need to listen to me. First thing in the morning, this is what you're going to do. You hear me?"

Loni waited Chelsea out through another bout of tears before she said. "At eight o'clock, I want you to take your custody papers and restraining order and go to the station and find Lola. Nobody else, do you understand?" Loni got another nod.

"Tell her to help you fill out a warrant. Tell her your ex-husband violated his restraining order and kidnapped your children, and you want them back. Are you with me?" Another nod. "Tell Lola to call me as soon as she gets the judge to sign, and I'll pick up the warrant and serve it. If all goes well, your kids will be home before noon."

"Are you shitting me?"

"No. Cross my heart."

Chelsea threw her arms around Loni, leaving tears on her collar. It took a few minutes to untangle from her. "Last thing," Loni said as she walked out the door. "Tell Lu to bring a U-Haul." At the woman's quizzical expression, Loni said, "She'll know what I mean."

Bobby's voice interrupted Loni's musings on Chelsea's joy. "It's done, Bobby. I sent the stupid ex-husband on his way. I'm on my way back home."

"Whoa there, you're not done yet."

"What?" she snapped at Bobby. She was desperate to get home to bed.

"I got a domestic at the Carter ranch. Off Wilson Road."

"Jeez. Two domestics in one night."

Bobby giggled. "How lucky is that?" He signed off still giggling.

Loni didn't even bother with a retort. She was too used up from her adrenaline high.

Turning around, she headed back up Harquah Hills Road toward a clump of buildings in the distance where a windmill slowly turned. The ranch sat on the north side up against a black hill to take advantage of the shade. The large main house was surrounded by three smaller ones where the hired help lived. Her favorite barn was behind the house. Its weathered red was almost rust-colored from years of heat and dust storm sand blasting. Standing majestic high, its twelve-to-one peaked roof had a pointed overhang with a pulley and ropes hanging into the large hay door. Below the hay door were the huge double sliding doors. One stood open, and a small backhoe sat in the opening. Loni wasn't sure whether it was coming or going. Limbs from mesquite trees formed a large corral on the back of the barn.

The main house was a fifties single-story ranch in a U shape. A few tired pomegranate bushes lined the rock walkway into the house. Surrounding the buildings were dusty, dry salt cedars.

She knew the people who lived there. Danny Carter was an energetic, hardworking man with a funny, highly volatile wife. She was a year ahead of Loni in school. They weren't exactly friends, but they still hung out together in study hall and the gym, sometimes catching each other's back against the rule-makers. They shared books, dirty jokes, and test answers. Loni hoped the call wasn't anything serious. Danny answered Loni's knock on the door and dragged Loni inside. He pointed at the floor. "Look! I want you to arrest the bitch."

"Hello to you too, Danny. How the hell are you?" She stared around at the scattered dirty clothes. "Where is Juanita?" Nothing else seemed to be out of order. Nothing on the tops of furniture but the usual lamps and clean ashtrays. Loni studied Danny. "What I see is dirty clothes all over the floor. Anything I'm missing besides Juanita?"

"Look!" Danny sputtered, pointing at the clothes. "She did this."

"Why don't you pick them up? They're yours, aren't they?"

"Are you that stupid? Look!" He pulled on a pair of Levis. They wouldn't budge. "They're nailed to the goddamned floor! The crazy bitch nailed my clothes to the floor and ran home to her mama!" Pacing and kicking at the dirty clothes, Danny worked himself up into a rant.

Loni fought a giggle. "Can I ask why?"

"She got tired of me stripping and dropping everything when I came in."

"Let me make sure I understand this. As soon as you hit the door, you start undressing and dropping clothes?"

"So? What's wrong with that? It's what I've always done."

Loni let it one go. "How long has she been doing this?"

"Four days."

"She's been nailing your clothes to the floor for four days?"

"Yeah. I'm about to run out."

"Yep." Loni counted. "Four Levis and four shirts. Four briefs. Eight socks." Loni had to tell him. "Danny, you know I can't arrest Juanita for this. But what I can do is save you the embarrassment by not writing up a report."

For the first time, Danny stopped and stared at her. "Loni? Is that you?"

"Yeah, Danny, it's me."

"You left for California twenty years ago. What are you doing back here?"

Loni corrected him, "It was only ten years, Danny."

"Heard you became a big-shot detective out there. Why'd you come back here?"

"My grandma had a stroke. Had to be here for her and my granddad."

"Life's a bitch, ain't it." He walked over to the door and opened it for Loni. "I'd appreciate it if you forgot about this." Danny ducked his head. "Not one of my better moments, huh?"

"Done, Danny." Loni punched his arm as she stared at the clothes nailed to the floor. "Got to admit, though. Juanita always was damned creative."

"Bye, Loni." He slammed the door in her face, and she drove away, still feeling good.

CHAPTER SEVEN

An hour later, Loni flopped into her chair and leaned back with her eyes closed. Her arms limply hung down at her side. "I am so glad to be back to work! This weekend was godawful," she said into the space. A few silent minutes passed before she opened her eyes and saw Junior staring at her. She closed her eyes again and muttered, "Maybe not."

Lola's voice was soft and sympathetic. "I heard about the Barclay boy. Carl's over there now."

Loni slumped forward over her desk and rested her head in her hands. "This time I'm glad it's not me telling them," she mumbled through her fingers. "Chelsea show up yet?"

"She's already come and gone. I gave her request to Judge Sal's clerk for the judge to sign. Tomas said he'd get it to her after the next hearing." Lola waited a beat. "So what'd you find out about Manny?"

Loni sat up in her chair. "I've got an appointment with the arresting officer Friday morning."

"Friday!" Lola's voice jumped several decibels. You're going to wait until Friday?"

"He wouldn't see me any sooner."

The morning dragged on and on. Lola huffed at her, Junior glared, and James was gone to testify in court. Loni tried to work through her old notes on last summer's drug bust until she admitted there was nothing to find. She stood and stretched before she wandered into Carl's office.

Carl jerked his head up with a startled expression when Loni knocked on his desk. "What the hell, Loni! Don't you know a door is to knock on?"

Loni pulled out the uncomfortable chair and sat. "Listen Carl. I've spent hours going over my notes and found absolutely nothing. I don't know where else to look."

"What are you going to do?"

"Wish I knew."

"Okay. Give the files to Junior for a few days. Maybe he can see something with fresh eyes." Carl leaned back and grinned. "At the least it should keep him busy and out of trouble."

Cold day in hell, Loni thought as she went back out to Lola's desk. "Lola, you know where Junior went?"

"No!" was her curt answer.

Loni gathered her files and stacked them on the edge of Junior's desk. With a feeling of satisfaction, she wandered back to her desk. She picked up a book and stepped back to Lola's desk. "Do you do any computer work with the Apache Web Server program? Or know anyone who does?"

"No. Why should I?"

"Maria's sister in LA ordered this book online and sent it to me for my birthday. She thought it would help me learn to cook with Shiichoo." Loni showed Lola *The Apache Cookbook*. "But when you open it up, it explains how to get the most out of an Apache computer language."

Lola broke up as she flipped through the book. She put her head down and pounded the desk.

"It's not funny!"

"Yes, it is." Lola handed the book back, swallowing her laughter. "It's a classic. Have you told Maria's sister yet?"

"I don't think she'll find it as funny as you do." By now Loni was laughing too.

Lola shook her head, and her dark red curly hair cascaded down her back. "You end up in the weirdest situations."

"Wasn't all me. Most of them Chief got me into."

"True. At least things are different from the first day you walked in here. Do you remember?"

"How could I forget? The first thing Chief said when I walked into his office was 'Holy shit, you're a girl!' He got up and left me sitting there."

Lola chuckled. "When he came out of his office and asked why I didn't tell him you were a girl, I thought he was going to fire me on the spot."

"The longer I sat there waiting for him to come back, the more I knew I was in deep shit. Especially after I read the framed posters on his wall. I can still quote his favorite saying. 'Women are as useless as rubber lips on a woodpecker.'" Loni added, "You know what? I know you've got my back, and I'm glad Chief didn't fire you for helping me."

Lola leaned over and hugged Loni.

Loni hugged her back in relief. "I'm working on Manny's case the best I can, I promise." She felt Lola's warm breath as she said softly, "I'm sorry I'm so worried."

Lola fit into Loni as though she's always been there. She felt so good, Loni wanted to hang on forever. Before she could draw Lola closer, she was jerked around and slammed into the wall. "You don't touch her, you freak." Junior bellowed at her.

"Damn it, Junior," Lola yelled at him. "Leave her alone! You sound like my bastard of an ex-husband."

"Heck, Lola. You don't want anyone thinking you're queer, do you?"

"Junior." Lola pointed her index finger at him. "It's none of your business what I am. Get out of my sight and make a few rounds around town until you decide to behave."

Junior stared at her until she yelled, "Out! Now!"

Pleased, Loni watched him leave. "When Junior comes back, tell him the stack of files is from Carl." Loni smirked. "And tell him the key to solving our newest cocaine problem is in those files, but Carl said I was too dumb to find it."

Loni took Coco outside for her usual morning sniffing around, reading her doggy newspaper. She leaned against a wall and watched a young girl knocking on the door to the police station. Her round face, almond shaped eyes, and the chocolate-colored skin of a Pima. Loni reached around her for the buzzer. She pulled the door open and asked for the girl's name. "Como se llama?"

The tiny girl shook her head. Loni couldn't guess her age. Her clean, full-skirted dress was yellow with large red polka dots, and her rubber flip-flops were covered with sequins. She hesitated to enter, and her eyes darted around the room.

"Por favor, entra." Loni turned toward Lola behind the booking counter. "Lola le ayudara."

The girl slowly followed Loni up to the desk.

"Hey Lola. She won't talk to me. Maybe she'll tell you what she wants."

Loni walked back to her desk and sat. Lola's soothing voice tried to comfort the girl who was frantically trying to make Lola understand her. Lola turned to Loni. "A little help here? I don't know this language." Loni joined them at the counter.

"*Mua at g Gaso g Chuk Baha ab e-kih-ab g wainomikaj.*" The girl shook her finger at Lola.

Oh, shit! "It's Pima language. She said somebody killed a man named Blue at his house," Loni said. "Or her house. I'm not sure which."

Loni turned to the girl. "*Kut heDai I mua g Chuk Baha?*"

"*Gaso! Gaso!*"

"Says someone named Fox killed him."

"Ask her where she lives."

"*Bah' o kih g Gaso?*"

"*T wo I men g Gaso.*"

"She doesn't want to tell us where she lives. Says Fox will run. Hell, he's probably already gone," Loni said to Lola. She turned back to the girl. "*Heg at wo I gei, heDai I meDk.*"

The girl glared at Loni several seconds. "I hate a smart ass," she said in perfect English before she rushed out the door.

Loni gawped and sputtered, "I guess her English is fine." She hurried to the door. "She's disappeared," Loni called to Lola. "Better call the cops on the Gila Reservation. It's their jurisdiction."

"What did you say to her?"

"It's an old Pima truism: 'He will fall who runs.' "

Lola faintly smiled. "What do you suppose she really wanted?"

"My guess is she's afraid of reservation cops. Whatever went down, she wanted somebody to know who did it, and she didn't want to be involved."

Lola smile grew. "First it was Spanish. You understand O'odham, too?"

"Just some words like yes, no, sit, move your butt, or eat shit."

"Sounds like you're a fine communicator."

"Pointing is good, too," Loni said with an impish grin.

"Good thing Papago and Pima are both O'odham."

"The Pimas I know mostly speak Spanish. Sometimes it's easier to talk to Willie than Bahb."

"He doesn't know English?"

"Not like Shiichoo. She was forced to go to the Indian boarding school when she was little more than a baby. Bahb managed to escape that hellhole until he was in his teens." Leaning on the counter, Loni tried to recall Bahb's voice. "Shiichoo made sure he learned enough English to get by, so it's pretty broken." Loni smiled. "Shiichoo understands O'odham better than she speaks it. She knows a bit of Apache. They both know Spanish."

"Do they talk to each other in mixed languages?"

"Sometimes I've heard them rattling words off to each other, and I swear they don't have a clue what the other's saying." Loni smiled at the image in her mind. "I asked Shiichoo about it one time. She said, 'I watch his body language to see how well I'm doing.'"

The phone buzzed, and Lola answered. Without a word, she disappeared through the door into the judge's chambers. With the courthouse backing up to the police station, they could easily go back and forth although the door was always locked. Loni tried to work until the sound of Lola's jingling bracelets interrupted her. A smiling Lola handed her a warrant. "You owe me," Lola warned. "Don't think I won't collect."

"Yes!" Loni jumped up, punched her fist in the air, and did a tap dance around Lola. "Something good's gonna come out of this day yet. Call Chelsea, will you? Tell her the kids will be home soon."

"Good luck," Lola said with an indulgent smile. "Let me know what happens, okay?"

"Of course." Loni pocketed the warrant.

Loni ignored the heat as she trotted to the police lot for her truck. She headed up Caliente Butte to get the kids, winding around one ostentatious house after another. At the Taylor house, she parked in the shade of a eucalyptus tree for Coco and left the windows open. White pillars flanked the porch entrance. Loni rang the doorbell and waited. No one came, but she sensed someone peering at her through the peephole. She pressed the doorbell button again.

"What do you want?" A shrill voice came from the intercom speaker beside the door. "I didn't call you."

"I've got a warrant, ma'am." Loni unfolded it and tilted it toward the camera eye at the top of the door. "I need you to step out."

The door opened a crack, and Loni saw part of Mrs. Taylor's face. Her sour expression hadn't changed since she was Loni's high school typing teacher. The skin was stretched across her face like a skeleton's grimace. "I called my son," she warned. "You better leave now."

Loni kept holding up the warrant. "I've come for the children," Loni said. Mrs. Taylor opened the door far enough for Loni to see her vehemently shaking her head side to side "If you resist, I'll haul your sorry ass to jail. Comprende?" Loni couldn't believe she said that. Embarrassed but still annoyed with the woman, she pushed into the house and shoved the warrant into Mrs. Taylor's stomach.

Two children stood at the top of the stairs. "Are you Max and Trina?" Loni asked. They solemnly nodded in unison. "Your mom wants you home and sent me to get you. Are you ready to go?"

Four frightened eyes turned to their grandmother.

"She won't stop you, I promise," Loni reassured them.

Soundlessly, they scurried down the stairs and out of the house with her. Four-year-old Max clung to his sister Trina, three years older. They both wore wrinkled white tees and dark shorts.

Loni lifted the two up into her truck and watched Max lean up against Coco. He weakly smiled when Coco licked his face. Trina kept her big blue eyes on the road ahead. Tears ran silently down her face during the fifteen-minute drive until she saw her mother waiting in the driveway for them. Chelsea opened the passenger door and lifted the excited children out of Loni's truck. She hugged them as though she would never let go of them again.

Chelsea let the kids go so she could come around to where Loni was standing and watching. "Thank you, thank you, thank you!"

Loni hugged her back. "If your ex shows up, please don't shoot him." Loni begged her. "call me."

Chelsea gave Loni a quick kiss on the cheek and agreed. Satisfied, Loni backed out onto the street and drove back to the station.

When Lola buzzed her into the police station, Loni walked toward the counter in answer to Lola's waving. Before she got there Lola tossed a set of keys at Loni. "Clive called. He's chasing a speeder coming fast from the south and needs help. Take James's car. He's still in court. I'll keep Coco."

Loni snatched the keys out of the air and said, "On it." She ran out to the car parked beside the police station. She sped out of town and pulled alongside the highway for the car. A yellow Corvette convertible flew by with Clive close behind, his siren blaring and his lights strobing. Loni pulled in behind him and stomped on the gas. The Corvette grabbed the road and took the left fork curving onto the dead-end road dropping down to the dry river bottom. It flew off the end of the road into the deep sand. The wheels continued to spin, throwing sand everywhere until the car was buried to the bottom of its doors by the time Clive and Loni reached it. Loni parked next to Clive, and they regarded each other and the car in the sand. In the river. The driver was trying to bury his car even deeper as he yelled, "Shit, shit, shit!" His squeaking was like a little girl's voice. He finally climbed over the door and staggered to the font of the car. The man banged on the hood and tried to kick at the sand before he fell on his butt.

"Hey," Clive poked at the perp to get his attention. "Hey!"

"What!" the perp turned his angry face to Clive.

Clive fanned his face and stepped back a few feet. "How much have you had to drink? Whatever made you think you could drive across this dry river bed?"

"That damn GPS, that's what. The damn thing said there was a bridge here."

"Guess not." Loni answered sarcastically. "Not that I remember anyway." She turned to the giggling Clive. "You remember ever seeing a bridge here?"

"I heard they moved up river to Why."

"Why don't you go to hell?" The perp slurred his words as he struggled to stand. "Think you're funny?"

"Yep," Clive told him. He and Loni pulled the drunk to his feet. "Hey Loni, can you take this here guy in for me? I've got to get to court and I'm late now."

"You'd better push it, or Judge Sal will have you shot."

"Nah. She won't bother having me shot. She'll do it herself."

Loni hauled the man through the station door and up to the desk. "He's got no ID, Lola. He's not saying anything either."

The perp checked Lola over and smirked. "Shoulda sent her. I'd tell her anything she wanted to know."

"Hey." Loni poked the perp. "Be nice."

Lola ignored him. "Let me get some fingerprints, and I'll do a search."

"Cool! You can feel me anywhere."

"In your dreams, little man. I'm talking about a computer search."

"All his prison tats should make him easy to identify," Loni remarked.

"How do you know they're from prison?" Junior's loud voice reverberated in the large room as he walked up and hovered over Loni. "You can't tell one tattoo from another."

Loni jerked. "Damnit, Junior. Get away from me."

"Just trying to help. Looks like you're letting a perp insult Lola. Although I agree with him." Junior smiled at Lola. "You smell real nice."

"You're so gross." Loni snapped.

"Stop butting in!"

"I wasn't butting in. I'm trying to arrest this guy while you stand here staring at Lola with your tongue hanging out."

"Was not!" Junior pushed into Loni's space and leaned over.

"Were!" Loni stood her ground.

"Not!"

"Boys, boys, boys. Shut up."

Junior smirked. "See, Loni. Even Lola can't tell the difference."

In disgust Loni backed away and jerked the drunk over to Lola. He swayed and threw up all over Lola.

"Shit!" Lola froze, staring in disgust at the yellow puke all over her purple shirt. "How could you!"

"Me? How'd I do that?" Loni stared at her in astonishment

"You kept jerking him around until he threw up on me!"

"Sorry. I've got a stack of T's in my locker." Loni offered. "Might be a bit big. What size are you? A six?"

Lola patted Loni's cheek. "How sweet. I haven't seen size six since I was ten years old."

Loni backed off from the smell of Lola's shirt. "I'll be right back."

"Wait," Lola stopped Loni. "Forget the shirt. Throw this asshole in the drunk tank, and I'll get to him later." She turned to Junior. "You! Wipe the drool off your mouth and clean this up. The bucket and mop are in the closet. I'm going home for a shower. Come, Coco."

Loni stopped on her way to the ranch to shop for her grandparents. Pat wrapped a thick steak for Bahb. "From all of us here at the store," he said. "Help Bob get better." She stopped at the bakery to pick up a loaf of bread along with a lemon meringue pie, her granddad's favorite. Dirk Flavo waited on her. "Hey, Dirk. Thought you drove the grocery truck that comes in on Thursdays? Aren't you here a little early in the week?

"I'm taking a few days off, helping out my uncle. Auntie's down sick. I'm thinking of moving here."

"You do realize the town is less than five thousand? Probably including the rattlesnakes and Gila Monsters."

Dirk shrugged.

"As long as you don't mind bars and churches for your only entertainment, you're good."

Loni briefly wondered about Dirk as she headed toward her grandparents' ranch. At the old barbed-wire gate, she stopped her truck to make out the faded words "Wagner Ranch" in her headlights. The rust-streaked sign was wired between tall, badly bleached and rotted weather-beaten posts. No matter where she'd been, this was still the only place she ever felt safe.

The ghosting form of the ranch house tucked up inside the crescent came into view around a black volcanic hill. The house was surrounded by a mismatched collection of dwellings built at different times and by different people. There was even a Papago sandwich house left over from the O'odham nation Bahb said was built in the early 1900s. She remembered wishing there was also a Hogan because her grandpa was half Navajo as well as half Papago.

A scattering of lights across the landscape brightened in the quickening evening. Three of the four cabins on the far side of the ranch house were occupied. A young Pima woman and her five children were staying in Pike Cabin. Loni picked the name because of its high peaked roof. The Boulder Cabin was made from ten-inch-round river rock. When Loni was little, those rocks were huge. An old Pima couple, Zago and Aja Gott, lived there. They stopped to visit several years ago and never left. Russell, his wife, and her three children lived in the rusty-colored house. Years ago somebody used up left-over red barn paint on the wooden cabin, and it faded.

The last quarter of a mile to the house was bordered by alfalfa pasture land left over from the homestead belonging to her dad's father, Ben Wagner. After Loni's mother died in childbirth, Loni's grandparents left the reservation to move to the ranch and take care of the newborn. Loni's dad disappeared to work in the salt mines where he died in a cave-in. At least, that's what she was told.

Old salt cedar and eucalyptus trees grew taller as Loni neared the circular drive in front of the main house. She admired the Spanish ranchero style with the walled court around the front and kitchen side of the house. The twelve-inch adobe bricks from the late 1800s still stood strong. Bunk beds ran the length of a screened-in porch added on the back sometime after World War II. More salt cedars sheltered the sleeping porch in a fluffy line of dark-green needles. They provided dense shade against the relentless sun and allowed cooler breezes at night. The oasis was an escape from the worst of the summer heat.

The old Samson windmill beside the barn slowly turned in the almost cool October breeze. Loni parked and checked over the corrals, fences, and gates about the barn for any necessary repairs. She took the long way around the house to the back door and left Coco outside. Stepping into the kitchen, she dropped the three sacks of groceries onto the wooden kitchen table. Beside it was the hulking black cooking woodstove several inches out from the sunshine-yellow plastered wall. Even though Loni had bought her grandma a new electric stove, Shiichoo insisted on keeping the old stove. Dim flickering lights on the huge wagon-wheel light fixture above the kitchen table illuminated the room.

Loni snuck up to her grandma who was singing to herself as she washed dishes. She grabbed the tiny woman by the waist and swung her in a circle. Soapy water splashed everywhere.

"Child!" her grandma flared. Apache ramrod straight in her colorful long dress, Shiichoo stood her ground. "You clean it up!" She was no longer as gaunt and rope-thin as she was when Loni came back home. Loni wiped up the sudsy mess with paper towels. She also checked to see if the woodstove was cool. Sometimes Shiichoo would sneak a small fire for her morning coffee.

"Willie got the painting done this morning. Your granddad's been waiting for you to put everything back on the walls." Shiichoo said.

"Wait, wait, Shiichoo!" Loni balked. "Don't I even get a hug back?"

Her grandma's smile melted Loni, and they clung to each other for a long minute. Shiichoo let go first. She hid her tears by flipping the Indian bread in a skillet. Loni hurried from her own tears by putting the groceries away. Staring into a large black pot simmering next to the skillet, she began to name the ingredients. "Green chilies, oregano, jalapeno—"

"Child! I know what's in it!"

Loni wandered out of the kitchen hunting for her granddad. She followed the sound of Russell's voice into her grandparent's bedroom. He was arguing with Bahb who wanted out of bed. Loni hugged Russell's wife and got one back that almost broke her back. "Damn Lil, I forget how strong you are!"

Lil covered her mouth to hide her missing teeth. "You forgot I made living on the reservation as woodchopper."

"Oh, yeah." Loni grinned back, remembering when Lil got thrown into jail for beating up a girl who flirted with Russell. He nearly went crazy. When Russell got her out, they came to live on the ranch and never left. Lil was famous for her temper, but she was short and round. Like Russell said, she was easy to outrun.

"Take me to the couch," Bahb insisted.

"You need to stay in bed!" Shiichoo insisted as she hustled in from the kitchen.

"No. I need to watch Loni put things back. Make sure she don't mess up."

Loni smiled to herself, knowing he was still on happy pills for his pain. "Let him come, Shiichoo. We can put him back to bed later."

A big man, Russell carried her granddad to the couch. Navajo strong and beautiful, spoke perfect English and had been a college professor. When Loni's studies got beyond her grandma, Loni got help from Russell. Shiichoo said he married a white woman, but they fought so violently he locked her in a closet, hopped a freight train, and wandered south. That was when he met Lil and her three children. He had an outstanding athletic citation framed on his wall Lil thought was his divorce papers. "Didn't you have an older son?" Loni asked him one day.

"I did. Paid for his seminar education. I went to hear his first sermon and realized he became a Jehovah Witness. I left." Loni remembered Russell's sad face and bitter smile. "Better he stayed Indian." Another time after Russell struggled to teach her geometry, she asked him why he didn't teach anymore. "You're so good at it," she told him.

He quietly answered, "The white man's cruelty was too much."

Bahb watched from the couch while Loni hauled a ladder into the living room to hang the blankets back up. The biggest room in the house, one wall was almost filled with a huge fireplace, and across from the two doors leading into bedrooms was a wide archway opening onto the dining room. Indian rugs covered the gleaming wooden floor. Loni worked her way around to the fireplace and picked up her grandpa's Talking Calendar stick.

"Be careful of that, child!" Shiichoo scolded.

Loni held it tenderly in her hands. The three-foot stick was made from a saguaro cactus rib and painted with soot and red clay. Small notches, dots, V-shaped cuts, and straight, deep lines were etched along its length. Shiny from years of handling, the cracks also indicated the stick was old. When she was little, Loni reached up on the wall to feel the carved marks along it. After supper, Bahb would tell her about the battles of his ancestors and other important events represented by each line. Loni carefully carried the stick and laid it on his chest. "Bahb, why don't you read me your talking stick as I hang pictures? I forgot some of it."

"Can't," Bahb reminded Loni. "You know I can't tell stories when sun lives." He held the talking stick in his arms until he drifted off to sleep as Loni quietly worked around him.

The children grew bored and left to play out in the shade of the eucalyptus trees. In the kitchen, the adults filled up with iced tea and Shiichoo's fine fruit tamales. An hour later after they thoroughly heckled Loni about her sloppy work, they decided Bahb was okay and dribbled out the door.

"Don't forget the cactus fruit from the barn before you leave," her grandma reminded Loni as she cleaned up.

"As soon as I feed the horses and Stonewall." Coco led Loni through the corrals to find Paint, Roani, and Stonewall. Her cell phone buzzed as she slid the halter to a gunnysack feeder with rolled oats over Roani's ears. Paint nuzzled Loni's arm while she searched for her phone. Loni jump around to escape the horse's busy nose. Stonewall impatiently pushed his refrigerator-sized head against her as Loni dodged his searching wet tongue and snorts. Slipping the sack over Stonewall's ears she found the phone and heard James' bellowing voice even before she got it to her ear. Paint nudged her, and she almost dropped the phone. She reeled a few steps before gaining her balance.

"Damnit, Loni! You got my sunglasses."

Slipping Paint's feeder on, she answered James. "You're the one who left them in the car," Loni shot back.

"Did you have to take my car out to the ranch?"

"What do you mean yours? It's a police car, for Christ's sake. The car belongs to the department, not you."

"Mine, do you hear me!" James yelled. "Mine, mine, mine!"

"Thought you were flying to Phoenix today. What do you need a car for anyway?"

"So you want to wreck mine now?"

"You could drive my truck."

"No, no, no! And hell no!" James screamed into the phone.

Loni was tired of James' tirade. "Buy a new pair of sunglasses."

"You're kidding me?" James squealed into her ear. "Those are Ray-Ban's."

"Hell, James. Come and get them if you want them so bad." She hung up.

Loni removed the gunnysack feeders and was talking to Stonewall when James came stomping around the barn. "You locked the goddamn car. Give me the keys."

"Say please."

"Fuck you, Loni. Give me the goddamn keys."

Loni gave him a skinny look and tossed the keys to him. "Lordy, Loni. How are you? Had a good day? Why, yes, James, it was very rewarding and how was yours? Fine, fine, fine."

"Oh, shut up." James said. Stonewall shook his huge head and flapped his ears forcing James to jump backward. "Jesus, those ears are bigger than a dinner plate!" James's blue eyes grew huge.

"You think those are big? Look at his hoofs."

James peered down and backed out of the barn. Loni heard his car start up and leave. She pulled the empty bags off the animals and hung them in the old barn. The tractors, a small plow, and old worn-out machinery were covered with years of dust. In the corner was one of Daniel's old cars he tinkered with while they were in high school. She wondered if he had forgotten about the car. A bench filled with tools ran several feet down one wall. At the end was a small door leading down into a four-by-four cellar room, dug in the early 1900s. Somebody told her people hid from Indian raids there. She made fun of Indians hiding from Indians until somebody reminded her the Wagner place originally belonged to her white grandparents on her father's side.

Quickly accessing the cellar Loni walked along the twelve-inch shelves along one wall that still held some of her grandma's large jars. Wine fermented in three of them while the others sat empty. On another wall were ten-pound bags of saguaro fruit they harvested last summer. Loni remembered reaching up with her long extension rod to yank the fruit off the tips of the saguaro arms with the pole's hook. Timing was everything. She had to run like hell to dodge the falling fruit coming down like bullets covered with long, sharp needles. The wine made a sweet smell as it boiled down to syrup.

Loni hauled a twenty-pound gunny sack of fruit to the kitchen and dropped it in the sink. Voices drifted out of the living room as she hollered goodbye and slipped back through the back door.

On her way home, Loni finished a tamale she had grabbed from the refrigerator on her way out of the house. Two miles down the road, she heard Bobby's slow drawl from the speaker on her police radio. "Burn victim at the old Caulwell farm on the southwest corner of Victor and 85."

"Ah, damn, Bobby. I'm sorry but that still begs the question. Why is a burn victim my problem?"

"Well, he isn't. Ambulance is picking up the kid. Your problem is the fire. Kid lit a match trying to steal gas out of a tractor. Got a bad hay fire now. We need all hands on deck."

Loni flung the remaining end of the second tamale into the brush for a coyote and pressed her foot on the gas.

The glow of the barn was visible five miles away. A hay fire was impossible to put out. Loni had seen a fire bury itself deep in a stack and smolder for weeks before it flashed up and burned all over again. Sometimes these fires were caused by lazy farmers who baled and stacked too green. She had heard of one of the farmers taking the insurance money, sold the land for half of what is was worth, and moved to Alaska. He said he'd rather freeze to death than burn in hell one day longer.

The yellow glow danced behind a silhouette of cottonwood trees. Loni herded traffic around the volunteer firefighters as they fought the flames, pulling the hay apart with iron rakes and pitchforks. They were lucky the farmer was too poor to have a big stack, but the sun still came up before the worst of the fire was out.

Bone-tired, Loni answered questions from early morning passersby, mostly about the boy. "Yes, he's still alive." "Yes, the burn was pretty bad, but he's alive." "No, he was by himself." "Don't know why Boyd wasn't with him." "I'm good. And you?" "Yes, he's alive." "Don't know." "Yes."

The sun reached high in the sky by the time firefighters could leave. Loni called one last time to check on the boy.

"Not good," Bobby reported. "Won't be able to light matches again. Might not see the flame anyhow, neither."

Loni was glad to leave the stench of smoke and wet ashes behind.

On the way home, she recalled the warm images of her granddad singing of clouds and rain and wind while he sipped his wine. Her rambling thoughts attempted to push away the evil of the past year. They came anyway, especially her images of her old Chief hanging on his bedroom wall like Christ crucified with his intestines at his feet. Only Jenny's sick imagination could do that. She had such a desperate need to get even for all the years he raped her. Refusing to let one more terrible thought in Loni hurried home.

CHAPTER EIGHT

A ll rise!"

The side door to the courtroom opened, and Judge Sal Suttig stalked in. Everyone focused on the figure in the black flowing robe. She was jaw-jarring, totally butch handsome with olive Mediterranean skin and sprayed, poofed-up, slicked-back black hair fitting like a helmet. She strode up the three steps to her throne-like chair. The judge's outrageous antics were known across the southern half of the state, and her court was part of the town's entertainment. The long benches rescued from a long ago abandoned missionary Catholic Church were always full when she presided. Judge Suttig glanced around and zeroed in on Janet Jace. "Oh, my god!" she said in a booming voice. "Janet, what the hell are you doing here?"

"Hello, Judge Suttig. I'm defending my client." Janet glanced back at Loni's surprised exclamation and gave her a slight smirk.

The prosecuting attorney hopped one step over to the other table and whispered to Janet. "It's Judge Sal."

"Sorry," Janet whispered back. "I didn't know."

Janet jumped when the judge bellowed. "Why don't you both shut up and sit down!"

Judge Sal glared at the snickering, and the court became deathly quiet. She told the prisoner to rise again and stared at him. "Chas! Read the charges," she ordered the gray-headed man standing beside her bench.

"Second Degree Robbery, Your Honor."

"What's your name, kid?"

"You know my name, Judge. I been before you before."

Sighing, the judge circled her finger at him. "It's for the record, Ronnie. Tell the court."

"Ronnie Dobbs, Judge Sal."

The judge glared. "Don't call me Judge Sal, Ronnie."

"Ain't that your name?"

The crowd tittered. Judge Sal banged her mallet and peered over her glasses. "Listen to me good, Ronnie. You call me 'Your Honor.' Understood?"

Ronnie ducked his head. "Yes, Your Honor."

"Your dad here, Ronnie?"

"No, ma'am. Said he got a lawyer for me and I didn't need him."

"Your Honor," the judge corrected. "You saying he wasn't with you?"

"No, Your Honor."

"How old are you now?"

"Turned eighteen last month on the second, Your Honor."

Judge Sal stared at Ronnie in surprise. "You committed a robbery on your birthday?"

"Yes, Your Honor."

"What? You didn't have enough sense . . ." The judge paused. "What did you rob?"

"A service station, Your Honor. Enough sense for what?"

"Don't ask questions! You didn't have enough sense to rob a service station the day before you turned eighteen?"

"Didn't need money then, Your Honor."

"What changed?"

"Wanted to get a woman in Mexico for my birthday," Ronnie said defensively. "Guess I should've filled up with gas before I robbed it."

"Sorry?" The judge looked confused.

"That's how I got caught. I ran outta gas a mile outta town. Tried to outrun her, but she caught up when the car quit and arrested me."

Judge Sal spit out a few swear words. "You mean to tell me you robbed a service station, and you got in a chase, but you got caught because you ran out of gas on the day you turned eighteen and were old enough to be tried as an adult? That about right?"

"Yes, Judge Sal."

"Your Honor!" Judge Sal corrected more loudly. "Did you give the money back?"

Ronnie Dobbs glared around the courtroom searching for Loni in the crowded audience. Finally finding her, he pointed. "She did, Your Honor, on our way back into town."

"Stand up, Loni." The judge stared at her. "Anyone hurt?"

"No, Your Honor," Loni said struggling to keep a straight face.

"Anyone mad?"

"Only me, Your Honor. Had to duck his shotgun."

The judge looked over at Ronnie. "You shot at a cop?"

"I missed, didn't I?"

The judge stared at Janet. "You came all the way from Boston for this case?"

Janet shrugged but kept her mouth shut. Loni wondered what Janet thought about the judge trying the case for her.

"You here for any other reason?"

Janet remained silent.

Picking up the mallet the judge slammed it down. "Case dismissed. Court adjourned."

"Wait! Wait! Judge Sal," the jury foreman hollered as he stood up. "What about us?"

"George, shut up and sit down. Bailiff, dismiss the jury." Judge Sal stood and pointed her finger at Ronnie. "You tell your daddy I'm finin' him ten thousand dollars." Turning to Loni, she said, "Make sure he's got gas in his car and send him home." She stuck her finger out at Janet. "In my chambers! Now!"

"All rise!"

Loni leaned forward to Janet as the people milled about to leave the courtroom. "So, I guess you already know Judge Sal. Ever been in her chambers before?"

"No. Something I should know?"

"Before you get too impressed, you might want to think about this." Loni nodded toward the district attorney shoving papers in his briefcase as he shot a dirty look at Janet. "That's her husband, George Suttig." Loni laughed at the deer-caught-in-the-headlight expression on Janet's face, grabbed Ronnie by the scuff of his neck. and pushed him out of the courtroom. She was still chuckling when she followed Ronnie's beat-up jalopy back to the gas station.

CHAPTER NINE

An hour after sunrise, Loni pulled up to a tired roadside bar and climbed out of her truck. A Tucson police SUV pulled up beside her, and a tall weather-beaten cowboy got out. Harry Beal's warm smile and crinkling eyes belied his tone when he said, "What the hell is that thing?" Harry pointed at her truck. "Don't tell me you paid good money for it."

Loni winced as she slid down from the seat of her tall truck. "Got a good deal on it."

She held out her hand, and his huge paw swallowed it. "How much?"

"It was free?"

Harry burst out in laughter. "Still got taken."

Loni grimaced. "So. We meet here because?"

"We found her body off San Pedro Road." He walked her over to his SUV and climbed back in. "A biker saw buzzards circling and got curious."

Loni got into the passenger side. "Buzzards do much damage?"

"Not much. She was pretty well rolled up in a horse blanket leaving her hair sticking out of one end. Feet were gone though."

Despite the gruesome description, Loni smiled to herself as she inspected the SUV. It was like the one she drove back when she was a highway patrol officer. Except the refrigeration worked in this one. "Can I see the blanket?"

"Sure. It's in the evidence lock-up at the station. Couple of boys Manny team-tied with said they thought it belonged to him."

Harry pulled out onto the long empty road to the crime site and talked about James and the good times they had in Mexico. Loni accepted the fact he knew a very different person than the James who made Loni's life miserable. After about twenty minutes, Harry turned onto a dirt road and followed a faint desert trail. Greasewoods scratching against the car reminding Loni of unoiled screen doors or, even worse, nails on a blackboard. They drove up to a deep wash, and Harry parked. "We have to walk in from here."

Loni trotted behind Harry, trying to keep up with his long legs as they climbed down and up the wash and striding through the brush. Stopping, he pointed to the ground. "Here it is. She laid right there. Nothing left to see."

Loni carefully walked around the area and inspected the ground. "Find signs of anyone else here besides the killer?"

"Only the footprints of the guy who found her. He didn't get too close before the smell backed him off."

"How'd he know it was a body?"

"He could see the bleached blond hair on the top of her head. Plus what was left of her feet. The killer did leave in a hurry though." Harry pointed down a few feet over, behind a tall saguaro cactus. "Spin marks. Four-wheel drive. He scattered rocks and plants getting out of here." Harry waited for Loni to finish her inspection. "Matched the tire tread on Manny's four-wheeler. Too rocky to match an individual tire for any nicks or cuts, but we got enough tread to match the make."

"Poor Manny," Loni said. "He keeps stepping in it." She squatted down to pick up a small plant. "He really peeled out of here." Loni fingered the small leaves. "Did you check in the tread of his tires or undercarriage for any debris from the scene? Maybe some of this plant is stuck somewhere."

"Nah. Probably burned away from road heat if it was in a tire. Don't see what it would prove anyway. The stuff grows everywhere."

"This one doesn't. My granddad says it's rare." Loni searched for others. "He was mostly raised on the O'odham Nation. I learned that knowing plants meant survival." Loni held out the small plant. "This is False Cloak Fern."

"Guess we could check. Maybe a leaf got caught somewhere."

"Any other suspects to know about?"

"Not really."

"What about the husband? Manny said they were getting a divorce."

Harry corrected Loni. "They were getting back together."

"Who said?"

"I guess it was him."

Loni snorted. "Sounds like a good alibi."

Harry called his partner to check for any plant debris on the Manny's tire treads. By the time they got back to Loni's truck, Harry agreed to let her follow him to the Tucson station to see what his partner found. Pete Sanchez was a small wiry Hispanic, wearing a green striped western shirt and Levis. "Manny's truck was clean. Not even pebbles in the tire." Pete pulled on the strings of his black bolo tie. "Don't look like it ever got off the highway."

"Could I see the saddle blanket?"

"You bet."

Harry removed its plastic casing from the tagged blanket and unrolled it on a table. Loni was glad she hadn't eaten breakfast. Her nose filled with the odor of decomposition, but she had to stand close enough to see. Loni locked her hands behind her back. "Isn't Manny's horse a grey and black appaloosa?

"I have no idea," Pete answered.

"And Manny's hair is black."

"So?"

"Don't you find it strange the hair colors on the blanket are blond and sorrel?"

Harry ruefully shook his head. "Didn't run a check on this blanket for the DNA, did we?" He took the small magnifying glass and tweezers out of his pocket kit and studied the blanket. "Got another bag?" he asked Pete, who fidgeted like he wanted to escape. Harry picked horse and human hair out of the blood stains and dropped it into the bag.

Pete whispered, "Harry messed up his smeller snorting drugs."

"I heard that!" Harry shot back. "I did not, you lying sack of shit!" He rolled up the blanket and shoved it back into its slot. As Loni and Pete left the evidence room, he said, "I think we might find a tag here. If not, we should have plenty of markers."

"Does her husband have a horse, too?"

"You know, I think so." Harry said thoughtfully. He turned to Pete. "Didn't Manny say something about meeting the girlfriend at a roping?"

"We could find out."

"Why not get the husband's DNA while we're at it." Harry clamped Loni on the shoulder as they escaped the smell in the cage. He grinned. "Now that you've given us more work, you might as well help us check his truck and the horse out."

Loni climbed into the backseat of the patrol car, hoping the husband had a horse. "Nothing's this easy," she said doubtfully.

"That's what we thought when we found Manny in her house. How stupid was that?" They were quiet a minute before Pete sighed. "I think we got used to stupid people making our job easier. Remember last week, Harry? That anti-abortion clinic we got called out on?"

"Sure. It did adoptions and provided clothes for the babies."

"And information on abstinence. They called us because it was tagged with swastikas and words like baby killers."

"And?"

"The tags were signed. And we knew the religious group who did it."

"Are you trying to tell me the right-wing protesters attacked their own clinic?"

"I am."

Pete snorted. "They had no idea what kind of a clinic it was. A sign over the door said Pregnancy Center, and they took it from there."

"Couldn't bother to ask?"

"The know-it-alls never do."

"I've got an aunt like that. The more you prove her wrong, the more she's convinced she's right."

"Did James ever tell you about the stupid thing he did with his old desert buggy down in Mexico?"

"No," Loni answered. "But I bet I could guess."

"He was way ahead of the rest of the cars so he decided to scare the shit out of us. He and the two kids with him turned the jalopy on its side, and they lay around like they were dead." Harry shuttered in memory. "We ran around them waving our arms until one of them started giggling."

"Bet you were ready to beat the shit out of them when you figured it out."

Harry hooted. "Nah, we got the last laugh. The gas ran out of the jalopy while it was on its side and we left them there. It was a four-mile walk to where we camped. In the hot sun."

Loni glanced around while she waited for Harry's raucous roar to stop. "Anybody know where we're going?"

Pete turned to her. "You lost?"

"Usually." Loni teased Pete. "Got no iron in my nose hair to tell me direction like you do."

"Well, looky here." Harry pulled into a driveway and stopped. "Soon enough for you?" He turned off the car.

Harry and Pete climbed out. Pete opened the back door of the SUV. "Want to come and help us? Better yet, do it yourself?"

Loni regretfully declined. "Too close to Manny. Might get accused of tainting evidence. I better stay here and wait." The two men knocked on the door of a yellow prefab house, and a blond man answered. When they went in the house, Loni climbed out of the car. A small barn and pasture land were behind the house, and three horses stood in the shade of a Eucalyptus tree. One of them was a sorrel.

A half hour later the two men climbed back into the car. Harry showed Loni a small plastic bag. "Wasn't any in the tire tread, but I did find this stuck up under the wheel well."

Pete frowned. "Cleanest damn truck I ever saw. Good thing he missed the underneath."

Harry talked nonstop as he drove away. "He had a sorrel horse in a back pasture. So now we have to get a subpoena to get the DNA from the horse. And Jacob." Harry gave the steering wheel a pound with the side of his fist. "And I was trying to show a fellow cop how good we are," he said teasingly to Loni.

Loni studied the battered plant leaves in the bag Pete held up. "Yelp, that's False Cloak Fern leaves."

"We'll send them in for a DNA match as soon as we can," Harry snorted in amazement. "Boy, I didn't expect that. Shit, Pete. I guess we messed up."

"At least we get a chance to fix it."

On her way home, she called Lola to leave a message about Manny. When Lola answered, Loni blurted, "Lola? Is that really you?"

"Loni?"

"What are you doing answering your phone?" Loni asked in surprise. "When did you start answering your phone?"

"If you call back, I could put the machine on."

"Funny."

"Not really. How's Manny?"

"He's going to be alright. I can't tell you how I know, but he should be home soon."

"Thank god." Loni could hear the relief in Lola's voice. "You sure?"

"Nothing's for sure, Lola. You know that."

Lola's voice had its edge back. "If you're not sure, maybe you should go back down there and make sure."

"Bye, Lola," Loni said and flipped her cell phone closed, grumbling to herself, "That went well."

CHAPTER TEN

Loni was not happy when she walked into the station the next morning. Seeing Junior sitting at her desk pissed her off all over again. "What the hell, Junior?"

"You weren't here."

"Use your own goddamned desk."

"Ain't proper for girls to swear." Junior admonished her.

Loni grabbed the chair where he sat and spun it away from her desk. "Get out of my chair now, Junior. And while you're at it, move your crap off my desk." Loni stopped. "Wait a minute. Are those my folders?"

"Nope." Junior deliberately picked up the folders and ambled over to his desk. "I've got those files at home, and I'm not giving them back." He sat and spread out the folders like a fan. "You know why you didn't solve this drug case? You rushed over all the evidence and didn't even see it. We need to move careful on this so you don't make any more mistakes."

"What do you mean any more mistakes?"

"Didja solve it? Didja?" Junior shot back at her.

"Tell me what you've done."

"I told you, Tonto, I'm not ready yet."

"Next time you call me Tonto, I'll shoot off your dick."

Junior sneered. "Temper, temper. Can't take a little teasing?" Guffawing, he added. "You'd need a twelve-gauge shotgun for my dick. Shooting that would knock you on your ass."

"I swear you're as dumb as old Tex who used to live up the river."

"Oh, yeah? What'd he do?"

"He tried to repair a combine one day while it was still running. Lost part of his finger. His brother walked up and said, 'Hell. How'd you do that?' Tex stuck his finger back into the combine and came out with another joint missing and said, 'Just like that!' "

"At least I got a dick. Where's yours?"

"You know what! You're as much a bigot as one of our past governors. When he got accused of racism, he said, 'I ain't no racist. Why, when I was little, I even played with pickaninnys.' Before long people had bumper stickers that said 'Pick a Ninny. Pick Meech for Governor.' I could make one up for you."

"How come I never understand a word you say?"

Loni dropped into her chair, still warm from Junior's butt, as she heard Carl call Junior into his office. Loni watched him leave while she restlessly tapped a pencil like a drum stick on a squat mug covered with playful dragons. She had filled it with malt balls, and the sound of the tapping against the cup produced a low tone so mesmerizing she didn't hear Lola for a few minutes.

"Would you stop that!" Lola's green eyes sparked as she pointed her index finger at Loni. Her agitated movements jangling her metal bracelets. "It's driving me nuts!"

Loni dropped the pencil like a piece of a hot coal and blushed. "Sorry."

"What are you thinking about so hard?"

"Nothing." She had a tough time facing Lola this morning, wondering if she should ignore what happened the night before? Try to apologize for something she wasn't sorry for? She didn't think so.

"If you're guessing helping Manny will get you back into my good graces, forget it. Junior's taken care of it."

"Took care of what? There was nothing to take care of."

"Do you see Manny home yet?"

Loni had her head down, working on the report she was trying to finish. A shadow loomed over her, and she glanced up to see Junior stuffing a handful of malt balls into his mouth. "Hey!" Loni grabbed her mug. "Don't eat those!"

"Why not?" Junior mumbled.

"Cuz I just picked them up off the holding tank floor." The dimples in Loni's cheeks deepened as she watched Junior spit out the brown goo.

"Loni, stop it!" Lola's voice turned shrill as she insisted, shaking her finger at Loni as her stacked bracelets exploded in ringing jangles. "That's the third time you pulled that shit! It's not funny anymore."

"Dadgum!" Junior sputtered, grabbing a Kleenex from Loni's desk.

Loni ignored Lola. "Also fished a few out from behind the toilet." Loni hassled Junior as she watched him brush crumbs of chocolate and smeared them into dark brown streaks down his red and white checked shirt front. One large blob of brown perched on a snap pearl.

"One of these times somebody's going to spit them on you if you don't quit saying that!" Lola warned Loni. "And I'm not going to clean you up."

"Or slap you silly," Junior warned.

The sight of Junior's glower made Loni's grin widen. "Only way I can keep some for myself."

"You could keep them in a drawer!"

"What's the fun of that?"

Junior opened his mouth when Loni interrupted. "Junior, I need my files."

"Why?"

"I need to check something in Chui's file."

"Why?"

"Why what? I'm tired of asking you. Give me back my goddamn files."

"No," Junior said defiantly.

Loni stood and jammed her fists on her hips. "What the fuck, Junior! You can't keep those files from me!"

"Watch your mouth, Loni. And yes, I can. I got them at home under lock and key so you can't mess with the evidence I'm gathering."

"Evidence for what?"

"None of your business." Junior stomped back to his desk.

Loni threw her hands in the air before she plopped back down in her desk chair in frustration. Shit. What's that about? She wondered what to do next.

Carl walked out of his office. "Hey Junior, I forgot to ask you. Did you find out whose billy goats were in the mayor's back yard?"

"Farmer named Carter. Darndest thing though. They were numbered. You know? In the left ear. Two, three, four. I searched everywhere but I couldn't find number one."

Loni intently stared at him. "You need to go find that goat, Junior."

Carl walked over to Junior. "Oh, god! How many people saw you looking for the goat?"

Junior frowned at Carl. "I asked everybody if they saw it."

Loni broke out in giggles. "Anybody see it?"

"Everybody. But they kept giving me different directions."

"And?" Carl struggled to keep a straight face.

Lola shook her finger at Loni and Carl as she said soothingly to Junior, "Don't worry. There is no Number One. Old man Carter always gives new cops a hard time so he can make fun of them."

Junior's eyes shot daggers at Loni. "The farmer said there was another one. Said if we didn't find it he was going to sue the city and the police department."

Carl grabbed a handful of malt balls and stuffed his mouth as Loni laughed so hard tears rolled down her cheeks. She didn't stop until she started to hiccup. Junior stomped back to his desk. Lola picked up a fax from her desk and handed it to Loni. "This should shut you up. Got a report back on Antonio Carillo. Looks like he's going to trial in Mexico."

"Good!" Junior sounded pleased. "I told them to keep him."

"What?" Loni was shocked. "Why?"

"What'd he do?" Carl asked.

"Nothing as far as I can tell," Lola answered with reluctance. "According to this fax, they're using a law I never heard of. Mexico's federal penal code, Article IV. Mexican judge can try a Mexican citizen for crimes committed in other countries."

"See how procrastination pays?" Junior sat back with a pleased grin. "We don't have to pay his bills no more."

"He won't have a chance down there, Junior." Loni groaned.

"Damn it."

"What birds can't fly, Loni?"

"Jail birds, and that's not funny."

"And you think I care?"

"I keep forgetting what a heartless right-wing sonafabitch you are."

"He's a wetback and don't belong here. I'm sick and tired of this politically correct crap. So get off my back."

"You do hate being a nice person, don't you?"

Junior strolled unrepentant out the door.

Half hour later, Lola answered the police radio. "Caliente Police Department. How can I help you?"

Loni watched Lola as she hung up the phone and turned to Loni. "There's a fight at the Last Stop Saloon."

"Early in the day for a fight," Loni commented as she called Coco from behind Lola's counter."

"Maybe a bus is in, and the passengers got drunk early."

Loni was glad to escape Lola's anger. She hurried out of the station and parked in front of the bar. Coco was at her heels when she slipped in the door of the bar. The room was quiet. The first thing Loni saw was two cowboys sitting at the end of the bar shoving each other and giggling like girls as they watched her. Someone stood in the shadows at the other end of the bar. Some of the small tables circling a tiny dance floor were filled. Everything seemed peaceful. "What's going on?" Loni asked the young man behind the bar.

His shit-eating grin was as big and bright as his sign outside, and he joined the two cowboys in giggling.

"What's so funny?"

"Nothing. It was a slight disagreement. Didn't amount to anything."

Loni watched the guy taking orders. Was it only her, or were kids getting younger every day? Seemed like this one didn't even have to shave his square jaw. Curling dark hair falling forward almost hid his blue eyes. She thought about carding him before she remembered it was his bar. He could own the place, but he couldn't touch the alcohol. "Who called, then?"

The bar owner pointed down a hallway. "He's in the john."

Loni checked around. "What happened this time?"

"Sam got a nosebleed." He tilted his head toward the shadowed man at the end of the bar. "He's too mean to hurt."

Loni walked to the end of the bar, stopping to study the man and his bloody rag he held to his nose. His pulled down hat over his forehead hid the man's face. When he finally looked up, Loni recognized him. The sad, defeated man had been a rancher famous for his rodeo skills. He team roped with his son, Phillip Daily, and they always won. Loni could see them in her mind's eye. Phil came out of the gate first, whooping and hollering as he swung the rope around his head, and his dad followed close behind. Together they were grace in motion. Phil was in Loni's year at school, and his folks came to every football game he played.

"Kith my ath," Sam flared at the bar owner. Blood spotted his dirty Levis, and his faded blue work shirt was stained with sweat and wrinkled as if he had slept in it for days. He rubbed his jaw and growled," Arres him." He pointed to a young farmer sitting with a woman at a table. "I thik he broke my nose." He opened his mouth and wiggled his front teeth. "Anth two foont theeth." He tried to wiggle another tooth. "Theee!"

Cringing at his bloody nose, Loni rubbed hers and turned to the barkeep, "Did he hit Sam?"

The bar owner shrugged. "Sam was having a coughing fit. Patsy there got a Kleenex out of her purse and handed it to Sam. 'It's alright, Sam,' she told him. 'I've got a cold, too.' So, Sam took the Kleenex, thanked her, and then he says, 'So, that was you I slept with last night?' Her husband there took offense and bopped him." He picked up another glass, rubbed the outside, and stacked it on a shelf behind him.

"Shith," Sam said, still feeling his teeth. "I wath so drunk lath night, I don't know who I wath with. Hey barkeep, who wath I with?"

"Your wife, stupid."

Sam took his hand out of his mouth and muttered, "Didn't know I had one." Taking his hat off, he shook his shaggy head and rubbed his jaw again, rough hands rasping like sandpaper over his three-day stubble.

Loni felt Sam's jaw. "You should get an X-ray to be sure it's not cracked." Backing off, she cringed. "Might get a bath, too." She scratched her head and wondered if he had fleas.

"Don't need one." Sam was insulted. "These Levis ain't even standin' up by themselves yet."

"How come you're in here, Sam? I never saw you drink before."

Sam turned back to his bottle.

Loni walked back to the bar. "Sam come here often?"

"Every day most all day 'til his wife drags him home."

Loni saw Junior walk out of the bathroom and scoot onto a barstool next to the two cowboys. Amazed, Loni confronted him. "You been here all this time?"

"So?"

"You called this in, you jerk." Shaking in anger, Loni pushed out the door leaving behind laughter, an idiot, and a broken man.

Loni shooed Coco in front of her as she went back to the police station and up to Lola. "You know why Sam Daily's hanging out in the Last Chance Saloon staying drunk?"

"Don't you?"

"Would I be asking if I did?"

Tears filled Lola's eyes. "Last summer he was stringing wire out on the Winghall place. He had the wire clamped in the slice box and chained to a fence post. When he pulled the pulley rope, he tightened the wire too tight and it snapped, whipping a hundred feet of barbed wire through the air. It cut Phil's head off. His wife, Emogene, didn't live long after he died. Sam claims her heart broke."

"But the barkeep said she would come and get him."

Lola shook her head. "It was the wife's twin sister who's trying to see after him. He buried his wife two months ago."

"Where was I?" Loni wondered out loud.

Lola reached her hand toward Loni. "He only had a short three-hour viewing in his living room before he took her home to her family in Colorado."

"Oh, God! He lost both his kid and his wife. I'd stay drunk too."

CHAPTER ELEVEN

Late morning found Loni sagging in her desk chair with her back to Lola. She was so lost in thought Carl's loud voice made her jump. "Loni! Get in here."

At least Carl's still speaking to me, Loni thought as she hurried into Carl's office. Carl's calm, weathered face left her sighing in relief. His broad shoulders had lost their hunching from last July's tragic mess at his ranch although his sandy hair had some new gray streaks. Loni worried about Carl's stoic denial regarding the O'Neals selling sex enhancing drugs planted in pots lined with heroin from his ranch. The court found them guilty. Loni knew Carl blamed himself, but he wouldn't talk about it. "Sit down and let me bring you up to speed." Carl opened a folder in front of him. "James left for Phoenix this morning to work with the narcs. Guess we're back on the case."

"Junior's got my files."

"You don't need them. We got way beyond that." Carl replied in disgust. "Keeps him busy anyway. I'm fed up with his fuckups."

"Why do you keep him around?"

Carl's stare told Loni to drop the topic. He handed her a map. She was relieved she wasn't the only one who couldn't stand Junior. She spread out the map on Carl's desk. A yellow line marked Arizona and Mexico border trails from Yuma to Sonoyta.

"Got this from Tully. It's the Sand Tank mountain range in the Cabeza Prieta Refuge. DEA thinks a motorcycle gang, pretending to be involved in the sand races, are actually bringing drugs in through this area, but they can't seem to track anything to Caliente."

Loni ran her finger along a line wandering up and around Sand Tank. "Last time I was there the windmill wasn't working. Didn't even have all its fan blades." She rubbed the bump on her nose. "Any sign anyone hanging out in the shack by the windmill?"

"Don't know. I'll ask."

Loni studied the map. She had forgotten how close the Devil's Highway ran parallel to the border below Cabeza Prieta. "I got a problem with this, Carl. How'd they decide to search here?"

"Picked up a sand biker with a bag of our same cocaine." Carl leaned back in his chair. "He's not talking, but his passport and the permit for the Mexico visa had him crossing into Mexico through Hermosillo several times over the year. They figured the bikers traveled a back way through Cabeza Prieta to Caliente from Hermosillo, Mexico."

"But coming here makes no sense. If they're coming through the Cabeza, the shortest way is straight on into Phoenix. Why go so far out of their way?"

Carl shrugged, rubbing his ear even harder. "I don't know, Loni."

"Let me get this straight. You think the dead biker and the biker who got arrested are both part of the sand dune cycle races over on the Yuma border. Right?"

"State does. Tully's staying at the Palm Tree Mobile Home & RV Park over near Yuma. State put a trailer in there for reconnaissance."

"So you got nothing from the biker connecting him except his permits into Mexico?" Loni's voice was thoughtful.

"Didn't say that. Got some phone numbers off his phone. One to a bar in Algodenes, Mexico. Another to the bakery here in town."

Loni's head jerked up. "Our bakery?"

Carl smiled at Loni's reaction. "Talked to Tommy already. He said they baked special cactus bread the biker boys loved. They'd call ahead and stop by occasionally to grab a few loaves."

"Strange," Loni thought out loud.

"What is?"

"Bikers, maybe, love his bread. But Caliente isn't a regular route for sand bikers, especially for the Yuma crowd. I don't even remember seeing sand bikers around here."

"You're forgetting our dead biker outside town."

Loni shook her head. "Still . . . "

"You ever taste Tommy's cactus bread?"

"Nooo," Loni muttered, "Wonder if Shiichoo would like it. Seems like everything she cooks lately is made of cactus."

Carl sat back. "'Bout this time she always gives me a bottle of cactus wine. Tell her I'm missing it."

Loni snorted. "Tell her yourself. I'm not breaking the law for you." She glanced down again studying at the map. "So what do you want me to do?" Loni wasn't sure she wanted to know.

Carl sat back in his chair and pulled on his ear. "James is coming home to follow a lead he picked up in Phoenix. Didn't say what. Tully wants you to go to Algodenes where the sand races are. Wants you undercover for a while."

Carl's ear pulling told Loni to be careful. "If you say so, Carl. But I have to say I think it's a waste of time. We could track it easier if we could figure out where it is here in Caliente."

"Tully thinks James can do it. He thinks the sand bikers are the key and he wants you there."

"Why me?"

"Nothing I can say, Loni. Tully heard you knew that country. Heard Bahb took you all over the border country looking for cattle to buy."

"True. When we bought any Brahma mix, we had to stay thirty days below the border to make sure they didn't have any hoof and mouth disease." Loni sighed. "Saw lots of Mexico then. When do I go?"

"Soon as James heads home. They're setting up a cover for you now."

"What's Junior doing while I'm gone? Working on my files?"

"Hell yes, Loni. He's dangerous on his own, so leave him alone with them, you hear? In fact, I need to see him. Send him in when you go."

Loni dragged her feet over to Lola's counter and tapped on Junior's shoulder. "Carl wants to see you, Junior. That is if you could stop panting and drooling over Lola long enough."

Lola sighed as she put her elbow on the countertop and rested her chin on her hand as Junior swaggered into Carl's office. "He's got the cutest butt."

Loni turned to Lola in amazement. "Drugstore cowboy asshole, maybe. Sounds like you're in lust."

Lola shot back. "Jealous much?"

"Not yet. Should I be?"

"Maybe you should find someone else to start dating."

"That what you're doing?" Loni shot back.

"Maybe."

"Maybe you're trying to piss me off."

"How's that working?"

"Maybe I'll ask Tori out?"

"Tori who?"

"The new veterinarian in town," Loni said proudly.

"Why would you ask her out? She's straight."

"No, she's not."

"Is."

"How do you know?" Loni asked suspiciously.

"She showed me a picture of her husband. He was killed in Afghanistan."

Loni was continually amazed at how much Lola knew about the town. "But Willie. Oh, shit. He caught me again."

"What are you talking about?

"Back when we were doctoring a cow that got into the jumping cactus, Tori came to help. Willie tried to convince me she was gay."

"Why would he do that?" Lola asked in amazement.

Loni shrugged. "How would I know what he thought? Maybe humiliation is good for me?"

"Good thing you didn't ask her out. Anyway, she's still grieving, and she won't go out with anybody."

Carl hollered for Lola, and she smirked at Loni before she joined Junior in Carl's office. Loni still wasn't used to seeing Carl in Chief's office, and she had a harder time seeing Junior at Carl's old desk. Loni was beginning to hate him, not occasionally but most of the time. If I hear how they do it in Texas one more time! Loni sighed. Maybe it's a good thing I'm leaving for a few days.

CHAPTER TWELVE

Loni hadn't seen this end of Highway 85 since she was a teenager and came with Bahb and Willie to help Essey Rigall gather his Santa Gertrudis cattle out of the Colorado River bottom brush. Nobody was better than Willie at finding them. As the desert rushed by, she noted the changes from the monsoon rains and the cooler fall weather. Colors were brighter after the vegetation soaked up the moisture. The saguaro cactus stood majestic in their new green, and the prickly pear sprouted new dark green pads. Greasewood leaves lost their withered silver reflection, and the thickets of mesquite trees along washes were colored in lacy lime-green colors.

Loni knocked on the door of a huge RV at the Palm Tree Mobile Home & RV Park. A tall, thin man with a dopey grin opened the door and grabbed Loni, dragging her through the door and giving her a long hug.

"Hey, Tully! It's good to see you again, too." She still couldn't believe the way he had changed from the sloppy, stupid cop he pretended to be when he was undercover last summer.

"Hey, Apache, I'm glad to see you." He joyfully dropped her in the middle of the living room.

Staring around, she couldn't believe what she saw. "Are your sheets silk, too?"

The huge smile on Tully's long, thin face showed gleaming white teeth in place of the false tobacco-stained ones she remembered from last summer. "Nice, huh?"

"Yeah. I suppose this came from a drug bust."

Tully kept grinning. "Sit."

"Well, I'm glad to see you regardless of why I'm here." Loni ran her hand along the back of the leather couch as she continued to look around. "Air conditioning. Don't suppose you brought me here to stay in this, huh?"

"Maybe you better wait on that." Tully patted her on the shoulder as he sat beside her. "We have a problem. How did you put it? The snake's not scotched after all."

"Carl told me we missed another connection."

"I can't believe closing down the greenhouses on Carl's ranch didn't fix it. Somebody's still moving big batches of cocaine through Caliente."

Loni rubbed her face hard to relieve her exhaustion. "Hell, Tully. Nothing is going to stop the drugs."

"I know, Loni. Doesn't mean we shouldn't try."

"I get it, Tully. I don't see how coming all the way over here is stopping the drugs in Caliente. So why am I here? "

Tully got up and pulled two sodas out of the refrigerator. He handed one to Loni and plopped back down on the rust colored plush couch. "We figure some of the motorcyclists down here are pretending to be racing so they can take drugs across the border. We just don't know where."

"Are you kidding me, Tully? The Arizona border's damn near four hundred miles long!"

"I know." Tully held up his hand to interrupt Loni. "If your granddad's people on the O'ohdam Nation would help us, it would cut out a huge chunk of the border we wouldn't have to worry about."

"No, no." Loni shook her head. "The border's too much of a goddamn mess, especially on the O'odham Nation, and they want everybody gone. Who's to blame them?" Loni took a deep breath to reduce her fury. "After George W. Bush's failed amnesty promise in 2004 for temporary workers, the O'odham Nation's been overrun with undocumented people, especially coming in around Sasabe."

"I know." Tully stopped her. "I know where the amnesty trail corridor crosses over into Arizona. We been trying to close several trails running through the ranches in the Alter Valley before they cross the O'odham Nation to Highway 85."

"Yes, and until they reach Highway 85, everybody's fair game. Don't they know there's no amnesty?"

"Somebody forgot to tell them?"

Loni sighed in defeat. "Hope kills more down here than it saves." She chugged down the rest of her soda and burped in Tully's grouchy face.

"It doesn't matter, Loni," Tully argued. "They're still illegal and have to go back."

"I understand. But the border patrol could at least return them in a humane way. I hate the way they get treated, Tully."

"They're breaking the law."

Loni leaned forward, elbows on her legs. "So is mistreating them. You got the cartel, coyotes, drug traffickers, undocumented workers, and the Federales on the Mexican side. You got our own Border Patrol with its Forward Operating Camps." Loni stood and waved her arms. "The right-wing Arizona politicians turn loose the self-appointed groups like the American Border Patrol who call themselves a watch group." Pacing around the tiny area, she kept ranting. "There's the Civil Homeland Defense. And my favorite of course, the Tea Baggers. Most heartless pieces of shit ever walked this earth."

Tully tried to interrupt, but Loni wouldn't stop. "There's the right-wing asshole white supremacist vigilante second pieces of shit, Minute Men, National Socialists, some of the ranchers, and Ranch Rescue. And don't forget the Joe Arpaio Walking Tallers. Some of our homegrown who've given themselves permission to travel the border and hunt human beings like they were sick dogs. Stand Your Ground, my ass!"

"Wow, Loni. All in one breath!" Tully laughed. "Preachy little shit, ain't yah?"

Loni got another soda from the fridge and held the cold can to her forehead before she spoke again. "Damnit, Tully! You asked."

"You're right. So, you're saying these crazies are running wild on the O'odham Nation border. Why don't the O'odham's stay out of their way?"

"Come on, Tully, what are they supposed to do? They got land and families on both sides of the Gadsden Purchase line, hunting and fishing grounds, and sacred places they need to visit."

"I know," Tully said. "The U.S. Supreme Court ruled the O'odham Nation border predated ours."

"But it doesn't matter to Arizona politicians. They unleashed the crazies on the O'odham Nation and invaded their homes, slaughtered their animals, terrorized their children and raped their women. Do you ever wonder why these people don't want anyone on their land? And most especially don't want a fence across the middle of it?"

"How do you know all this?"

"My granddad buys lots of Brahma-mixed steers from families he knows." Loni took another long swig of her soda. "Bahb's friends told us horrible stories about beatings, people left in the heat and lying in their own piss, no water or food, wives and daughters raped, and homes vandalized. Those state-sanctioned animals stripped them of everything they owned and turned them loose to die. The O'odham Nation police are helpless because they can't arrest non-Natives."

Tully shrugged in defeat and changed the subject. "How well can you ride a bike?"

"Putt-putt or pedal?"

"Putt, of course."

"I'm okay." Loni hesitated. "Daniel taught me years ago. Mostly dirt biking. Rode them some on the streets in LA." She confessed, "Scared me enough that I told them I didn't like to play with their toy and they could have it back."

"Suck it up, Loni." Tully poked at her. "You can do it. Need you to meet with an undercover FBI agent."

"Why me?"

"Because you know the border better than anybody I know." Tully added, "Who I know and trust. Besides, you have an uncanny ability to see through bullshit."

Loni kept shaking her head. "Let me tell you what I keep telling Carl. Caliente is where the snake is. That's where we should be searching."

"Searching for what?"

"I don't know, Tully. Every truck and car in and out, every biker. Knock around the farms and ranches. We got a rattler in Caliente at least fifteen feet long. We can't miss it forever."

"Sorry, Loni. People at State don't agree with you."

"We all have a different truth, don't we? Like I told Carl, we need to follow the money."

"What'd he say?"

"What else? We have no legal right. But I think we better find a way."

"Sorry," Tully said. "Carl's right. We need something before a judge will let us subpoena bank records."

Loni gave up. "Where do I get the bike?"

"Sitting right outside." Tully grinned at Loni's horrified expression. "State fixed up the crashed one. Nobody claimed it. James thinks maybe someone will recognize it and want to question you. Might give us a lead on a possible perp."

"If it doesn't get me killed first. How do I explain where I got it?"

"Say you stole it off a police lot. They'll love you for that."

"Who was it registered to?"

"That's the thing. Some Mexican export/import business way down Hermosillo way that doesn't exist." Tully handed a file to Loni.

"Paperwork he used to enter the races gives his contact information and address in the states. All bogus. Ran his prints. Seems he's a petty crook from LA area."

Loni studied the photo and said. "He's just a baby. LA cops give you anything?"

"No, but trying to get information from them is like pissing upwind."

Loni flipped a page. "James thinks he's working with other bikers?"

"Yes. He's convinced if we find his buddies we can figure out how these drugs are getting to Caliente." Tully reached over and took the file out of Loni's hand. "I need you to listen to me now. I want you to work his last known hangout."

"I'm going in without a partner?"

"No. You'll partner up with the FBI agents. One of them's a woman and you're going to be her girlfriend who finally showed up."

"She's in a motorcycle gang? In the middle of the Arizona desert?" Loni said in amazement.

"Actually California right now. Crossing borders makes it an FBI problem.

"Is she cute?" Loni grinned.

"Cute and straight. Sorry."

"Getting to be the story of my life." Loni shrugged.

"She and two other undercover FBI agents hooked up with a gang that crossed into Mexico for cross-country racing around Algodones."

"Algodones, Mexico? Are we working with the Mexican police on this as well?"

"No!" Tully's responded with force. "Strictly undercover, so stay out of trouble there." He shook his index finger at her. "I won't be able to help you, understand?"

Loni dropped the file on the coffee table. "Let me get this straight. You want me to get on a bike and travel the back way to Algodones, meet up with FBI agents, and stalk bikers along the border across the open desert where I hope to catch them with drugs and follow them to Caliente. That about right?"

"Close."

With a snort followed by a sigh of resignation, Loni picked up the map. "I know the O'odham Nation doesn't let bikers on their land so we can skip that section of the border. Getting on the Goldwater Proving Grounds takes an act of god. Or at least Congress. So you're right. Probably the best route would be somewhere across the Cabeza Priete Refuge to Highway 85."

"Liv thinks so, too. But we haven't caught any bikes with drugs. So far we have no idea how they move them out of Algodones. Maybe the two of you can find the trail to Caliente." Tully tapped the map with his index finger. "If you cross the Colorado below Yuma, it's a straight shot to Algodones. Shouldn't take more'n three or four hours."

"The FBI agent. What's her name?"

"Liv Ludd."

"Where do I meet her?"

"At a biker bar at the town's edge called Diablo. You can't miss it when you get through the town."

Loni studied the map. "Could be okay."

Tully stretched out his long legs. "Remember how the border between California and Arizona jogs at the Colorado River?"

"Sorta. I was there only once. Went with Bahb and Carl to help another rancher dig cattle out of the bush along the Colorado. Saw where the river broke through into Imperial Valley, flooding everything. Carl said it was the 1905 flood. The only way they could stop it was to fill railroad cars full of rocks and back them into the break until they filled it up. Couldn't believe it, all those stacked cars. But that was years ago."

"Yeah, yeah," Tully said. "Kinda like No Man's Land. They put so many dams on the river it dried up below the canals. We think it's one of the main routes. They travel under the radar into Arizona and cross somewhere along Devil's Highway. Once they get there, they disappear into the Cabeza Priete Refuge."

"How come nobody spots them?"

"I wish I knew. We know they can't cross on the sand dunes at Algodones. The fence stretches for miles. But we're still left with more than a hundred miles of fence to monitor."

"Maybe they get somebody to lift the fence up at night. I know one of the guys who lifts and moves it every time the wind shifts and builds another sand dune to cover it up. Did you check that out?"

"Yep. Looked into it. But you know a third of the fence in Arizona is mostly a couple of strung barbed wires. Easy to cut." Tully wagged a finger in Loni's face. "Remember when you get there, don't mix with the local cops."

Loni reluctantly nodded. "What's the name of the bar again?"

"Diablo."

Loni laughed. "Why am I not surprised?"

"Here's the agent's picture."

"It's black and white," Loni complained.

Tully retorted, "Listen! She's got light red hair and blue eyes, and the back of her black leather vest has BOSS written across it. Remember, you're going to be the girlfriend she's been waiting for."

"Sounds like fun. So do I get to kiss her?"

"If she arrests you for sexual harassment, don't call me. You push on her, and she might bop you one."

Loni rubbed her nose. "Won't be the first time."

"Just sayin'." Tully sounded serious.

"Damn, Tully. When'd you ever see me hit on anybody straight?"

"What about Jenny?"

"No, no, Tully. She wasn't straight," Loni said. "Besides, she came on to me."

"How about Lola?"

"What about Lola?" Loni flashed in exasperation. "Never met a bi woman before?"

"She was interested in you last summer."

"Not anymore."

"What happened?"

"Her brother got into trouble, and she decided I didn't help him enough."

"Did you?"

"Move on, Tully. When do I meet this Liv Ludd?"

"Tomorrow afternoon at one o'clock." Loni listened as Tully handed her a few more photos. "These bikers are keeping records of possible mules running drugs." Waiting for her to memorize them, Tully took out more papers from an envelope. "Here's your passport and the permit for the FMM along with a short bio for you. Learn your new name." Tully tapped on the permit with his long index finger. "This is good for up to a hundred and eighty days."

"Oh, please, Tully." Loni's sarcasm came through loud and clear. "Cold day in hell before I renew this."

Tully laughed out loud at her. "But it's so easy to do. Return to the States, grab a cup of coffee and a new FMM, and cross right back over for another hundred and eighty days."

Loni agreed. "These assholes cross back and forth forever, and nobody to stop them."

"There's you," Tully reminded her with a shit-eating grin.

Loni's slight smile brought out a small dimple as she shook her head. "There you go again, Tully. There's your truth and there's facts. I'll bet you my new boots we're going in the wrong direction."

"I already heard you, Loni. But we need you to do this anyway. Give me your keys, and I'll see that your truck gets dropped off at the Caliente police station."

CHAPTER THIRTEEN

Loni left early right after breakfast to avoid the afternoon sun as she headed toward Algodones. The worst of the heat usually broke after Halloween, but this year was different. And the reflected desert sand could still boil Loni in her heavy helmet and leather chopper gear. The motorcycle was built for a taller person, and Loni was soon worn out from reaching out to grab the long handlebars. She leaned into the wind, bug splatters hitting her helmet visor without protection from a shield. Loni swore as the splatters smeared when she swiped at them. Her biggest problem was remembering to keep her mouth shut or else eat them. A couple had been bitter gross.

Bikers had dug deep into an animal trail that crossed the sand and salt-weed ridden river flats. Loni followed it out and up until she crested above the river basin. She turned off the engine for a minute to rest from the horrible racket, she let the silence settle over her. Behind her, the Colorado River fizzled out before it even reached the ocean. All the tributaries disappeared in the sand or were dammed to death.

Loni spent what seemed like days bouncing across rock spurs and up and down jagged wash banks. Mesquite, catclaw, and other spiny plants grabbed for her legs. At the border to Old Mexico, she idled the engine while she waited to pass through. At the check point towered the narrow border fence, fifteen feet tall and specially built to move with the ever- shifting sand dunes.

Algodones was a four-block area of medical buildings for doctors, dentists, opticians, and pharmacies. A flood of people came there for big savings and better medical care. The town was like any other town on the north side of the border.

Loni followed Tully's map to the edge of town. The Diablo bar stuck out like a sore thumb. Its garish red sign of the devil sat on top of an adobe building that had seen better days. She parked her bike alongside a dozen others and sauntered through a swinging door into the bar's cool space. Relief at escaping the heat and taking off her hot helmet and leather jacket almost overcame her anxiety. Her feet stuck in dark blobs mired with dirt on the floor as she moved to the bar. I do hope it's not blood, she thought.

Bikers sitting at some of the tables stared up at Loni as she walked toward the bar. The blurry mirror distorted faces as Loni studied the three bikers perched on high stools. One of them had long pale red hair curling down the back of a vest dotted with rivets reading BOSS. That's my girl.

"Hi, honey," Loni announced herself, spinning the stool around. "How about a kiss?"

"You're late, you bitch, and you don't deserve a kiss. Get off me," Liv snarled. "You were supposed to be here a week ago."

Loni took a step backward. "Liv, you never change. I missed you, too."

"Well? What took you so long?"

"My husband got sick, and I had to stay until my mother-in-law came."

The guy sitting next to Liv smirked. "Does he know what you're doing, hanging out with a girlfriend biker?"

"Hell, yes. He was going to hang out with his boyfriend 'til he got sick. Really, really bad flu."

"Sure it's flu?"

"Ah, hell, Howard." Liv climbed down off the barstool and grabbed Loni's hand. She dragged Loni into a hallway. The sound of catcalls followed them into a filthy single-stool bathroom, and Liv chortled at Loni's displeasure as she peered around. "Michael and Howard are good. They're undercover. Glad to have you aboard, Loni. Tully says good things about you."

"He thinks you're gosh golly swell yourself."

"Bet those were his exact words, too." The dimples in Loni's cheeks deepened as Liv smiled back. "Bet you don't work undercover much with those dimples. Too distinctive."

"No problem," Loni frowned. "I don't smile much anyway. So what's the plan?"

Liv's crooked grin matched her sarcastic answer. "Find drugs?"

"There is that," Loni said thoughtfully. "Though I did think you might already be hunting for them."

"Not really." Liv shrugged. "We have no idea. Drugs are all over the place, but nothing big like we're looking for. Believe me. We've scoured this country looking for the Caliente source."

"Tully did say the federales were undercover here and never found anything either."

"Only place we have left to check out is the Cabeza Prieta National Wildlife Preserve. We're headed there now."

Loni was confused. "Why didn't we meet up there?"

"We wanted to check once more across the Colorado River area before we head north."

A sudden bang against the bathroom wall jarred both of them. Liv opened the door and stepped out into a tall, skinny man wheeling a dolly toward the back door. "You always run into walls, bud?"

Loni jumped back, ducking behind the bathroom door. "Shit!" She whispered. "I know that driver. It's Dirk Flavo with the Thursday grocery delivery truck."

"What?"

"The truck. It comes to Caliente on Thursdays," Loni said impatiently.

"So? If it's a delivery, how come they're loading on instead of off?"

"Ask him!"

Liv yelled at the guy as she peered out the back door. "Whatcha loading?"

The driver slid the back door down and locked it before he answered. "Bad batch of flour."

"Appears you're about empty. Where's your next stop?"

"Caliente." Dirk didn't look back before he climbed in the cab and drove north at high speed.

Liv stepped out the door waving and hollering to the back of the truck. "Have a good trip."

Loni joined Liv and watched the truck disappear. The dust covering it hid most of the color, but it could have been dark green. She followed Liv back around to the bikes and watched her climb on a purple chopper.

"Well? You coming?"

Loni winced at the loud noise as Liv gunned the engine before turning to her own bike. "I don't know how to race this thing."

"We're done racing. Time to head toward the refuge."

The idea of getting back on the bike and traveling back across the Colorado basin did not appeal to Loni. "Think I'll meet you there."

"Sorry? Meet us where?

Loni thought a minute. "How about Tule Tank."

"I don't understand. I thought you were supposed to work with us."

"The basin's full of salt cedar, and I'm allergic."

"That's a lot of bull crap."

Loni shrugged. "It's my story, and I'm sticking to it."

Liv snorted. "I take it you didn't care for your trip across the basin?"

Loni rubbed her butt. "Nope. I'm taking the highway this time."

Liv released her kickstand. "Why didn't you ride with your Thursday Caliente truck? He could've taken your sorry ass all the way home."

"Thought about it."

"Shit!" Liv spun silt all over Loni as she disappeared in a cloud of dust.

CHAPTER FOURTEEN

Loni crested a hill and gazed down into a desolate valley shaped like an oval platter. A sad-looking lopsided windmill missing several blades slowly turned in the hot breeze. Next to the windmill was a metal tank with a cement basin at one end for animals to water. Beyond, a barbed-wire fence stretched over to a roofless one-room adobe shack. Sparse greasewoods, barrel, and prickly pear cactus spread over the hills. The blue flag sticking a good twenty feet in the air interested Loni. Clean water.

At mid-afternoon Loni arrived at Tule Tank. She was ready for quiet after the incessant noise of the chopper. Leaving it in the shade of the shack, she walked over to the barrel. She filled her helmet half full of water and dumped it on her head.

"Wasting water. Shame on you!"

Loni jumped and swung around to face a huge man with a bushy, flaming red beard. She hoped he was smiling. His eyes crinkled before he let out a roaring laugh. Red hair as thick as a pelt curled out and about his shirtless bib overalls.

"Shit, dude! You scared me." Loni's heart pounded.

"Meant to." He flung back. "Hate to see water wasted out here."

"You belong to Humane Border group?"

The man tilted his head in curiosity. "What's that?"

"People who placed these water barrels and those poles with the blue flag on top." Loni pointed.

"I wondered where the drinking water came from. They got a club for backpackers?"

"No. They're the good guys trying to keep people crossing the Mexican border alive. Especially undocumented workers."

The man stared at the flag. "I wondered. Many of these around?"

"Over a hundred, last I heard. The project's got people leaving water and food along regular routes the undocumented take." Loni frowned. "Sometimes ranchers empty the barrels or move the flag. They say they're tired of travelers trashing their property. But other ranchers trying to help have to be careful and not get caught. I heard one rancher got arrested for putting water out."

"Not the first good guy I heard of that payed for it." He stared at Loni a few seconds. "Even more of a reason to not waste water." He pointed at a tall tank next to the windmill. "Tank's empty, but the windmill's working. Sort of. There's some water in a basin over there to pour on your head.

"I don't think so," Loni defended herself. "There's a body in it."

The skin Loni could see around the man's eyes turned pale. "Come on." He said in a half laugh. "You're kidding."

"Nope. Back when my granddad and I brought cattle up from Old Mexico, we met the man who found him. Said he was floating in the water blown up like a balloon so he left him to it."

"Eeuuu. eeuuu, sick, sick, sick!" The big man shivered. "I took a bath in it!"

Loni was surprised to see the bear of a man use feminine words. "So. You camping here?"

"Not anymore."

"You alone?"

"Aren't we all?"

Loni snorted. "I mean is anyone with you?"

"Why? You going to beat me up and rob me?"

"I'm beginning to like you."

He reached over to shake Loni's hand, and his eyes crinkled again. "All the girls tell me that. Call me Red."

"Why?"

"You must be color blind."

Loni laughed and shook his hand. "I'm Loni."

"So, Loni, how'd a woman alone get out here on a cycle and not get knocked in the head a time or two?"

"Rode up washes at night?"

"That's stupid. You think nobody in the middle of the night could hear you?" Not waiting for an answer, Red said, "Lucky you got a full moon or you'd be dumped on your ass out there. Can't see shit without it." He inspected her bike all over. "Sand bike, huh? You part of those racers across the border?"

"Was. Heading for home now. I'm taking a shortcut."

Red crossed his arms over his chest. "You running drugs?"

"No." Loni grinned. "Search me if you want." She turned around to get a drink from the cup hanging on the side of the water barrel.

Glancing back at Red, she said. "I got my clothes folded up neat in my saddle bags so don't mess them up."

"Nah. You racing or are you a cop?"

Loni shrugged. "Cops stay away from the flags. They don't want people to die either."

"Our cops? Arizona cops? You serious?" Red was upset. "I spent a few days over at the Charlie Bell tank." He pointed to the north. "Watched border patrollers take an axe to the spigot. Left the flag."

"I know, Red, but have faith. Some of them care."

"I don't want to get in a fight with you, but where the hell you been lately? Our crazy politicians reward cops for kicking immigrants around like a pile of horse shit."

"That good?"

"Not reason enough for you?"

Loni leaned against the tank and crossed her arms. "My granddad says we never grow up. Most of us learn how to hide our sickness in public." She studied the big man. "You got a reason for being out here?"

"Yep. Wildlife photographer. Camped over the hill over there. Early morning I sit on the hill and wait for animals to come to water."

"Interesting." Loni hung up the cup and glanced around. "Any human traffic?"

"Only a teenager with maybe a ten-year old boy. Filled their canteens. When they saw me, they ran. You might catch up with them."

"Pretty much as I remember it. You see signs of anybody living in the shack?"

"Not since I been here. Lotta trash around, but not people."

Loni strolled over to the shack and reached into the scattered debris. She picked up an empty tortilla plastic bag. "I think you just missed some hikers. Probably undocumented workers. Stayed a few days from the mess."

Red gawked over his shoulder. "Think they'll be back?"

"Not unless they're mules. If that's so, they'll head back in a few days."

Red thought for a minute. "It was nice while it lasted. Want some coffee before I pack up and go?"

"Sure." Loni followed Red around a small hill. A pickup was hidden in a grove of mesquite trees. The red color had turned to washed-out rust. Above it was a mesquite tree with rags hanging off the branches. Loni cried, "Oh, god. A rape tree!" She pedaled backward and reached for her gun before she saw the sun had faded the tattered underwear.

"What do you mean, rape tree?" Red's eyes darted around.

"Check out that underwear hanging in the tree, Red. Coyotes smuggling women into the U.S. often rob and rape them," she sputtered. "They hang the underwear in a tree for trophies and dump the women to die in the desert."

"Can't the women climb up there and get it back?"

"You ever tried to climb a mesquite?" Loni asked scornfully, thinking about its thorns.

"Oh, god." said Red. "I didn't know. I figured they were some kind of flags showing the trail. I never imagined. Please. I'm sorry." Red jumped onto the hood of the pickup and tried pulling the half-ratted underwear from the mesquite tree.

"Leave it, Red. Those mesquite thorns are gonna cut you to pieces."

He climbed off his pickup and pulled on his beard. "How could anyone do that?"

Loni had no answer. "You've picked a main trafficking route for undocumented immigrants and drug runners to do your picture-taking. It's really dangerous along here."

"I'm beginning to feel like I'm in the middle of a war." Red gave a sour smile. "Funny thing. This war on drugs is a big joke, and border security is the other joke."

"You need to be careful anyway, Red. Check around for smugglers. Don't even trust those self-appointed phony cop sickos our politicians turned loose. If you see a body, don't go near it. That's how they ambush you. Maybe they won't kill you, but by the time they strip you of everything and leave you to die, you'll wish they had."

"You know, when I drove up here I came through an auto graveyard. Had to stop and take photos. Everything was abandoned there." Red pointed off to the nearest hill. "I even saw a car with Arizona license plates reading SMUGLR." Red studied her again, "You're saying I shouldn't trust anyone out here, huh?"

"Not on this border. My granddad always said violence never resolved who's right. Only who's left."

Red left fresh coffee in her thermos, and Loni settled in with her fake MRE lunch. She kept them in her apartment freezer for when she worked overnight or on short trips. The sound of bikes came as she finished. The three motorcycles circling Loni threw dirt in her face before they turned off the noise makers. "You expecting company?" Loni's sardonic grin stayed on her face through the antics. "Made enough noise to bring the second coming."

"Nope." Michael sat down cross-legged beside Loni and grabbed the thermos. "Just left a nasty scene."

Alarmed, Loni blurted. "Was it Red?"

"You talking about the hairy red monster in the beat-up pickup?" Michael giggled.

Loni playfully shook her finger at Michael. "Don't make fun. That's his coffee you're drinking."

"He went by us so fast I thought he was going to flip. What'd you do to him anyway?" Liv asked.

"Wasn't me." Loni grimaced at the rape tree.

"Shit." Liv rubbed her face. "Does it never end?"

"She's still stressing about the scene we left at the border."

"What happened?" Loni said.

Liv tried to wipe her tears away as she shoved her kickstand down. "I suppose the bathroom's out there somewhere."

Howard winked. "There's a million acres, girly. Help yourself."

"Smart ass." Liv slapped him across the back of his head and hurried down the wash snaking by the windmill.

"So, Howard. Talk to me."

"You know those catapults that fling things through the air?"

Michael interjected, "I keep telling you, it's a trebuchet, not a catapult!"

"And who the fuck cares?" Howard shot back.

"Call it a slingshot," Loni suggested. "Tell me."

Howard toed the dirt with one foot. "It was up against a border fence on a flatbed towed by a big beat-up Mack cab. The sling was a big sucker made from wood. I'd guess the federales caught them tossing bales of marijuana across the fence." Howard swallowed hard. "Guess they decided it would be great sport to trade the bales for the smugglers. They strapped smugglers into the contraption and flung them over the fence. That was after they shot the smugglers on the American side of the fence who were catching the bales."

Michael cut in when Howard paused. "Liv went ballistic. She rode into them firing into the air and threatening to shoot the lot of them. She made them untie the smuggler in the sling and put him in their car along with the two who were left. Still waving her gun in the air, she followed them for a mile, making sure they drove back toward town."

"What'd they do with the bodies?"

"Nothing. They would have left them for the coyotes and cougars to drag the carcasses back to their lairs. Liv made us bury them. She burned the sling shot. We had to go more than twenty miles to find a barbed wire fence to cut so we could circle back."

"Good thing part of our border has barbed-wire instead of those big ass-jerk fences. We'd never got back to bury them." Michael's high stressed-out voice grated on Loni's nerves. "I just got back from a tour in Afghanistan, and I'm beginning to feel right at home." He reached over and gave the thermos top to Howard who gulped the last of the hot coffee down.

"He already worked for the FBI before he went in so they gave him back his job," Howard explained as he returned the lid to Loni.

Michael's laughter sounded like a small barking dog. "Never said I was smart."

"So that's why you're late," Loni said, ignoring Michael's retort. "I got to ask. How'd they camouflage a trebuchet?"

"Easy. They built it to imitate a cotton trailer. Opened the back and pulled off the canvas top."

Liv walked back into camp and glanced around at the group before she settled on Loni. "Who's cooking?"

"I already ate. Sorry. Was I supposed to wait for you?"

"Hell, yes." Liv declared. "We've got packets of jerky and energy bars, but we could sure use something else."

Loni shrugged. "I've got a few more MREs."

"Oh, God no," Michael groaned. "I had all of those I could stomach in Afghanistan. Please say you have something else."

"I could toast some prickly pear pads for you. They taste kind of like green beans."

"What pears?" Liv stopped in the fire circle.

"That cactus right over there." Loni pointed to a clump a few yards away. Large glove-sized oval-shaped flat pads grew out of each other. Sharp yellow clustered needles covered the dark green pads.

Pushing off the rocky ground, Loni groaned, realizing how sore she was from riding her bike. It was worse than a horse, she thought. She stretched her muscles before she walked over to a mesquite tree. Carefully, she pulled off a dead club-like limb along with two long smaller limbs and shaved off the thorns with her knife. Using the bigger stick, she knocked the greenest pads off the prickly pear plant. Using the small sticks, she skewered four pads on each stick. Handing them to the men, she said, "Hold these over the fire until you singe all of the needles off. Pulling those suckers out of your mouth isn't fun. And be careful you don't burn yourself!"

"When you get them cleaned, grab my GI Joe plate over there to cut them up and fry them in," Loni said to Liv when she handed her the knife.

"Got any salt?"

Loni snickered. "Lick it off my arm."

Liv snapped back. "You wish!" She glared at Loni in the growing dusk. "What else is out there to eat?"

"Beans off the trees in spring and most of the summer. Not great, but edible."

"Do water stills work?"

"Some." Loni frowned. "If you line them with cactus chunks to get more moisture. If you're not careful, you can waste more body water chopping up the cactus than you can get from a still."

They sat around the fire, not full but not as hungry as they were. Liv's voice came out of the dusk. "Loni? Do you think the drugs are coming in on the hogs?"

"You want the truth?

"Of course! Why else would I ask?"

Loni threw a stick onto the fire. "No."

"What about that one you found in Caliente?"

"I think that was a fluke. We checked every hog for weeks and found nothing. But the drugs still showed up in Phoenix."

Howard's droll voice came through the darkness. "Gee, Loni, tell me why I been wasting days of my time, hot, sunburned, beat all to hell from bouncing all over that damn desert, half deaf from a roar that keeps following me into hell, with sand up my ass ground in so hard I know it'll never come out."

"Well, they didn't travel through this way. I didn't see any bike tracks anywhere around here, and I rode in a loop for several miles. All the traffic is on foot or four-wheel drive. Also, Red didn't hear any bike sounds or any other motor in the two weeks he was here."

The camp was quiet for a long time. "Shit." Howard groaned.

"But, look at it this way." Michael sighed in relief. "We can go home now."

The camp was silent the rest of the night.

CHAPTER FIFTEEN

W e need to get up," Liv said into the dark dawn sky. No one made a sound. She said it louder the second time before she shouted, "Get the hell up." She climbed out of her sleeping bag. "Damn! It's cold." Just as she dumped a big log on the hot coals of the night fire, a shape appeared in its flicker. Liv screamed.

Loni jerked up with a gun in her hand aimed at the small figure.

"Shit!" Liv patted her chest and gasped for breath. "You scared the bejesus out of me!"

"Please help us." The form became two. A teenage boy was carrying a child on his back.

Michael and Howard jumped to their feet and quickly searched the children. "They're clean except for this," Michael held up a hunting knife.

Howard hovered over the two. "What do you want?" Loni thought his deep voice sounded almost kind. Howard led them to the fire to get a better look at them. "You're just kids. What the hell you doing way out here, for Christ's sake? You crazy?"

"No." The boy slid the child down his body, and they both sat on the ground close to the fire.

"What's your name?" Howard demanded.

"Gabriel Salazar." The teenager put his hand on the child's shoulder. "This is Izzy."

"Is not!" The child was belligerent. "My name's Isabella."

"What did I tell you?" he scolded her. "You're supposed to be a boy!"

"I forgot."

Gabriel hugged her. "Guess I'll call you Dizzy."

"Take that back!" Izzy punched Gabriel. Gabriel rocked her back and forth.

"Where you from?" Howard asked.

"Globe. My dad worked the mine until it killed him. When they found out our papers were fake and took us back to Mexico."

Loni had heard these stories for years. Thousands of undocumented workers sold everything to escape Arizona prisons. Families who raised families and run businesses disappeared in an agonizing exodus, leaving whole neighborhoods and businesses to predators. She didn't know which was worse, forcing Native Americans into reservations for a destitute life or running off undocumented workers like wild dogs. The families were robbed of everything like the Japanese in the western states of the country during World War II. "What kind of help do you want?"

"Some clean socks. Maybe food." Gabriel sounded hopeful. "Maybe even a ride?"

Loni looked at their tennis shoes covered in cactus needles. She reached for her first aid kit from the motorcycle and squatted beside Isabella. "Hey. Can I take your shoes off?"

Izzy turned her big frightened eyes toward her brother. He was muttering to himself and didn't look at her. She turned back to Loni and slowly dipped her head.

Loni handed her flashlight to Liv and carefully peeled off Isabella's shoes and socks. "Michael, could you get two meals from my bags and feed these kids?" She held Isabella's calf and pulled needles out of her foot with tweezers. Loni ignored Gabriel's frazzled voice in the background and got out as many needles as she could. She tore off a short piece of duct tape and pressed it on Isabella's foot. Before Isabella could react, she jerked it up. Isabella started to cry, but Loni said softly, "Look! I got all the needles out." Isabella stopped crying as she studied the tape. Loni reassured the little girl before she checked the foot with her.

"Hey!" Liv poked Gabriel, attempting to stop his babble. "Hey, you're safe now!"

Gabriel broke. Through heartbroken, wrenching sobs, he continued, "We had no family in Mexico. We couldn't make it. Too hard! I looked for work. Nothing!" He scrubbed his tear-filled eyes with his fists. "No one would talk to me. Gringo's puta, they kept calling me. Nobody would help! I'm so scared! Please, take us with you."

They let him cry it out as Loni took the cactus needles out of Isabella's other foot. When she finished, Isabella climbed into Loni's lap and buried her head in Loni's neck. Loni rocked her as she looked around, "Anybody got any extra socks?"

"I do." Liv answered. "Where's she going to get shoes?"

"First things first. Her feet are cold."

Michael gave pear pads and jerky to Gabriel while Liv cleaned his feet. Loni pulled the socks onto Isabella's feet. She played a game with the little girl until she finally got a smile.

"How'd you avoid the Border Patrol?" Howard sat beside Gabriel and put his arm around him.

"They make so much noise it's easy to hide from them." The boy's sobs lessened. "Then we heard the rattles from snakes. So many of them. I was so scared. I smelled your smoke so I came back."

The adults packed and cleaned up the campsite. Loni crouched in front of Gabriel. "You know we should turn you over to the Border Patrol. We could get fired if we help you," she quietly told him.

"Maybe the Border Patrol will help them?" Liv looked hopeful.

Loni didn't agree. "Even if they wanted to, and some do, they can't break the law either."

"Jesus," Michael protested. "Who made these crazy laws?"

"Right-wingers. Who else walks this heartless among us?"

"It's illegal for any of us to transport them." Howard reminded Loni.

"Yeah, but I'll do it anyway." Loni sat on her bike. "Climb on. kids. You're going home with me."

U

Loni left the kids at Maria's Hacienda and picked up her truck so that she could get Coco from her grandparents. The hangar was dark and quiet when she got home. She leaned against the huge hangar, waiting for Coco to finish her nighttime rituals. When they got upstairs, Loni was exhausted, but she had to laugh at Coco. She had hopped onto Loni's bed and stretched out on her back, legs in the air and head on Loni's pillow. Loni heard the sound of snoring before she got Shiichoo's leftovers into the microwave.

CHAPTER SIXTEEN

Loni!" Carl yelled out of his office. "Get your ass in here!"

Loni shooed Coco under her desk before she slid on the wooden floor into Carl's office. "God, Carl! You sounded exactly like Chief. You might welcome me home." At the grim expression on Carl's face, she looked down at herself. Clothes clean, checkered Western shirt snapped, Levis zipped, boots on. She waited.

"Heard you aborted the investigation." Carl's voice was tight. "That true?" Carl was rubbing his ear harder than usual.

What the hell? Loni thought. She kept it simple. "Yes."

"Sit!" Carl barked. "Tell me what happened."

Loni wiggled into the misshapen chair and tried to explain. "Nothing, Carl. That was the goddamned problem and I told you so. After a month running races all along the border, they came up with nothing. Well, not nothin' nothing. There were plenty of drugs out there, but they weren't our cocaine or anything else headed toward Caliente. My gut tells me it's not bikers bringing our cocaine across the border."

"So you're saying the whole trip was a bust."

"Yes, Carl. There you have it."

"Out!" He pointed at the door.

"Wait a minute. What'd James find out?"

"Nothing. Out!"

"You mean his trip was a bust too?" Loni backed up a step.

"Out!"

"Want me to shut your door behind me?"

"Out!"

Loni carefully closed Carl's door and moved over to her desk. Coco settled on Loni's feet, and Loni reached down to rub the brown curls. The cell phone buzzed. "Detective Loni Wagner speaking."

"Loni?"

Loni sighed. Her granddad always questioned who she was. "Yes, Bahb, it's me."

"You go Minnie's Well now. Dead child needs to come home."

"How do you know?"

"Matt Barlow brought couple here for you to come and get. Coyotes deserted them at Minnie's Well. When baby died, they headed north. They got to Matt's place."

"Undocumented?"

"Yi."

"They're at the ranch now?"

"Yi."

Loni listened to the dead sound of the phone for a few seconds before she speed-dialed Doctor Benjamin. She gave the coroner directions to Minnie's Well and said, "I'll meet you there." Once again, she heard the dead sound of the phone and thought, Doesn't anybody say goodbye anymore?

At the well, Loni stood over the baby. The ambulance arrived soon after she did, and she watched Lu and Doctor Benjamin climb out of the ambulance and walk over to her.

"How you doing, Loni?" Doc stared around at the frozen windmill and dry tank.

"Been better, Doc." Loni said. "Hate to see this."

"I know." Doc squatted and uncovered the tiny body before he slowly stood and quietly watched Lu pick up the baby. She held the baby close and walked to the back of the ambulance.

Doc placed his hand on Loni's shoulder. "Heard about your friend Jenny O'Neal. Real shame she and her dad are gonna spend the rest of their lives in prison for nothing."

"She was more like an acquaintance."

"Anyway, it's a real shame they didn't wait."

"What do you mean?"

"She means Jenny and her father didn't need to bother to kill Chief," Lu quietly told Loni.

Surprised, Loni gawked at Lu. "Huh?"

"It's a damn shame." Lu ducked her head.

"Why?" Loni was totally confused.

"Didn't you read my autopsy report?" Doc asked her.

"No. Why should I? He couldn't get any deader."

"True, but he would have been dead in weeks anyway. He had advanced small-celled lung cancer."

"You're shitting me!" Loni squeaked.

"Nope."

"It was all for nothing?"

"Yep."

The ambulance left a trail of dust, and Loni sat in her truck and cried. The parents hadn't been prepared for the desert. In a nearby dugout under a thin-leaved mesquite tree, pieces of a barrel cactus showed they tried to suck on cactus parts. There wasn't enough for them. The plants had shriveled from the unusually hot summer temperatures.

Loni followed the path of the ambulance and heard a loud explosion as she slowed down to turn onto the highway. The truck jumped, and she slammed on her brakes and fought the wheel. It swayed and bucked before it lurched and shuddered to a stop. Ready to attack, Coco put her ears back as she slammed against Loni.

"Stay, Coco." Loni left the poodle in the cab while she walked around the truck. The front right tire was shredded in a thousand pieces. Even the rim was bent from the force of the explosion. Jesus! Loni shivered from fear. What if I'd been going faster? she thought. She leaned down and studied the wheel. Sniffing a piece of tire, she recognized the smell of explosives. Loni learned about them from a workshop she took in LA. She dropped pieces of the tire into an evidence bag.

With a deep sigh, Loni kicked the spare. She took out her cell phone, hoping a tower signal reached this far south. She got lucky. "Shiichoo, I can't make it to the ranch today. I got a flat."

"Where are you?"

"On my way home from the Well That Minnie Dug."

"What are you doing way out there, child?"

"There's this nice woman?"

"She going to change your tire?"

"No," Loni smiled. Hearing her grandma always made her feel better. "You think I don't know how to change a tire?"

"Yes," Shiichoo teased. Suddenly Loni heard a loud voice, "Damn it, cat!" For a minute all was quiet until Shiichoo got back on the phone. "I knew it was going to be a bad day. I just kicked the cat."

"Kicked the cat?"

"It was an accident. She won't stay out from under my feet."

Loni laughing for several seconds before she gasped and said, "Never heard you swear before!"

"You think it's funny? It's your fault the cat's under my feet all the time."

"Why me?"

"You're the one that drug it in the house, don't you forget."

"I had to. Lola about ran over him, and I was worried."

"Piffle. You wanted to annoy me."

"Worked, huh?" Loni giggled.

Shiichoo hung up. She called Lola and got the same response Shiichoo gave her. "You even know how to change a tire?"

"I'm not even going to grace that with an answer." This time she hung up on Lola's laughter. No way could she admit she had never changed a tire on this monster. Sighing again, she dug out the jack and wondered what an oversized tire was going to cost. And rim. Don't forget the goddamn rim.

CHAPTER SEVENTEEN

Loni didn't get back to the station until mid-afternoon. Lola was leaning on the counter waiting for her when Loni came through the door. "How bad?"

"One toddler. A boy."

Lola sat back down, tears in her eyes. "Oh, god. Will it never end?"

"At least the parents are still alive." Loni fished a form out of Lola's basket to fill in her report and slumped at her desk. "They stumbled into Matt Barlow's place in bad shape. After what Junior said to Matt the last time, he took them to our ranch for me to help."

"Damn!" Lola rubbed her arms defensively. "What'd Junior say?"

"Said he'd take the next wetbacks he picked up to the desert and shoot them."

"He wouldn't do that!" Lola scoffed.

Loni rubbed her eyes. "Matt wasn't so sure. Neither was I. After all, he called them wetbacks."

"Can't we get somebody to fix the windmill at Minnie's Well?"

"Maybe I could get Uncle Herm to do it. I don't think the state will pay for it, though."

"I know. The local politicians have all pretty much written off undocumented people as good road kill."

"Do you know who owns the ranch?"

"Doesn't your granddad know?"

"No. Heard him say one time it was owned by a big business back East. Western something? Typical behavior for big business. Nobody fixes anything. Nobody's responsible for anything." Loni sat forward in defeat rubbing her nose. "Too big to fail, my ass. Too big to care."

"Want me to find out who's in charge?"

"One time I tried. But if you can find anybody, maybe they would at least let someone else fix it. Too many travelers see the windmill at a distance and end up dead trying to reach water."

Lola's voice was determined. "There has to be a CEO at the company who'll help us."

Loni sat back in defeat. "Other day I was reading this study on psychopaths."

"And?"

"Not counting those in prison, most of the rest are either extreme right-wing politicians or CEOs. I'm adding coyotes to the list."

Lola snorted. "Why don't you tell me how you really feel!"

"I'll tell you how I really feel. I'm going to ask Carl to let me do some night surveillance at Minnie's until I catch those sons-a-bitches. They are the worst I've ever run across." Loni stood and thumped the counter with determination. She hurried into Carl's office. "Got a minute?"

"I'm not sure. Every time you come into my office I end up with a whole lot of trouble."

Loni thought he was in a better mood. "Should've stayed on the ranch if you wanted a peaceful life."

Carl leaned back in his chair. "What is it this time?"

Loni decided to stand rather than try to fit into the chair in front of his desk. "I'd like to sit on Minnie's Well a few nights to catch those coyotes working out of there."

"You think you can?"

"Don't know why not. This is the fifth time the past three months we've dealt with undocumented people who got dumped there. I know there have been others that didn't make it to help. From the load of trash and tire marks everywhere, they spend a lot of time hanging out and they don't seem to be very careful."

Carl took several minutes to answer her. He leaned forward, his elbows on the desk. "It's worth a try. I think you need to wait a night or two before they come back. I also want you to take James with you. It's too dangerous alone."

"Shit, Carl. For the first time in my life I got on his good side. He'll hate me after this."

"Blame me. Tell him I ordered it."

Loni hesitated. She reached into her pocket and pulled out a baggie with pieces of her blown-out tire. "Before I forget. Can you ask Harris Harris to send this to the Phoenix lab for me? I don't want Lola to know about it."

"Whose tire?"

"Mine."

Carl almost exploded himself. "God, Loni! What have you gotten yourself into this time?"

"I'll let you know when the results come back in," Loni said and scurried out of his office.

Loni walked back to her desk to finish filling in her report. She jerked up from her work when she heard Lola on the phone. "I'm sorry, say that again?" Loni's ears perked up at the stress in Lola's voice. "You say she got into Old Man Morris's car?" Hanging up, Lola turned to Loni. "You need to find Old Man Morris. He's driving away with a woman who robbed the convenience store."

"Robbed what? Who?"

"You know his black Caddy, don't you?"

Loni hurried out of the station to see the ancient car slowly rolling by. "Shit!" she sputtered out loud to herself, not believing her eyes. The Caddy failed to obey the stop sign and crawled around the corner, and Loni sprinted forward. She was out of breath by the time she caught up to the car. She banged on the driver's window with the butt of her gun and motioned for him to stop the car. He slammed on the brakes and stared at her through slitted eyes.

"Mister Morris! Roll the window down." Loni pointed her gun at a gaunt and tired woman in her late fifties. She held a brown paper sack in her lap.

The old man rolled the window down an inch and hollered, "Not letting in the heat. What you want?"

"Mister Morris. Roll down the goddamned window!"

The window went down two more inches, and the old man snapped, "Don't be rude, young lady. Your grandma raised you better than that. And get that gun outta my face!"

"Mister Morris. For the last time. Roll down the window."

Five inches later, the old man yelled, "What!"

"Who's your passenger, Mister Morris?" Loni's gun was still pointed at the passenger.

"My boarder, Mrs. Piller. Why you pointing a gun at her?"

"Mrs. Piller, get out of the car. Hands out first so I can see them."

"Can't you ask her polite? You crawl out of the devil's bed?" the old man bawled.

"Maybe so," Loni muttered to herself. She edged around the hood to the passenger's side. "Hands, ma'am. Show me your hands."

The frail woman calmly opened the door and slowly pushed her way out.

"Hands please, ma'am. Now!"

"What the hell are you doing, Loni? That's no way to treat a nice lady!" Old Man Morris screamed at Loni.

"Are you part of this?" Loni spoke through the open passenger door.

"Part of what?"

"The robbery."

"What robbery?"

"The convenience store. You were just there, right?" Loni was getting impatient.

"She was. I waited outside. Said she needed milk."

"Seems she robbed it while you sat and waited for her."

"What! What! No, no, no! That can't be." He pushed open the door.

"Stay where you are, Mister Morris. You need to stay out of this."

"Holy shit!" Morris sputtered as he folded back into his seat, eyes darting around nervously.

The afternoon was hot, and Mrs. Piller's heavy coat made Loni wonder what weapons the woman had. She grabbed the sack from the woman and tossed it on the hood. When she lifted the brown tweed coat, she found a sawed-off shotgun and hunter's knife attached to a wide belt. Loni hoped there wasn't anything else. "What the hell were you thinking?"

"I couldn't think of a better way to get arrested."

"Sorry?" Loni sputtered, confused.

"I'm sick, and I can't afford to pay for my medicine."

"Ah, shit." Loni held onto the woman's arm. They went back to the station with Old Man Morris following in his car. Lola buzzed them in.

"Sit there, Mister Morris, and give me a minute." Loni pointed to a long bench. She introduced Mrs. Piller. "Here's your thief, Lola. She needs to be booked."

"You're kidding?"

"Am I smiling?" Loni dumped the contents of the sack on the counter in front of Lola. Coins spun and rattled around the paper money, and Lola's eyes widened.

"Did you read her rights to her?"

"On our way back."

"She confess?"

"Yep. Said she was sick and needed nursing care. Too young for Medicare."

"I'm standing here, young lady." Mrs. Piller huffed. "I can confess for myself. You ready to fingerprint me?"

"Good god," Lola half-chortled. "I don't know whether to laugh or cry."

Loni shrugged. "How about I take her over to Maria's Hacienda? Bet Calli can help her."

Lola gave Loni a long, hard glare. "You pray we don't get caught."

"Deal."

"You going to settle it with the store?"

"Double deal."

"I'm not going to jail?"

"Not today." Loni led the woman out to her truck.

They stopped at a solid wooden gate, and Loni smiled as she keyed in a code. Only three months ago the old adobe wall was full of crumbled places and holes to patch. And there was no gate. Now they looked good. The abandoned motel at the edge of town had been a blight on the main approach to town, but the strong, light-red adobe walls glowed behind the graffiti. The roof with the clay tiles from Old Mexico running in even red waves across the horizon held up well throughout the years. Loni and Lola convinced people in the town to help them with the repairs. The graffiti was gone, the roof tiles were repaired, and windows and doors had been replaced.

In front of the office, Calli met them. Her beaming face brightened Loni's world. She introduced Mrs. Piller. "Can you call the doc and get medicine for her?"

"Bet your sweet bippy, Loni," Calli burbled. Small-boned and slim, she exuded warmth. Short light-brown hair framing her animated heart-shaped face bounced as she sat Mrs. Piller down at the kitchen table. She placed a cup of coffee and plate of muffins in front of the older woman. Calli sat next to her and motioned Loni to do the same. "Where you from?"

"The Oregon Coast." The woman gazed at Calli with sad, watery blue eyes as she swept her long, stringy grey hair back off her leathered face.

"Really? I'm from the Oregon Coast. That's where Loni and I met." Calli exuberantly pounded the table. "I lived below Yachats out on one of those headlands sticking into the ocean."

For the first time, Mrs. Piller smiled. "I know that place. I remember it's called the Jewel of the Pacific coast. Beautiful little town."

"Yes. Did most of my shopping there."

"How could you stand to leave such a beautiful place?"

"Lost my husband."

"I'm so sorry." Mrs. Piller patted Calli's hand. "So did I."

"It's okay," Calli cheerfully reported. "We had a bad accident, and he was in pain all the time. Had a head injury so he didn't remember much either. Drugs don't help that." Calli threw her head back and laughed again. "That's how I met Loni. Remember? Kate invited you for breakfast and I was there too." Calli patted Loni's arm with affection. "We were renting rooms for the night and took turns staying at home taking care of guests. I wanted to go to Kate's house for breakfast so I gave him an extra dose and was out of the house before he woke up. He couldn't remember it was his turn anyhow." Calli became quiet for a minute before she finished. "When I lost him, I decided to totally change the way I lived so I moved to the Southwest. Variety's the spice of life, right?"

"I loved it there. Except for worrying about tsunamis."

"Oh, my, yes." Calli's loud laugh was accentuated by her pounding on the table. "I remember this time we got a call to evacuate. So I told Will, that's my husband, to grab the Indian rug. I'd find the cat and meet him at the car. By the time I was out the door the car was gone. He already forgot what I told him and drove up the hill without me."

Mrs. Piller's smile brought some life to her pale face. "What did you do?"

"Nothing. The cat and I sat and waited, and the tsunami came in two inches high. By the time he came back home he forgot why he left."

"That's why you moved here? Getting away from tsunamis?"

"No. Sort of got in trouble with my advertising. My website said, 'No children, no Hummers, and nobody who voted for Bush.'"

Loni said, "She's right. I was having coffee with her one morning when a Hummer pulled in. She ran out the door waving her arms hollering, 'No Hummers. No Hummers. No Hummers.'"

"A right-wing paper from back East wrote a nasty article about my website and called me a bigot. I got so many threatening calls I had to disconnect my phone."

"What happened to your business?"

"That was the problem. Without a phone I didn't have any. So I called the paper and got handed off to a fancy lawyer. I told him I was a little old lady with a sick and dying husband trying to rent a room occasionally to pay a few doctor bills. Told him I had to remove my site, change my phone number, lost my business. I was thinking to sue."

"What happened then?" Mrs. Piller's face got more animated.

"They sent some money." Calli's smile left her face. "My husband died soon after, so I used the money to move south. Thought seeing the sun might be a fun change. So," Calli said, "tell me about your family now.

"All I got left is a daughter. Heard she was living somewhere around Caliente so I came to find her. Wanted to see her one last time before I died."

"Did you?"

"Not yet. She got married after she left home." After a short hesitation, Mrs. Piller said, "My husband beat me and ran her off. I don't know anything about her husband except his last name and he was from Caliente. Can't afford to search anymore. I ran out of money." She turned to Loni, "Do you know a Jonathan Brown?"

"Sorry." Loni shook her head.

"Jeez, Loni. This place is small enough you should be able to find her daughter. Did you try to help her?"

"Nope," Loni shrugged. "Didn't know anything about it until now." Loni spent the next half hour making notes. She promised to do what she could. As she left, Loni watched Calli lead Mrs. Piller to one of the units. On her way back to the police station, Loni returned the money and explained why the woman robbed the store. The owner agreed to forget it ever happened.

Back at the station an hour later, she found Mister Morris where she left him. She sat down on the hall bench beside him. "I'm sorry I left you so long. Can I get you a soda?"

"No, Lola there took good care of me. Am I in trouble here?"

"Not really. I wanted to talk to you about your renter. You know her long?"

"No. Met her at the clinic yesterday. She said she had nowhere to live so I took her home with me." Mister Morris's sad face made Loni want to cry. "I'm lonely, you know? I outlived three wives and all my kids."

"How old are you, Mister Morris."

"Be ninety-six next month."

"Good Lord, Mister Morris. Letting someone move in that you don't even know is not the best way to find a new wife."

"Wasn't wanting a new wife. I'm not really looking."

"Think you'll be looking by the time you're ninety-six?"

The old man gave Loni a small grin. "Maybe."

Loni helped him out the door and back to his car, but she couldn't bear to watch him drive away. He was one of those old timers who stared straight ahead when he drove and never stopped for anything.

At her grandparents table, Loni listened to Mister Ybarra tell his story between tears of agony at his loss.

"They slept all day," Shiichoo told Loni. "I forced water down them."

Mrs. Ybarra's grateful smile lit up her a cherub face, soft and quiet. "Yes, and good thing we're in the desert, or I would float away."

"How long did you wait at Minnie's Well?"

"Five days. We ran out of food on the second day and water on the third." Mrs. Ybarra began to cry again. "Our Miki couldn't . . . " Her words broke off with another sob, and Loni thought about the dead baby.

Her husband held her. "When they left the highway, they told us they were picking up another family. As soon as we crawled out of the back of the truck, the one called Jesus pulled a gun. They tied us up and robbed us of everything before they left us there."

"Can you describe them?"

"I'll try." Mister Ybarra closed his eyes. "It was around midnight. There were two of them. The driver was tall. Maybe six foot two. Skinny, dark complexion, acne scars down his cheeks and neck. He had tattoos on his knuckles, you know, but they were so old I couldn't read them. Clean shaven, short haircut. Big feet. He had on work boots. The second one was also tall. Could have been his brother they were so much alike. Much younger. Maybe in his late teens. He was nervous, maybe scared like he never did this before. He was always telling Jesus to hurry. I think his name was Pablo." He turned to his wife. "That about right?"

Mrs. Ybarra nodded. "We didn't see much of them. They loaded us in the back of the truck and shoved boxes around us. We traveled all night and all the next day. It was late when we reached the border. I saw the older one hand a guard an envelope." She slowly sipped her ice tea and wiped tears from her plump cheeks.

Loni studied Jose and Mary Ybarra, impressed with the clear description. "When you're up to it," Loni quietly said, "I'd like to hear your story from the beginning."

"You take care of these two," Bahb told her as they left the house. "We are judged by how we treat those in need. Do not forget everybody counts. Everybody."

Loni left the couple with Calli at Maria's Hacienda before she drove toward home. Right before the turnoff from the highway, she saw a battered red Mazda. Black smoke poured out of the engine, and a teen-aged girl dressed in yellow shorts and a skimpy orange halter stormed around the car kicking at the tires. Her long, straight blond hair swirling around her head, and her swearing at the top of her lungs added some words to Loni's vocabulary.

The girl opened the back door to the car and pulled out a huge purse. She used it to pound on the car, wildly swinging it and bringing it down with a whap. Shrieking, she banged on windows and doors. Loni got out and leaned against the fender of her SUV. She grinned to herself, wondering if she could arrest the girl for assault and battery.

When the girl headed for the trunk, Loni decided to stop her. She stepped forward and held the trunk lid down. "Enough!" Loni held the lid against the girl's pull. "Enough."

The girl sagged as the crazy leached off her face. She collapsed on the hot earth and hid her face in folded arms on her bare knees. Loni let her sob while she lifted the hood to check for flames. She walked to the girl and gently pulled on her arm. "Come on," she said. "I'll take you home." Inside the truck, Coco licked at the girl's tears. "What's your name?"

"Fairy Mae."

Don't laugh, Loni told herself, don't laugh. "Where do you live?"

"Down behind the seed store." The girl had a weak depressed voice. "I can show you."

Loni handed her a tissue, and Fairy Mae blew her nose. "I don't know what happened." She wiped her eyes. "I spent the night at my girlfriend's. You know the Spencers?"

"Sure. They have one of the farms back there."

"I promised my dad I'd be home before he left for work."

"Do you need to call him?" They were nearing the town, houses filling up both sides of the highway.

"No. I already did when I left." She shed a few more tears. "I don't know what happened."

"You ran out of oil. You ever check the stick?"

"Why should I?" the girl objected. "It came with oil!"

"You're right." Loni tried to stay expressionless. "Of course, it did."

At the girl's house, her father was standing in the driveway, and Fairy Mae let out a wail equal to Loni's siren. The big, burly man opened the door and pulled her out. When he enveloped her in a hug, the wail ratcheted up a few more notches. Loni solemnly pulled around a corner before she howled in laughter.

Loni was almost asleep when a buzzing penetrated her fog. She fumbled for her phone.

"Loni?"

"I think so. Let me check."

"Sorry?"

Shit, it wasn't Lola. "Hey. I thought you were someone else."

"This is Chelsea."

"Of course. What's up?"

"We've got another rape victim here. Can you help? I called Junior, but he said he was too busy."

Loni sighed. "I'll be there as soon as I can."

A Mexican girl with a torn, bright-red tank top under her white shirt was in tears when Chelsea let Loni in. Loni thought she was probably cute when she wasn't in such misery. Blood caked the insides of her legs. Loni took Chelsea aside and whispered, "What's her name?"

"Carmen Gomez."

Loni sat beside the girl and spoke in Spanish, hoping it would make her more comfortable. "Carmen, mi nombre es Loni. Te acuerdas de nada?"

The girl ducked her head and kept crying.

Loni gently brushed the hair away from Carmen's eyes. She stood and sat by Chelsea. "Same as the others. She doesn't remember anything. Did she tell you anything?"

Chelsea sighed. "I can't even talk her into a rape kit."

Loni turned back to Carmen. "You sure?"

"No! No! No!" Carmen shook her head violently.

"You could get a disease. Or get pregnant and need the pill."

Carmen sobbed. "They'll find me there."

"No. I'll be with you."

"I'll be here, too," Chelsea reassured her.

The only sound was Carmen's sobbing.

"Can I take you someplace?"

"My aunt," Carmen whispered.

Loni drove Carmen to a small wooden house behind the remains of the Catholic Church. A woman reached for Carmen and folded her arms about the sobbing girl. Loni followed them through the dark into the warmth of the house. "I need her clothes," Loni said cautiously.

The aunt nodded, and the two of them walked out of the room. The woman returned and handed Loni a paper bag.

The day's sadness followed Loni on her drive back to the hangar as thoughts chased each other in a crazy circle. If they didn't catch the coyotes, the Ybarras couldn't stay in the states. Luckily the bigoted anti-immigrant Arizona legislators didn't change the IU Visa law that allowed her to provide a visa to anyone who helped catch a coyote. If she caught them. Mixed in with these worries was the fury that Junior ignored all the rapes.

Loni drove by a car on the side of the highway. She turned around to see if anybody needed help. Inside was one of her high school classmates, a big football hero and one of her torturers. He had to get married every before he graduated. The smell told her he was drunk. She poked at him and told him to get out of the car. He woke up and seemed sober enough to drive. Loni knew he couldn't afford to miss work at the seed mill. He couldn't afford to get drunk, either and he certainly couldn't afford six kids. She followed him home and made sure he got into the house. He flipped a bird at her before he disappeared through his front door. She turned around in his driveway and spun back out onto the highway, half grinning to herself. Next time she found him drunk, she decided she would throw his sorry ass in jail.

Loni parked beside Daniel's pickup and searched for him while Coco wandered. He came crawling out from under the other side of his pickup. "How come you're so sad?"

"Daniel? Could I have a hug?"

Daniel smiled and stepped toward Loni. He held her until she sighed and stepped away. "Thanks." She opened her mouth to explain when James drove into the hangar and parked next to them. He rubbed his temples and squinted his blue eyes at the bright light while he slowly climbed out of his truck. Loni and Daniel laughed at him.

"Oh, god, don't. It hurts my head."

"What's wrong with your head?"

"I celebrated too much."

"I'm glad that's done because you and I are spending the next few nights at Minnie's Well," Loni told him.

"Huh? What the hell, Loni!"

Daniel laughed.

James quickly grabbed his head again. "Ow, ow, ow. Not so loud."

"Got a couple of sicko coyotes using Minnie's Well to rob and dump undocumented travelers."

"What did Carl say? You sure he approved of this?"

"Of course! It was his idea." Loni was obdurate.

James grabbed his head again. "Ow, ow, ow. I said not so loud, damnit." He glared at Loni through his fingers. "What about my wife? I just got home again."

"You got tonight."

"She's gotta work tonight."

"Well, now, that's a real pisser, huh James." Loni's voice reeked of sarcasm. "Why don't I throw down an ice pack for your head?" She sprinted up the stairs and tossed it down where it landed at James's feet. He leaned over to pick it up and went to his knees, groaning in pain as Loni bounced back down the stairs.

"You know what, cuz?" Daniel picked up the ice pack and placed it on James's head. "You better go on a stakeout. Otherwise living is going to kill you." Loni and Daniel dragged him into the office and shoved him onto the rickety couch.

Loni retrieved the icepack and stuck it back on James's head. "Carl said we could only stake it out for three nights at the most. Pick me up here about eight tomorrow night."

"Shit." James continued to rub his head as Daniel drummed on an old green barrel. "Would you stop that noise?" James snapped.

Daniel picked up a big wrench and banged on the side of the drum.

"Stop!" James yelled and grabbed his head.

Daniel giggled. "Cuz, I hope you had a good time last night because I hate like hell to see you feel this way for nothing."

"Do you have to make so much noise?"

"What noise? You mean like this?" He banged once more. "That's not noise." Daniel grabbed a pipe in his other hand and banged on both sides of the drum. "This is noise!"

"You're about as quiet as a squalling elephant in heat. If you don't quit, I'm gonna have to hurt you."

"Way you're feeling you couldn't hurt a pissant." Loni teased him. "When did you hear an elephant in heat, anyway?"

"Never, but I can imagine it." James shook a finger in Loni's face. "I could start with you," James warned her.

"In your next life."

James poked at her, barely missing her nose. "Gee, Loni," James grabbed at her nose again. "Where'd you get the hump on your nose?"

"Which one?" Loni knew where James was going.

"The biggest one."

"You're such a shit, James. You know you broke my nose in high school when you shoved me into a locker."

"Oh my, oh my. Did it hurt much?"

"Fuck you!"

Daniel nearly fell off his barrel from giggling so hard. Soon even James was laughing.

James grabbed her chin in his large hands and turned her to the light. "Where'd you get the other hump?"

"Domestic." Loni squirmed away. "I lost."

James smiled. "Sure wish I'd seen that one."

"Once is enough, James. That's all you get." Loni stood. "I gotta go get a shower and get back to the ranch tonight."

Loni was wrapped in a towel when she heard Coco's excited barking. She threw on a shirt and jeans before she poked her head out the door. James squatted at the foot of the stairs and growled. Coco barked back from the top landing. Loni yelled, "Stop pestering my dog!"

"She started it. She won't let me by."

"I hope she finishes it by biting you. What do you want?"

"What he always wants," Daniel answered walking up to the bottom of the stairs. "My beer."

"You drinking Daniel's beer again. What happened to your headache?"

"A beer helps. And anyway, how do you know I didn't bring it?" James insisted.

"Daniel, tell him to drink his own beer." Loni said.

"What do you care what I drink?" James retorted.

"Because you buy the cheapest piss-smellingest crap there is and leave it in my refrigerator where it sits and I want it gone. Not even the cockroaches will touch it."

James shrugged. "Can't help it if he makes me replace his beer. Didn't say I would drink that crap."

Shaking her head, Loni walked to her refrigerator and grabbed one of James's cheap beers. She stood in the doorway and shook it before she tossed it down to James.

"Loni! You shit! I can't open this now."

With a big grin, Loni grabbed a box of sopapillas her grandma made for Uncle Herm. Leaving her door open, she hurried down the stairs, Coco following. As she passed James she said, "Sic him, Coco."

James leaped up the stairs two at a time and slammed her door behind him. After a minute, he carefully opened the door sticking his head out. "When are you leaving?"

"I'm waiting for you to come back down."

"So what is this? Pick on James day?"

"What do you think, Daniel? Shall I tell him or should you?"

"You can do it."

Halfway down the stairs, James turned around. "Tell me what?"

"I'll tell him later." Loni opened the truck door for Coco and followed her in. She slowly drove by James who pounded on her door and yelled, "Tell me what?" Feeling much better, Loni drove to the ranch to finish evening chores.

CHAPTER EIGHTEEN

For the third night, Loni and James parked on a slight rise with a good view of Minnie's Well and the road coming into it. Except for the occasional panting from Coco, the desert silence felt ominous. A bitter chill caused the frigid cold to hang around them. They frequently warmed up the car to keep the fog off the windshield as they challenged each other in a running bet of scissors, paper, and rock to see who got the binoculars. Loni usually lost, but it didn't matter because she couldn't see through her side window because Coco's breath kept it a foggy mess.

The car was Carl's favorite, a bright yellow 2004 Ferrari 612 Scaglietti he picked up in a drug bust. Someone had raised the chassis for off-road travel and modified the front with a large bull bar adding to its bumbling ugly shape. Carl said the bar was there to push things, but Loni didn't know what he planned to push. To add to the car's abuse, Carl bolted a bar of four spotlights to the top. Loni figured the bull bar gave James the idea to ram the coyotes' truck. In a Ferrari for god's sake. Loni tried to talk him into throwing out tire spike strips or simply shoot out the tires. She finished her complaining by saying, "But nooo! You got to cowboy it, James. What if it's a huge truck?"

"So?" James's head was settled back against the headrest, his eyes closed and his bored voice rolling over Loni. "Why don't we talk about something else?"

"Like what?"

James decided to tease Loni. "Heard once that people average twenty-eight first kisses. How many have you had? Anybody I know?"

"Move on, James."

"How come Lola's mad at you all the time?"

Peering out into the pitch-black night, Loni shrugged. "She thinks I'm not helping Manny enough."

"Harry told me he was cleared."

Loni snorted in disgust. "He is, but Lola won't believe it until Manny's home."

"Sorry about that. I thought you and Lola would make a cute couple."

"Time to change the subject again."

"Okay. How about war stories? Funny things perps did, who we shot, who shot at us."

"You start."

"Okay. You remember our free enterprise teacher in high school? Doctor Tucker?"

"Boy, that takes me back. He left town years ago."

"Only recently. He went broke farming."

"Farming? I thought he taught school?"

"Did. He quit and bought a small farm down in the alkali flats on the bank of the Salt River. Didn't know it was too salty to grow anything. Didn't bother to ask. His son-in-law saved seeds from his pot smoking, so they planted the seeds down in the riverbed among the salt cedars. That was the year we had the bad floods, and they lost their whole crop. Watched it washed right on down the river. He complained to anyone who would listen about the five-thousand dollar crop they lost so I had to arrest them for planting it in the first place."

Loni laughed until she hurt. "That's a good one. Couldn't happen to a nicer guy."

"You are so right. I'll never forget the time I was late for his class and he grabbed me by the front of my shirt, shoved me up against the wall, and called me every name he could think of. Then he threatened to beat the shit out of me. I was never late again."

"Did I ever tell you about the bank robber in LA Maria and I arrested?"

"Maybe. Tell me again."

"He walked up to the teller and shoved a gun in her face asking for her money. She said she needed to see his ID first. So he gave her his driver's license and she gave him the money. When he got home, we were waiting."

"Good one! You remember the bartender who shot herself in the leg?"

"Oh, God." Loni groaned. "I had to interview her at the clinic."

"Really? Did she tell you why?"

Loni shrugged. "Said before she shot herself in the head she wanted to see if it would hurt."

James kept a straight face. "That's so sad it's funny. Anyway. She was in the other day to fill out a complaint against her boss. In the middle of it she called me over and said, 'I can't find any place where this form has a box for marking asshole.'" Grinning, James turned his head as his expression turned quizzical. "So? How many people you shot?"

Head down, Loni answered quietly. "I almost shot somebody once."

"Almost? Almost doesn't count."

"It does when somebody grabs you and has to take you down to stop you from shooting them."

"What happened?"

"A rookie cop thought my partner was the perp and shot her in the back. I never wanted to kill anyone so bad."

"How'd that work having a partner be your girlfriend?" James's voice dripped with sarcasm.

Loni frowned at James. "None of your business."

"Is that what brought you home? Getting your girlfriend killed?"

Loni teared up. "Sometimes I wonder what I could have done to change it. Anyway, it was part of the reason. Partly Shiichoo was sick. And partly I couldn't be a cop in LA anymore."

James was silent awhile before he spoke again in a soft voice. "You know? I always wondered why Daniel hung out at your ranch so much."

Loni scoffed. "I bet you did. He never told you, did he?"

"Come on," James begged. "Tell."

"Why not," Loni decided, liking James better. "Our old barn was the perfect place to rebuild his old cars to sell before you had a chance to wreck them," Loni said, making fun of James. "Kept him in pocket money. The other day I ran across one of his old cars he never finished."

"Anything else?"

"Between Russell, me, and his mom, he had the best tutors around." Loni reminded James. "You know how much he hated school!"

"Yeah. I remember when he graduated. They handed him his diploma. He left the stage, found his mom in the audience, handed her his diploma, and said, 'Here, Mom. You earned it.' The school was pissed that he didn't stay with his procession Almost took his diploma back." James turned to Loni. "Did you know he was up on the stage drunk on his ass? He was gone the next year, and you didn't have anybody to protect you anymore. Guess I was a little hard on you."

Loni shrugged. "Everybody has to have somebody to look down on. I was your somebody."

"I guess." He poked her in the ribs. "So what's it like to be raised by wild Indians?"

Loni snorted. "I wish I had been more like my grandparents."

"What! A wild Injin?"

"No, of course not. I do wish I'd followed the old ways better."

"Such as?"

"Such as getting along with others. The success of the group instead of the success of the individual. Stuff like that."

"You mean like it's not what you know that gets you by in this world, it's who you know?"

"Close."

"What else?"

"Always be polite and never argue. Treat everything with great respect. Be good to everything, especially animals." With a straight face Loni declared, "They have supernatural powers, you know. You mistreat them and they can make you sick."

"What a bunch of crap!"

"What's your problem, James? You're part Indian too."

"Yada, yada, yada." James changed the subject. "Sure wished I'd known about his cars."

"I'm glad you didn't. You'd have been dead by now. How many cars did you total growing up?"

"Need to know, and you don't need to know."

Loni giggled before a memory turned her somber. "Daniel told me about one wreck you escaped, thank god." Uncomfortable with the conversation, she asked anyway, "Tell me about Harvey Herring. Did he really kill himself?"

"I'm pretty sure he did." James seemed to search for words. "We always drove around after school for a while, picking up girls. This one day he said he didn't feel good so he took me straight home. Funny thing. He got out of the car, hugged me, and said goodbye to me." James paused before he spoke again, even more quietly. "He'd never done that before. He spun out of my driveway and jumped to a hundred miles an hour in seconds. Quarter mile down the road he hit that canal abutment, and I watched his car shatter into pieces." James stopped a minute and sighed. "The crash threw him so high in the air I could see him above the tamarack trees. The fall crushed his chest." James rubbed at his eyes fighting tears. "I never saw it coming. At his funeral the preacher kept ranting about people committing suicide burning in hell. I hated that man for trashing Harvey's memory."

"I understand," Loni said softly.

"Harvey used to rag on me about my behavior. I'm sorry for the way I used to behave. So much I didn't see."

"You already apologized before, James. I still accept it."

"I don't mean I'm sorry for what I did to you. You deserved it." Loni punched him on his arm and James laughed at her as Coco gave a hushed woof. "On the other hand, everybody needs somebody they can admire. Who do you admire, Loni? Besides me, of course."

"Listen, you simple shit—"

"Shhhh!"

Coco woofed again, and James whispered, "They're coming." Coco must have spotted the jiggling light in the distance.

"Why are you whispering?" Loni whispered back before she hollered at him. "They're still two miles away."

"Yeah." James giggled. "Freaky."

The bouncing lights grew larger. "You remember the plan, right?"

"Yes, James." Loni sighed. "We wait until they drop off their passengers. When they leave and get far enough away, we ram the side of their car. Coco and I get out, run around to the passenger side, and arrest anyone there while you arrest the driver."

"Good girl," James patted her on the head. "I'll make a good cop out of you yet."

The lights slowly danced in front of them as the vehicle dipped and bumped along the old desert road. Thick dust obliterated the taillights, and they couldn't tell if it was a car or truck. "Head for the front tire, James. The headlights are hanging pretty high for a car."

"Maybe we can tell more on its way back."

Twenty minutes later the lights raced away from the tank, catching James unawares. He quickly shoved the car in gear and spun down the hill. The car slipped and slid as it fought for traction. Loni held on to Coco so hard the dog yelped. James hit the brakes before the crash, and Loni's head slammed back. She almost lost her grip on Coco as the car pushed the delivery truck against a saguaro cactus and settled back down in the dust and debris. Loni managed to open the door at the same time James did, and they both fell out.

Loni scrambled to her feet with Coco and yelled, "Hunt!" She followed the dog to the other side of the truck where the sprawled passenger was trying to crawl away. Coco growled as she bit down and shook the coyote's wrist. He dropped his gun. Loni climbed through the open door into the cab and held her gun on the driver. James was waving his gun through the window at the driver on the other side. He slowly followed Loni out of the truck. They cuffed both men and called for backup. Pushing them into the back seat of the Ferrari she settled Coco between the two. The dog swung her head back and forth between the two men, staring them in the eyes and snarling. They didn't move or say a word while James drove back to the well to help the couple and their five children. He explained what happened and they would get their money back. Somebody would be back to get them.

"Lucky for you your plan worked, James," Loni said when he got back. "I can't believe you can still drive the car. Don't know how you're going to get that truck out of here though. You did a number on the tire."

"Not my problem." He poked at Loni. "See how much fun cowboying is?"

"It would have been if you hadn't broken my nose for the second time." Loni complained as she rubbed her nose.

"Let me see."

"Get away from me, James!"

Loni didn't get back to the abandoned family for two hours. On the way to Maria's Hacienda, Loni explained to the father about the IU Visa. "You get one because you helped capture the coyotes." Loni could tell from the blank stares that the others didn't know what she was talking about. "It protects victims of trafficking and violence. People who put criminals in jail can live and work in the United States toward a green card. You can also add family and get help."

"You're kidding?" The father blurted. "You can help us stay?"

Loni nodded in agreement.

With a wide grin, the father translated to his wife what Loni told him. She gawped at Loni in disbelief. Tears rolled down her plump cheeks as she repeated, "Gracias Dios." The kids cheered.

CHAPTER NINETEEN

S it, Loni," Carl ordered. "What's going on with your undocumented workers?"

      "I found a home for the two kids I brought home from the
Cabeza with the Ybarras."

"That's illegal as hell, Loni. What were you thinking?"

"No, no. We added them onto their IU Visa as family. They were
delighted, especially with getting a little girl."

"I hope you're right."

"About the trip to the Cabeza Refuge, Carl. The biker? I've been
thinking. There's something bugging me. Something is off, but I can't
figure it out. Can we talk about it?"

Carl let go of his ear. "You're talking about the dead biker with the
cocaine in his saddlebags?"

"A fluke? An anomaly? A strange coincidence? Something doesn't
add up."

"I know how you feel about coincidences."

Loni squirmed and waited until Carl tilted his chair back. "Maybe
it's not a coincidence. Maybe our real dealer plowed into the bike.
Maybe it was planted on him to mislead us. Did you find out what hit
him?"

"No." His sun-brown skin on his forehead crinkled into a frown.
"Didn't even think to check."

"Me neither until now. Did anybody keep the paint transfer from
the bike?"

"I don't know that either." Carl sighed and pulled on his bolo tie.
"It was Junior's case. Guess I should've checked." The gaudy turquoise
blob twisted as he adjusted it. He sighed again and stood to tuck the
back of his Western shirt into his Levis. "Let's get the evidence box
from Lola and find out. We could send it off for analysis."

"Can I see the accident photos?"

"Why not? Should be in the box." Loni followed Carl out of the office and up to Lola's counter. "Lola. Get me the file and the evidence box from the motorcycle accident last month where the kid was killed."

"You talking about Ralph Manor?"

"That's the one."

Carl waited until Lola disappeared into the evidence cage. "What do you think you'll find?"

Loni didn't want to say. She waited for Lola to set the box on the counter and dug out an envelope of photographs. Scattering them along the length of the countertop, she put them in order. She felt as if she was hovering above the scene and traced the tire marks with her index finger from one photo through another. "See this, Carl?" She walked along the counter, pointing out more tire marks. "There's nowhere that the driver skidded to a stop before he hit the bike. He didn't hit the brakes. He hit the gas. The kid was deliberately run down."

"Shit! That makes it murder. No wonder we never found the vehicle."

"Add conspiracy, Carl," Loni decided. "I think he was set up to send us somewhere else."

Carl turned to Lola. "Did you send the paint transfer scrapings to the lab?"

"I did. Got a fax back on it a couple of weeks ago and tried to give it to Junior, but he wasn't interested." Lola handed him the fax from the file.

Carl grabbed the paper and held it close to his face before he pulled glasses out of his pocket. Balancing them on his skinny nose, he read the report. "Says here it was a dark Woodland Green. Maybe from a 2008 to 2010 Jimmy truck." Handing the fax back to Lola, Carl rambled on. "I can't think of any green truck around here. You seen one, Loni?"

"Nope. You, Lola?"

"No."

"What now?" Carl sounded lost. "Shit, shit, shit." He tossed the photos back into the box.

"Don't do that." Lola slapped his hand and took the photos from the box, carefully putting them back in order.

"Damn, Lola, I'm glad I don't live with you. You're so OCD I bet you'd even count out how many sheets of toilet paper I would use."

"Twelve." Lola flipped back at him.

Half laughing, Carl repeated, "What now?"

Loni didn't know if the question was rhetorical, but she answered him anyway. "I guess we start all over." Loni glanced around. "I wonder if the truck will be mentioned somewhere in my files. Where's Junior?"

"He left early this morning." Lola answered. "Said something about going out to your ranch, Carl."

"Do you know where Junior left the files?"

Lola turned to answer Loni. "At his home I guess. He told me he'd done too much work on them to leave them here for anybody to mess them up."

"What the hell?" Carl exclaimed. "What made him think he could take files home with him?"

Lola avoided eye contact with both of them. "He's asking weird questions too."

"What kind of questions?"

Lola shot Carl a quizzical look. "Mostly how well you knew the O'Neals and the couple from Fresno who died up on the butte. Did you ever visit Fresno? How did you find your renters? Did you keep anyone from checking the ranch out? Did you have anything against the Barclays, especially around the time they lost their son, Todd. Did you lose or change any evidence? That kind of stuff."

Carl glared at Lola. "That sonofabitch! Why would he want to know? It's none of his business anyway!"

Lola's nervous shrug set off her stacked metal bracelets. "He didn't say, Carl."

"You said Junior went where?"

"I told you, to your ranch. You renting again?"

"Yeah. Winter vegetables. The greenhouses are still there. This time I was real careful when I checked them out. Did he say why?"

"Something about how he needed to examine one more thing before he arrested somebody. I couldn't get any sense out of him before he rushed out."

"So, what'd you tell him?"

"Nothing that wasn't in the file."

Carl stretched and took a deep breath. "It's been a long day, and I'm looking forward to an even longer weekend. What do you say, ladies? Let's start again Monday."

Watching Carl stalk back into his office, Lola cautiously asked Loni, "You going to the ranch this weekend?"

"Bahb wants me to move some mother cows to the north windmill. It got a little rain and the six-week grass is up."

"How's he doing?" Lola's voice softened.

"Compared to what? If you're talking about a bear, run. If it's a skunk, duck." Loni turned to leave but before she got the door open, Lola called her back. "Loni! Telephone!"

"Loni here . . . Sure. How old . . . ? See you." Loni handed the phone back to Lola. "Chelsea's got an undocumented girl at the clinic."

"And she called you why?"

"Remember last summer when we got her kids back and put her ex-husband in jail?"

"Of course." Lola said. "He was as mean as my ex. I'm glad I never had kids with him."

"You never said much about him."

Lola frowned at Loni. "We were talking about Chelsea. What about the girl?"

"Last summer I told her about Maria's Hacienda and asked her to keep a lookout for anybody who could use our help. Somebody found a young girl out in the desert under a mesquite tree nearly dead. The girl said there were five of them in her family, and the rest of them died. She walked as far as she could."

"You're taking her to Maria's?"

"Chelsea said she had her on an IV, but she's in fair shape and doesn't need hospitalization. Said she'd be ready for Maria's in another day."

"Chelsea's a special NP. If anyone can save her, she will." Lola paused her green eyes soft. "You know it's not even been five months since you bought Maria's Hacienda. I can't believe how much work we got done."

"Thanks to people like your dad. You wield a good hammer too." Loni grinned at Lola.

"Only thing that saved the motel was its good bones."

"And your mother badgering the good townspeople to donate time and materials to fix it up."

Lola nodded. "Worked, didn't it?"

"Glad she had the churches on her side."

"I'm pretty proud of what everybody's given to Maria's."

Loni agreed. "It's still pretty rough but having even six units up and running is pretty good."

"It's a great place to take the girl. Calli will take good care of her."

"And put her to work."

"And send her to school with papers."

"God bless Judge Sal."

"I heard the Ybarras are working in a grocery store for her brother. Are they really taking in those two kids you drug in from the Cabaza Refuge?"

Loni smiled. "Six degrees of separation. The Ybarras wanted children, and now they have them."

"You did good, Loni."

Loni stared at Lola. "Why are you all of a sudden being nice to me?"

"Got a call from Manny. He convinced me he would be home soon and you saved his ass. Said to tell you thanks." Lola smiled at her again. "Sorry for being such a bitch." Lola's green eyes were sparkling again. "I was wondering if you'd like to do something this weekend. Besides working on Maria's."

Loni returned her smile. "Wow, wish I could but I've gotta help Bahb this weekend. Rain check?" Ecstatic about Lola's attitude, Loni left for the ranch.

A mile from the ranch road turnoff, a car was crossway blocking traffic on the bridge over a dry wash.

"What the . . ." Loni walked through the cars until she got to the bridge. A woman was standing over a buzzard, hollering, "Do something!" Mrs. Ballard's booming voice could wake up a dead sidewinder buried in the sand. Loni's cell phone buzzed and she tried to listen to Lola as the huge woman's voice bombarded Loni's ears.

"I'm getting calls, Loni," Lola hollered over Mrs. Ballard. "They're saying you got traffic stopped from both directions. What the hell are you doing on that bridge?"

"I'm trying to get to the ranch, but Mrs. Ballard is blocking me."

"What?"

"You tell me, Lola. Listen." Loni held out the phone so Lola could hear Mrs. Ballard's diatribe. Tired of waiting for her to wind down, Loni said, "I know traffic is blocked, but I can't get Mrs. Ballard to move her car off the bridge."

"Why not?"

"Why not?" Loni almost screamed at Lola. "Because there's a goddamned buzzard here with a broken wing, and she wants me to take it to the vet. And she won't move until I pick it up."

"Well, pick it up and take it to the vet."

"And be the butt of everyone's jokes for the rest of my life? I don't think so."

"Do something and get the traffic moving." Lola's voice rose in both pitch and volume.

"I know I need to do something but I can't figure out what."

Loni heard Junior's voice in the background. "Shoot it!"

"No, I can't shoot it." Loni shouted back in exasperation. She turned off her phone to avoid the catcalls from people standing around Lola at the station. "Heel, Coco," Loni ordered. "Heel the bird." Coco looked back and forth between Loni and the bird. Loni pointed to it. "Heel!" The brown poodle carefully danced around the bird. She dodged its sharp curved beak and darted in between the bird's jabs. Loni grabbed a blanket from behind the seat of her truck and slowly circled behind the hissing bird. She marveled at how butt ugly its flaming red head was.

Coco stared at the bird rocked back and forth. Loni tossed the blanket over its head and bundled its body. She tied a rope around the bottom, capturing the buzzard's feet in the wrap. Stunned, it lay quiet. Loni laid the bird on the back seat of her king cab truck and got Mrs. Ballard off the road. As Loni waved the traffic on, she tried to ignore the people making fun of her. Shit, I'll never live this one down, she thought.

The ride to the vet was quiet. A crowd surrounded Loni when she unwrapped the bird on the vet's table. She told her story and moved to a side room to wait. With no room to pace, Loni perched on the edge of a chair and admired the animal portraits on the walls. A small rock waterfall trickled in a corner. Loni decided this must be the room where Tory gave people bad news. All the trickling water did for her was make her want to pee, and she wasn't going to cry over a buzzard.

Forty minutes later, Tory came in laughing. "First time I ever splinted a buzzard's wing."

"Yeah?" Loni grinned back. "It's the first time I ever caught one."

"What are you going to do with it?"

"Take it to Maria's."

"That shelter in the old motel outside of town. Heard you are beginning to open rooms for undocumented people to stay. You're adding a buzzard?"

"The woman who runs it. Lucky for me she has a soft heart."

"You hope. Heard you named it after your late girlfriend."

"Yes," Loni said pensively as she watched the waterfall. "She loved everything. Always dragging somebody home or somewhere to find a safe place. She would have loved Maria's Hacienda." Loni was quiet a few seconds before she looked at Tory. "Listen. I heard about your husband. I'm so sorry."

"Thanks."

A broadly smiling teenager walked in and handed the wrapped bird to Loni. She tried to avoid the snickers around her as she held the tranquilized buzzard like a baby and left the office. In the truck, the bird woke up and pecked at her ears while Coco barked at the bird's insistent squawking. Its broken wing, heavy with a splint, hung down as it hopped back and forth, shitting all over her back seat. Loni pushed her truck as fast as she dared, relieved to see Maria's Hacienda ahead. She dumped the bird off on a young girl in the office and sped away before Calli could catch up with her.

Loni was exhausted and ready for peace and quiet. She was fed up with being ridiculed. Time to head home. Her phone buzzed. What this time, she thought.

"Loni, can you come get me?"

"Who the hell is this?"

"Phillip."

Loni groaned to herself. She liked Phillip Brushard, but he only called her when he needed something from her. "Okay, Phillip. What do you need?"

"I rolled my car on Arling Road at the hills. Can you come pick me up?"

"You mean Gillium Dam area?"

"Yep. North side right at the last curve. Or is it the first?"

"That's a long way off, Phillip."

"I'll make it worth your while."

Loni thought, Oh, sure. He never had before. "Okay," she said. "I'll head out there now." She sped along the road and scanned for landmarks. Her grandma had written her a farmer plowed under the two huge piles of Indian trash left from centuries of camping on the river. She felt ill as she drove by the field. All that history destroyed for cotton farming which no longer existed due to underpricing from India.

The dam loomed over her, and Loni slowed down for the crossing on its apron. The dirt dam no longer backed up any water, but it created a small lake below. The bottom filled in with silt from nine major rivers that merged and dropped over on its way to the Colorado River. Loni drove over it as the SUV climbed out of the river bottom.

At the crest of the first hill, Loni saw a red sports car on its side at the edge of a cholla patch. She pulled up and spotted a man leaning against a Palo Verde tree. Walking up, she said, "Shit, Phillip. How many totaled cars does this make? Five?"

"Nine. You missed a few while you were gone." Bloody scratches and red blotches covered his pale-white shirtless chest and back. He could have stood in for a pin cushion. Loni watched him pull another needle out of his arm. "I was trying to pass on a curve, and that asshole in the pickup over there wouldn't let me by. Look." He pointed at his car. "Shot straight out there and rolled seven times."

A heavily tanned and muscled man glowered at Loni as he leaned with his arms crossed against a black pickup. "He's young, so he's got an excuse for being stupid. What's yours?"

Phillip glared at Loni in disgust. "Have you got any tweezers? Help me out here." He yelped as he pulled out another needle with a beat-up pair of pliers.

"Hell, Phillip." Loni shook tweezers out of her flat desert survival can. "I'm beginning to think you've got a death wish."

"Nah. Only testosterone overload. I wouldn't back off, and he wouldn't either."

Loni found a flat rock to knock cholla balls from his Levis. "Lucky you're wearing boots. This is the second time this week I've spent my time pulling out needles. Had a cow in a cholla patch. Thought about shooting her."

Phillip snorted. "Leave the gun in your holster and get those balls off me."

"It's a thought. Want me to call the ambulance?"

Phillip shook his head. "My ribs are sore, but they're probably not broken. I don't have any insurance." The diagonal bruise from the seatbelt strap across his chest was already deepening in color.

"Yep. Damned thing saved your sorry ass."

"Fuck you too."

Loni pulled a group of needles out of his Levis with his pliers. "You wanted a drive home?"

Phillip nodded toward the pickup driver. "Nah, he said he'd take me home. Conversation should be entertaining."

"I need to talk to him."

"Wasn't his fault."

"He could have gotten you killed."

"Coulda. Woulda." Phillip shrugged and worked his way onto his feet. He carefully walked over to the pickup driver and stuck out his hand. "No hard feelings?"

The pickup driver was obviously relieved. He shook Phillip's hand and muttered, "No hard feelings."

Loni glared at the pickup as they drove off and called a tow truck. She figured she would photograph and scene and file a report because she was there. Loni answered questions from the gawkers while she recorded the scene. "Yes, he walked away fine." "Hell, if I know how he did it." "He caught a ride home." "Yes, he's fine." She was more than ready to leave by the time the tow truck rolled up.

Loni drove into the hangar and parked. As she climbed out of her truck, she half-smiled about the ribbing she'd gotten for saving a buzzard. Daniel grabbed her shirt on her way to the stairs, stopping her cold.

"Mom's taking us all out for Dad's birthday tonight." Clean shaven and his black hair slicked back, he was all dressed up in new Levis and a gleaming white Western shirt with pearl snaps. Most of the black grease was scraped away from under his fingernails.

"Wow, how come you smell like bubblegum?"

"Loni!" Black determined eyes stared down at her. "It's Halloween and you have to come."

"Oh, God. How could I have forgotten?" Loni was walking backward as Daniel pushed her toward her stairs. "But I have to get the ranch now!"

Daniel grinned at her. "Come on. Maybe we can find an outhouse."

"I wonder how many outhouses are still around for kids to dump on the streets?"

"Daniel held her against the stairs until she agreed to go with him. It's dad's birthday. You have to go."

"But I don't have a birthday present."

"I figured you'd say that so I put your name on mine."

"What'd we get him?" Loni was ready to cringe.

"A case of peanut butter."

"What!" Loni didn't believe Daniel. "You putting me on?"

"What's wrong with that? He loves peanut butter. Especially on watermelon."

"I forgot. I'll go. But I'm denying any part in buying this. I'll get my own present. When's this shindig?"

"Now."

"What do you mean now?" Loni frantically tried to jerk away. "I can't get ready that fast."

Daniel examined her up and down. "Smells like you had a shower. Your hair's still wet, and you smell funnier than my bubblegum. Go put on a dress shirt and clean Levis."

Loni sighed. "Where?"

"The Oasis." Daniel checked his watch.

"But it's karaoke night!" Loni objected.

"So?"

"I hate listening to screechy off-key voices."

Daniel giggled. "Get drunk like the rest of us, and you won't care."

"I couldn't get that drunk if I tried," Loni tried to jerk away, but Daniel held on tight.

"Are you going to get ready?"

"No!"

"Mama told me not to come without you."

Loni groaned. "Now you're trying to guilt me."

"How's that working?" Daniel giggled.

"Maybe a smidge," Loni admitted.

"Lola promised to sing tonight."

"Really?"

"Really." Daniel smirked at her.

"In that case . . ." Daniel finally released her, and Loni ran up into her apartment. Ten minutes later she was sitting beside Daniel in his pickup. She laughed at the package between them. "Nice colors. At least you used the Sunday comics to wrap it with. Where'd you get that bow?"

"What bow?"

"The thing on top of the box."

"Oh, that's the card. I folded up a rolodex card but the damn tape didn't want to hold it on the package so I stapled it."

"Jesus, Daniel! You need to get married."

"So do you. We should get married together."

"Don't wait for me." Loni liked being a passenger for a change. It gave her a chance to people watch as they drove through town and out the other side. She saw the bar's blinking sign ahead. The Oasis was a bar where she spent more times arresting people than enjoying herself. "You remember Len and Sharon Hinkle? They had that chicken ranch up north?"

"Sure. Len is older, but I went to school with Sharon."

"Did you hear about last summer when I got a call from the Oasis about a woman climbing on the top of the bar and refusing to come down? I asked the barkeep what he expected me to do and he just said, 'Get your ass over here and talk her down!'"

"You telling me Sharon climbed up top of that monster bar?"

"Yep."

Daniel snorted. "Good god, that thing's more than twelve foot tall!"

"Probably." Loni agreed. "When I got there her husband was yelling at her to get down. Seems she grabbed one of the barkeep's large sloppy wet sponges and took it with her, threatening to throw it at her husband. By the time I got there everybody was chanting 'Jump! Jump! Jump!' I stood there wondering what the hell to do when she dropped the sponge onto the floor. Then she said, 'Watch this, everybody! I'm going to dive into that sponge!' There she was, all two-hundred pounds of her perched up on one of those carved colonnades, her frizzy blond hair flying as she started a countdown." Loni smiled in memory. "The bar counted with her while her husband hollered, 'No! No! Come on, Sharon! Stop!'

"She stopped counting and shouted at him, 'Why should I?'

"'Because,' Len hollered back at her, 'you can't swim!'"

Holding onto the steering wheel, Daniel weaved back and forth in giggles. "I never heard that one." He was still giggling when they parked behind James's huge black pickup, blocking him in. Anything to irritate James, Loni thought.

Daniel leaned over to Loni with an innocent expression. "Just making sure he doesn't drive away drunk."

"He's got a wife now."

"Ever seen her at a bar? She can out-drink him."

"That bad?" She knew Daniel would be the happy drunk before this night was over, and she would be the one driving them home. Good thing they both lived at the airport.

They pushed into a loud noise and a crush of bodies. Loni didn't know so many people lived in Caliente. People were dressed in Western tuxes, matching square dancing costumes, wildly colorful Western shirts, and Levis. The old-fashioned juke box flashed red and green as it blasted through the vibrating corner speakers around the room. Daniel trailed Loni as she wormed her way through the big smiles and hugs. She waved and started toward Lola until she saw she was sitting with her family. Lola's oldest brother, Miguel, stared knives at her.

Aunt Mae and Uncle Herm's table was covered with streamers, and balloons hung overhead. Daniel put his present with the others on the middle of the table. "This here's from me and Loni," Daniel yelled at his dad as he held onto Loni, giving her a knuckle rub on top of her head. "She picked it out!"

Loni sent an elbow into Daniels ribs before she pulled up a chair next to her aunt Mae. They did a jiggle hug in their chairs. "I love you," her aunt shouted to her with a kiss on the cheek.

Daniel disappeared, and the racket of music suddenly stopped. He spilled suds everywhere from a beer mug as he leaped up on the ornate bar. People ducked and wiped. "Everybody!" Daniel waved his beer like a flag. "Can any of you country bumpkins out there sing Happy Birthday?"

The crowd tittered. "Why don't you show us how," someone hollered.

"Ready?" Like a band conductor, Daniel led the waving crowd through the song as Uncle Herm waved back. He hopped down from the bar, grabbed four pitchers of beer, and slammed them on the table in front of Loni. Herm was already ripping paper off the presents. Dancers kicked the colorful scraps of scattered paper around the floor.

Loni joined the groups of step dancing singles until Lola moved onto the floor with Junior. He pushed into Loni's space until he kicked her behind the knee, forcing her to the floor. Daniel grabbed her as she started after Junior and dragged her back to the table. Loni played with the gag gifts and half-heartedly blew party horns until the hot and sweaty dancers were ready for karaoke.

The church singers predominated, but a small Western band and three jazz players took turns with the jukebox. Lola was the biggest surprise. Loni had heard her humming around the station, but her actual singing was mesmerizing. Her voice combined the mellow of Nora Jones with the pitch of Barbra Streisand.

Daniel yelled in her ear, "Not heard her before, have you?"

"Not for karaoke." Daniel's punching elbow gave her sore ribs. She pushed her chair back, said goodnight, and hugged Uncle Herm and Aunt Mae. Slipping her hand in Daniel's pocket, Loni grabbed his keys. "See you tomorrow," Loni told him with a bite on his ear. Moving into the crowd to find Lola, she got caught in a line dance. The second time around the room, Loni caught up with Lola and shouted, "I want to talk to you."

"I want to talk to you, too."

Loni pulled her out the door into Lola's three brothers.

"Where the fuck do you think you're going, Lola?" Miguel grabbed her arm.

Lola jerked away from him. "Back off, boys. This is none of your business."

Miguel grabbed Lola around the waist and dragged her, screaming and kicking, back into the bar. Her twin brothers circled Loni and held her until the door closed behind Lola. Loni trembled in anger and despair as the twins disappeared back into the bar. She leaned against the truck, but Lola didn't come back. Loni opened the door to Daniel's pickup. James rushed out the door and jogged up to her.

"No goodbye hug?"

"Sorry James. You were busy dancing."

"But I haven't had my dance with you." James grabbed Loni and swung her around a couple of turns before he sat her back on her feet. "I've been wanting to tell you I'm glad you came home."

Loni had tears of both joy and sadness as she drove back to the hangar. She was grateful for James and Daniel. If only she could find peace with Lola's family.

CHAPTER TWENTY

P aint was down. Tears ran down Willie's brown face as he held the horse's twitching head in his lap. Bahb worked to cool the horse by streaming water over him from a hose. Loni felt Paint. He was on fire, and his sides heaved as he panted for breath. Saliva bubbled out of his mouth, and muscle spasms racked his beautiful painted body. "Bahb! What the hell happened?"

"Indian chase with pickup. Paint got too hot."

"Did you call the vet?"

"She on way."

A streak of fear shot through Loni. "Where's Roani?"

Bahb didn't answer.

"Bahb!" Her voice quivered.

"He gone." Loni heard the sorrow in Bahb's voice.

"Five came in two pickups with trailers. I could not stop." His sorrowful voice stabbed through her. "I could not stop." The tremor in his voice broke Loni's heart.

"Who, Bahb?"

"They gone now, two hours."

"Goddamn it, Bahb. Who? Please tell me it wasn't the Pimas."

"No. Not Pima."

"You sure? You haven't heard of any funerals?"

"No."

"Please, Bahb, I can't let them push him off a cliff."

"No, I tell you." His face rock hard, he insisted, "They bad boys running the wild Santa Cruz over on the Colorado. They come before. They know the best horse."

"Why are you so sure?"

"One in rust-covered pickup had painted face. He ran Paint hard." Bahb scrubbed at his face with the back of his hand. "We at Topaz Tank fixing gate when your grandma call. Not back in time."

"Why didn't you call me?"

"They bad boys. They hurt you."

Loni sagged against the corral railing and buried her face in her arms. "Roani can't do that anymore." She pushed herself up from the railing and trotted back to her truck, swearing the entire way, "No one's going to steal my horse again!" She pulled open the door and shouted, "Take care of Coco!"

"Hela! They hurt you," Bahb shouted at her back.

Not if I see them first, Loni thought grimly. She shoved the truck into first. Spinning tires shot fine silt everywhere as the truck fishtailed its way back to Old Highway 85. Loni slammed a portable red and blue flashing light to the roof and turned west. She was breaking the law, and she didn't care. She would bring Roani home.

Ninety minutes later, Loni saw the village ahead and stopped. She pulled her gun out of its holster and tossed the belt behind the seat before she drove on. The truck crawled along, and she watched for any signs of life.

The sixteen square, government-built cement-block houses clumped together and surrounded a church and school building. Painted in a variety of faded pastel colors, they all reflected empty. Scattered among ironwood trees behind the houses were sandwich houses. The truck dipped down a wide gully as the road crossed the dry sandy wash. Brilliant yellow blossoms barely hung onto the Palo Verde trees. There were no street signs. Loni saw missing doors and windows left dark, empty holes in the block houses. Below the blank spaces, broken glass sparkled in the hot sun. A skinny red chicken hopped up on a window sill and cocked its head, watching Loni drive by.

Beds under sparse mesquite and ironwood trees indicated where people slept in the heat. Furniture and abandoned cars littered the ground, and a trash mound rose behind the Catholic Church. Pickups and horse trailers crowded around the schoolhouse ahead.

An old woman in a long, dark blue dress threw scratch to the few scraggly black-spotted hens hurrying toward her. Two of them flew out of an old, crooked mesquite tree. Another one ran out from under an old faded couch with holes in its ticking. The old woman ducked her head down as Loni passed her.

Loni smelled cooking. Under a huge mesquite tree, she spotted a fire under a grocery cart on its side with a big aluminum pot sitting in it. The odor of menudo wafted through the stench of hot dust. No dogs barked, and she wondered what was in the stew. She remembered the time she went with Willie and Bahb and ate at a La Paz village. They were miles away before Willie told her she ate dog. "Didn't see that old blue hound around, did you Bahb?" She vomited and stayed angry with him all day.

Roani's ugly tail was hanging out of a horse trailer hooked up to an old Datsun king-cab pickup. Loni breathed a great sigh of relief and stopped a few car lengths back, she got out, facing the schoolhouse. Focus! She eased past Roani and opened the door to the pickup. Climbing in, she crouched down and curled up on the board seat behind the driver, sharing the seat with a saddle. God help me if they're already on peyote, she thought.

Loni watched for signs of movement Loni wondered what ever happened to the murder on the reservation. She knew Caliente police weren't allowed on the reservation when the young girl had come into the police station to report it. Blue had been in town a few days earlier. Maybe it hadn't happened.

Hours seemed to pass before the schoolhouse door opened. A stream of dogs, kids, and adults poured out. Sweat rolled down her body covered with a smelly horse blanket. The driver's door opened, and someone sat down heavily, bouncing the pickup. It started, and voices faded. Careful of the mirrors, Loni pressed her gun into the hollow where the head connected to the neck. "Stop!" she ordered. "Don't move! Put it in neutral. Take your foot off the gas. We're going to talk."

The La Paz raised his arm to swing at her. Loni jabbed him hard in the throat, stopping his arm in midair. "What's your name?"

The smell of anger and fear radiated off him. "Name!" Loni jabbed him again.

"Merve," he grunted. Loni glanced around again. The dust from the cars and trailers pulling away was so heavy they wouldn't notice he wasn't following them.

"Okay, Merve, hands on your head. Then get out." Loni unwound her long, lean body and followed him. She pressed her gun in his back as she handcuffed him to a Palo Verde tree. Trading her truck for his pickup, she locked the hitch on the ball. Merve's dark eyes sullenly watched her every move.

Fear replaced the arrogant expression on Merve's face when Loni stuck her gun in his face. "Your trailer will be at the Caliente Police Station with your pickup keys. Take this horse again, and you will not live to ride him." In her rearview mirror, she watched him struggling with his handcuffs until the village disappeared from view. The ride home was uneventful.

Loni unloaded Roani and opened the gate. He went directly to the water trough. Exhausted, Loni leaned against the rails as the surging adrenaline faded. Her grandparents came toward her with sorrowful faces.

"Paint's dead." Shiichoo turned and went back into the house.

Loni turned to Bahb. "He drink too much water before we could stop him."

"Where's Willie?"

Bahb shrugged. "He broken now. He go off like old sick dog."

Loni sighed. "I'll find him." She searched Willie's house. Most of his treasures were gone except for his tomahawk on the kitchen table and the biggest two ollas in his pottery collection. She checked his secret hiding places. The stack of gold coins, the pocket watch she never saw him wear, and the few Pima trinkets she didn't understand were all gone. In his closet, his gaudy turquoise string ties, even the expensive ones, were all missing.

In the field near the hump of dirt, Paint's new home, Loni fell to her knees and wept.

The weekend on the desert seemed to last forever. Bahb's broken leg stopped him from riding, and Loni had to push a herd of mother cows to the north windmill. A deep ache accompanied her on the long ride. Loni missed Willie, and she missed her granddad. She couldn't match them, no matter how much she tried. With a heavy heart, Loni drove home.

> FROM: Loni Wagner
> TO: Sandi@gmailyahoo.com
> DATE: October 20
> SUBJECT: Still here
>
> Reason #6 why I don't ranch: Losing old friends to the fierce desert heat is too hard.
>
> Willie lost Paint today and I almost lost Roani. Bahb says we may lose Willie too, but I'm going to find him and bring him home.
>
> I don't understand such cruelty. Bahb always said gentle treatment is important because if you are good to a horse and you get sick or hurt, the horse will come to you and you will get well. But if you mistreat a horse and you are sick or hurt, the horse won't come willingly, and you will probably die. He means that applies to all pets

and people, too. As I stood by Paint's grave, Bahb's loving attitude didn't help. Sorry, I can't deal right now.
Take care of you and yours.
Loni

"Coco?" Loni called to her beloved poodle. Burying her face in the kinky wool, Loni let her tears flow.

CHAPTER TWENTY-ONE

Late Sunday afternoon, Loni faced her granddad's silent disappointment after she admitted losing three mother cows in her push to move them to the Carter windmill. She promised she'd be back the next weekend to find them.

Dirty and tired, she wanted to shower and climb into bed, but she needed to find Willie. On the trip into town, she kept flashing back on the fax report listing traces of flour stuck to the drug package they found on the biker. It niggled at her all weekend below her misery. She figured since she was hunting for Willie, she might as well ask the cooks around town.

The last bar on the street was the Last Chance Saloon. Loni pushed through the doors, close to admitting defeat. She perched on the bar stool and ordered her fifth Coke in a little over an hour. Petting the yellow-striped cat strolling back and forth in front of her gave her a chance to watch the bartender. Elmer Bowe was a big man, both tall and broad, with an arm span that made it easy for him to reach across the bar and smack a badly behaving patron. "Hey, Loni. Guess you want the usual." he growled. She knew he was a softie under his gruff exterior.

"Seen Willie lately?"

"Last night late. Damn shame about his horse."

"He say where he was headed?"

"Not really. All I heard was he was on his way hunting."

"You think he said happy hunting grounds?"

"Why? Something wrong?"

Loni rubbed her face hard. "Losing his horse sent him on a bad drinking binge."

"He did look rough." Elmer peered at Loni, questioning, "Sure you wouldn't rather have a drink?"

"Nah. A coke would be fine. With lots of ice. And maybe a treat for my friend here," Loni said, pointing at the huge cat sitting in front of her. "What's his name?"

"Jalopy."

"Isn't that a car?"

"See how big he is?"

"Good choice."

"Did I hear right? Did you really wreck another police car and lose a bus along with the Mexican Mafia? Bet that was a real proud day for you."

"Why don't you sit on your thumb?"

"I'm trying to cheer you up. How'm I doin'?"

"You're about as cheerful as that dirty dishrag you been pushing around."

"Speaking of dirty, how come you're covered with so much dirt? Didn't know cops did any work. Or even knew how." She gave him a disgusted glare, and he slid a tall glass of Coke in front of her. "Maybe you should stay downwind from my customers."

Loni lifted the cat's head out of her drink and picked up the glass. She turned the stool to gaze around the empty bar. Nothing changed since she had come to find Willie and haul him home. Bright halogen lights couldn't brighten the gloomy room with grime engrained in its walls of dark pine tongue and groove boards and wide floor planks. The windows covered with advertisements didn't let any outside light in. She turned back to stare at Elmer.

"Church ain't out yet." Elmer yawned at Loni revealing a mouth full of gold teeth. "Only heathens hanging around now." Elmer put his money in his mouth, swearing his retirement money was hid where nobody could take it from him.

"Okay, you've made enough fun of me. Tease your cat for a while and answer a question."

"Maybe. What you want to know?"

"How much cooking flour do you use?

The hostile expression on Elmer's face was priceless. "What kind of question is that?"

"Only wondering. Do you use five pounds a day? A barrel a week? What?"

Elmer couldn't seem to stop laughing. Finally he grunted, "This here's a bar, Loni, not a fancy restaurant." Elmer pointed to the grill at the end of the bar. "Wine, burgers and chips, that's it. And no, I don't make my own buns." Wiping down the tired bar again, Elmer threw the rag in the sink and wiped his huge hands on a towel flung over his bulky shoulder. He picked up Loni's glass, refilled it, and slid it back to her. "Only flour I use is Wonder flour for gravy and that's at home. I buy all my buns, pickles, and hamburger from Pat's store."

"You don't get any flour from a delivery truck?"

"Nope."

"So you don't get any deliveries from a green truck?"

"Didn't you hear me say no? Drink your damn Coke and stop asking me stupid questions." Elmer walked to the other end of the bar.

Loni was ready with smart remark when a slap on the back of her head made her jerk around. Janet Jace hopped up on the stool beside her.

"What was that for?"

"Making sure I have your attention."

"Think about a gun in your face the next time you do that. Would that be good enough attention for you?"

"Oh, bullpucky, would you listen up? I have to ask you something, and you have to promise not to laugh."

A yellow butterfly above Janet's left breast showed through a thin tank top, and her matching black shorts showed a lot more skin. Loni took a deep breath and forced her eyes up to meet Janet's amused face. "Hello, Janet, how the hell are you? Where'd you come from? How'd the Tony Branger case come out, and how come I never got called to testify? Do you hit everybody you sit beside and how the hell did you find me?" Janet tried to interrupt but Loni stopped her with a finger on her lips. "Here's what I want to know." Loni leaned over and whispered in Janet's ear, "How many tattoos do you have, and when can I look for the rest of them?"

Janet pushed Loni back and gave her a fake smile. "I'm good, back door, Sal dismissed it as you well know, and no, I only hit you because you'll need it for something like the last question, and who could miss the ugly monstrosity you pretend to drive." Janet crossed her eyes as she grinned, finishing with "Too many butterflies for you to ever count."

Loni couldn't stop her blush. "She dismissed? You're kidding, right?"

"Nope. She told Carl he needed to get her more evidence."

"You're talking about the kid who ran his girlfriend out of her own apartment and threw her clothes out the window to her front yard with beaucoup neighbors watching. The one who called her on his phone when she got to her parents' house and sent her photographs as he burned everything? That kid?"

Janet snapped back, "Since when do you speak French?"

"Just answer my questions."

Janet gave her a weak smile. "Yep."

Loni patted Janet on the shoulder. "Good luck finding more evidence with that one. It's one of mine. I cuffed him still trying to light more fires."

"Back to why I followed you into this dive. Do you think Sal's husband would shoot me?"

"What for?"

"To put it bluntly, he caught us in his bed and kicked Sal out of the house. Then he threw out all her clothes."

Loni burst out in loud laughter before she could stop herself. "Damn! Did he burn them too? Sal could be her own witness if she's sure she saw enough while she stood there watching and all."

"It's not funny, Loni. Would you lower your voice? I don't want everyone to know."

"Shit, Janet. Would you stop worrying?" Loni paused a few second, "Besides, the town newspaper doesn't come out until tomorrow." Loni watched Janet's eyes get huge before she realized Loni was joking.

"Shit!" Janet slugged Loni on the arm. "That's not funny, either."

"How'd you end up here in bed with Judge Sal? Aren't you from Boston?"

Janet sighed. "We met last year in Boston at a seminar on criminal justice. One thing seemed to lead to another. You know?"

"So, naturally, you followed her all the way out here and she didn't even know you were coming." Loni got her chortling under control. "If you two are worried about him taking a gun to you, how come you're still in town?"

"Shhhhh!" Janet furtively checked around and waved Elmer off. "Charlie Thorton's trial goes to summary in the morning, and we can't leave. You know she's the judge, and I'm the defense attorney."

"Of course, I do. I had to testify, remember? But I heard it was over. So what do you want from me?"

"Come to the trial," Janet pleaded, and keep an eye on her husband so he doesn't cause any more trouble?"

"Why don't you tell Carl?"

"Because Carl would tell his wife, and June would have it all over town. I'd feel better if you did it. Will you come? Please."

Loni sighed and nodded in agreement.

Janet disappeared out the back door as the opening front door cast a bright light across the floor. Squinting to identify the two silhouettes, Loni recognized them. Just shoot me now, she thought.

"I need to talk to you." Lola said as she headed on to the restroom at the back of the bar. "Don't leave."

Junior stopped behind Loni. "Heard about the buzzard you rescued. Been glad to grab my shotgun and take care of that bird for you." Junior's loud cawing laugh bounced around the room.

Loni spun her stool around to face him and snapped, "No thanks, Junior. Do appreciate the offer though. Didn't want you to miss and be embarrassed."

"No way. A Texan never misses."

"That's true. I heard about this Texan that never missed. Wanted to get rid of a wart so he shot it off along with his finger. I figure since you Texans don't care what you shoot, I don't want to be anywhere near you."

"You're crazy, Loni." Junior shook his big head in disapproval. "Heard you're tryin' to find me."

"Yes, Junior. The next time you fob off a rape, I am gonna shoot you."

Junior's face wrinkled in a frown at the drink in her hand, and said, "Shame, Loni. You know Injins can't handle liquor. Better give that to me."

"Too late now, Junior. This is my fifth."

"Give me that, Loni." Junior reached for her drink.

Loni swung away and snarled, "Get away from me!"

"Okay, give me your gun, or so help me God I'll take it away from you."

"Touch me again, and you're gonna need God's help." Loni slid off the stool and backed away. "You know what else, Junior? Next time you ignore a rape case it'll be your balls I shoot off."

"What's going on?" Lola rammed herself between them.

"Your stupid boyfriend is trying to take my gun away from me."

"He's not my boyfriend!" Lola put her hands on her hips and turned toward Junior. "Why do you want her gun?"

"Because, Lola," Loni shrieked in frustration, "his head is so far up his ass his brains are scrambled and he thinks his shit don't stink."

"See what I'm sayin' here, Lola? She's an Injin, and everybody knows Injins can't handle their liquor. She's so drunk and filthy she looks like she wallowed in buzzard shit!"

Angry, Lola grabbed Junior's belt and jerked him around so he faced away from Loni. "One!" She reached up and grabbed Junior's nose. "She doesn't drink. That's a Coke, asshole. And two! What you're saying about Native Americans isn't true. And three! She's been out at the ranch helping her granddad. She might be dirty, but it's from hard work and, let me repeat, she isn't drunk!"

"All Injins drink! Even worse, she's queer!"

"Junior, don't ever call her that again!" Lola's voice climbed to a screech. "I'm also part Native American. What's more, I'm gay."

Junior snorted. "You can't be no queer. I don't date no queers."

Shit. A date? A good time to leave. Loni quietly slid off her stool and left the bar listening to Lola's loud voice informing Junior they were not dating, never had and never will That was the last Loni heard as she slipped out the door.

Loni's brain reeled from Lola's revelation and Junior's declaration. She stumbled into the Oasis, the last place left where she could might find Willie. He hadn't been there. And nobody bought flour off a truck. Loni's fear spiked as she drove home and parked inside the hangar. Coco bounded past her into the dark, and Loni stood by the hangar door to wait.

The moon was still chasing the sun early in the morning eastern sky, and she missed its soothing glow. A coyote yipped in the distance, and Coco dived through the door. The fuzzy brown poodle huffed as she shot up the stairs.

After a bowl of Shiichoo's menudo, Loni fell into a restless sleep with Coco curled up next to her. Her dreams turned soft as she felt Maria surround her. Suddenly she jerked awake and sat up. Oh, my god! Loni realized Maria's face had morphed into Lola's.

CHAPTER TWENTY-TWO

Loni was early, but the courtroom was already overflowing. The whole town must be at court, Loni thought. There were always problems finding a parking space on court days, and this murder trial made it even worse. Loni worked her way up front until she sat directly behind Sal's husband, Wesley. Relief crossed Janet's face as she gave Loni a little wave. Wesley turned from Janet and locked eyes with Loni.

Seeing the pain in his drawn face, Loni leaned forward and whispered, "I'm so sorry, Wes."

"So am I, Loni. So am I."

"All rise!" The bailiff bellowed. The side door opened, and Judge Sal stalked behind the bench. Her black hair spiked out around her taut face. Sal studiously avoided her husband as she faced the packed courtroom and sat down.

"Please be seated!" the bailiff called out.

No one settled. The milling people talked as if they were waiting for something to happen.

Sal banged her gavel three times and shouted, "Sit down and shut the fuck up." The room was instantly silent. "Defense. You're up."

Janet took a deep breath and stood facing the jury. "Against my recommendation, my client insists on his own summation."

Janet sat, and Charlie took her place. He was in his fifties and owned one of the biggest feeding pens close to town. His good looks faded from a good life, and his gray sports jacket couldn't hide the paunch under his yellow shirt. He smoothed down his tie and quietly gazed around, making eye contact with each jury member. A few of them gave him slight smiles while others turned away.

"You all know me," he said as he paced up and down in front of the jury, his boots echoing on the wooden floor. Sorrow filled the warm brown eyes almost covered by the curly brown hair falling on his forehead. "You know my folks and how tight a family we all are. In fact, Maud there," Charlie pointed to a stocky grey-headed juror in the back row who lifted her head a bit, "was my mother's midwife. You all watched me and my brothers grow up here. Hell, we all look alike!"

Three of the older jury women gave Charlie big smiles as they nodded in agreement. A man in the back row chuckled. "You know they would do anything for me." Again, Charlie got several nods from the jury. "Even lie for me." The jury members fidgeted, and a few of them frowned. I plead innocent because I wanted my say in front of everyone, including, God help me, the lord almighty. But I'm not innocent."

Wondering where Charlie was going with this, Loni leaned forward on the railing separating her from the action in front of her and tried to watch his eyes.

Charlie turned to Judge Sal. "They hired me a lawyer when I said I didn't want one. I even tried to fire her, but she wouldn't quit. Said I wasn't the one paying her."

The restless wave passing through the audience quieted when Judge Sal lifted her gavel and stared out at them. "The facts of this case as I see them, since I was the only one there as a witness, are these. We went to a party at the McCluars. You all know them." Charlie searched for the couple in the audience and pointed them out. Jury members smiled again at the McCluars.

Charlie gestured as he paced in front of the jury. "I drank too much at the party and, even though my wife tried to stop me, I kept drinking while I drove home. Barbara got mad because I wouldn't let her drive. She tried to take the bottle away from me while we drove over the bridge on the Santa Cruz River. I lost control and we went into a spin. When we stopped, the passenger door was open, and Barbara was gone." Tearing up, he stopped and stared into space for a few seconds.

Loosening his tie, Charlie turned back at the jury. "Here's the thing. My family wants you to think it was an accident, that when I hit the bridge the door accidently opened, and Barbara fell out. Did it happen that way? Or did I shove her out as the prosecutor claims." Charlie hung his head for a few minutes before he straightened up. "But it doesn't matter. It doesn't matter whether she fell out or was pushed out. The point is I was drunk. I was stupid drunk. I am, therefore, totally responsible for her death. It doesn't matter how she died. I was drunk, and it's my fault. I am guilty as hell and deserve to go to prison." Charlie sat back down behind the table.

Pandemonium reigned in the courtroom. No one paid any attention as Judge Sal banged her gavel. The bailiff released the jury and took Charlie away in handcuffs. Wesley followed and closed the door behind him. Loni joined the exodus into the street.

Loni missed lunch, but she wasn't hungry. She spent an hour wandering through the town bars, and alleys behind the bars, desperately hoping to find Willie. No one had seen him. It was as though he dropped off the face of the earth, like losing Maria all over again.

Loni stayed busy at her desk by making a list of things to do in her search for the green truck. She took the paper and grabbed the tape dispenser off Lola's desk. Intent on fastening the paper on her organizing board, Loni didn't notice Lola. She jumped at Lola's angry voice. "Loni! Put that back where you got it!"

"Geez! I only wanted to tape this list up."

"Use your own tape." Lola stalked over to Loni and snatched the tape dispenser. Back at her desk, she moved every item in jerky moves.

"Gad!" Loni said to Lola's back. "I have to agree with Carl about your counting-each-sheet-of-toilet-paper fetish. Did anybody ever talk to you about your OCD?"

Lola ignored Loni as she buzzed Carl and Junior through the main door into the building. They were yelling at each other. "Goddamnit, Junior!" Carl growled. "I don't care what you did in Texas. Here you pay for your goddamn coffee."

"Why? I'm a cop, for god's sake. It's what I deserve for serving and protecting."

"That's why, you dumb ass. It's like taking a bribe. You accept nothing free, do you hear me?" Carl turned to Loni with an irritated glance back at Junior. "El es codo duro."

Junior dropped his big Stetson hat on Lola's counter. "What did he say?"

Loni turned toward Junior with her sweetest dimpled smile as she purred, "It means, Junior," her voice slowly rising in pitch, "you're a cheap sonofabitch! And now that I have your full attention," Loni's voice rose a few more notches as she stepped into his space, "give me back my goddamn files."

Junior turned to Lola. "Help me out here, Lola."

Twirling the bracelets on her arm, Lola frowned. "Why can't you give her back her files?"

Junior shook his head so hard Loni thought he might damage his brain. "Come on, Junior," Loni insisted. "I need the file on Chui's Mexico contacts. I want to ask them if they remember seeing a green delivery truck anywhere along Devil's Highway."

"I don't care what you want!" Junior bellowed. He grabbed his hat, stomped to the door of the police station, and slammed out of the building.

Loni stayed furious. "You know what, Lola? You should pick your company better. No wonder you married a loser."

Lola's green eyes sparked in anger. "I don't see your ring on my finger."

"Are you kidding me?" Loni flared back until she saw the hurt on Lola's face. Loni's entire body sagged, and she dropped her head into her hands.

Lola's voice softened. "He was only buying me a hamburger to thank me for my help. More than you've done lately."

"Sure. He's so grateful for your help he buys you a cheap burger at the Last Chance."

"What are you saying Loni. That I'm a cheap date?" Lola's bracelets chimed like church bells. "I'm not marrying him, for god's sake."

"Or having sex?"

"I didn't say that, but no. I happen to love wine hamburgers."

Shit! Loni lifted her head. "Forget I said that." "I know we need to deal with this thing between us but not here. Maybe meet up after work?"

Lola considered Loni's request. "Not tonight. I'm no longer sure what talking would accomplish." Lola paused before she changed the subject. "Junior says he's close to getting the rest of the evidence he needs to crack the case."

"Oh, bullshit!" Loni stomped out of the station house and back to searching for Willie. She drove by the grocery store and noticed a small sports car in the parking lot that reminded her of the one Phillip Brushard rolled, but it was gray instead of flaming red. Loni drove by it. The car was covered with duct tape, and Phillip and a tall teenage boy stood behind it.

Loni turned around to go back. Arriving back at the car, she yelled out the window, "Got those cholla needles all pulled out yet?"

Phillip grimaced. "Nope. Especially where I can't reach. How about a ride home? You could—"

Loni said, "You've got a car."

"Not anymore. I sold it." He pointed to the kid who was inspecting the taped driver's side door. "The motor mounts popped and I didn't want to be in that piece of shit when the motor drops."

"You tell the kid that?"

"Told him baling wire should hold it."

Loni inspected the car. "You missed a few spots."

"Nah. Tape's already peeling."

"You bought cheap tape?"

"So?" Phillip pulled a money clip out of his pocket to put some bills in. He brushed the white fuzz flying from it. "What is this crap on my money?"

"I'm sure it's cobwebs." Loni laughed again. "Happens when you never spend it." Grinning, Phillip stuck the money in the clip. "How much did you get for it?"

"Four hundred dollars."

"You should give him four hundred bucks to take it!"

"How about buying me lunch? You can take me home afterward."

"Sorry, Phillip. Busy."

"How do I get home?"

Loni gestured at the kid and said, "Have him take you." She drove off with Phillip hollering, "I just said I'm not getting in that piece of shit again."

Willie was out there somewhere. She found the shade of a cottonwood tree where she sat in her truck and called bars. The sixth one gave her hope. The barkeep at Voltap, a redneck spot at a crossroads forty miles from Caliente, said, "Sounds like the drunk in the back."

Loni got there in thirty-five minutes. She showed the barkeep her badge, and he pointed to the back door.

It wasn't Willie.

Loni leaned down and tried to wake up the man. His skin was dry and pasty. He pushed Loni's hands away and rubbed his head. "Got a drink?"

"No. But I'll take you to a doctor."

"No doctor. Stay here." The drunk rolled back onto his filthy blanket and passed out again.

She stopped at every bar back to town and finally found him at the Oasis.

Willie leaned his head on her shoulder. "Loni. Paint dead."

"I know, Willie." Loni hugged him. He reeked of alcohol.

"My Paint gone." Tears ran down his leathered face.

"Come on, Willie. Time to go home."

"Ni, ni, ni, ni." Willie stumbled away from her and crawled back onto a barstool.

Loni wrote her cell number on the back of her card and handed it to the bartender. "Call me when he passes out."

For the next few hours, she drove around sick at heart, Willie's pain mixed with despair over her fight with Lola. Fear and grief slammed her like a sledgehammer and froze her to the steering wheel. She could have dragged him home, but he would only leave again. If only she could drag Lola home with her.

A red streak flashed from a dirt side road onto the county road in front of her. She considered chasing it, but the sports car was already out of sight. It might be more important to see why they were in such a hurry. She called Bobby about the speeder and drove along the rutted track where the low-slung sports car left clouds of dust in the air. In the beam of her headlights, she saw a girl on the side of the road, struggling to stand. Loni jumped out of her SUV and ran to her. As she reached out to touch her, the girl swung at Loni, screaming "No" over and over.

"You're safe now, you're safe now," Loni repeated in a calm voice. "I'm a cop."

Long, black hair was stuck in the congealing blood from the girl's bleeding slashed cheek, and her split lip puffed out to one side. She was naked beneath the torn purple shirt she held over her breasts. Her thighs were covered with bruises and cuts as if she'd been thrown out of a moving car. The girl collapsed into her arms, sobbing. "They raped me! Oh, god! They raped me again!"

Loni helped her into her truck, scrutinizing her in the overhead light as the girl buried her face in Coco's furry neck. Loni dug a pair of shorts out of her emergency bag and handed them to the girl.

"What's your name?" Loni carefully drove up the road as the girl wiggled into the shorts.

"Chickie Bodia."

"Chickie, can you tell me who did this?"

The girl hiccupped through sniffles. "It was Billy Joe." She paused and cried out, "I hurt!"

"I know. We're almost to the clinic."

"Find Chelsea. I need to see Chelsea."

At the clinic's emergency entrance, Loni opened the door, but Chickie refused to let go of Coco. Loni took out her phone and dialed Chelsea. "Hey, it's Loni," her voice low and quiet. "I'm at your door and need your help."

Chelsea was at the passenger door before Loni could finish. "Chickie?" Chelsea gently pulled the girl out of the truck. Loni followed them as they slowly walked into the clinic and disappeared behind a curtain.

Loni paced until Chelsea reappeared. "She was the first girl these bastards raped," she muttered. "She works in the clinic during the day. Admittance." She glared up at Loni. "Can't you stop these animals?"

"I plan to," Loni answered with determination. "I'm picking them up right now!" She slammed her flashing red light on top of the cab and sped to Wagner Road. Before she pulled up to Dorothea's house, she shut off the rack lights quietly pulled into the driveway. Dorothea answered the door, still half asleep. "Where's Billy Joe?" Loni pushed by Dorothea with no explanation.

"Why?" Dorothea said defensively. "It was an accident. He didn't mean to kill Jimmy."

"No, it's not that."

"It's not about Jimmy?"

Dorothea grudgingly motioned toward the living room.

"Which way is his bedroom?"

"Last door straight ahead." Dorothea pointed down the hall. "It's probably locked. He's got an outside entrance."

Loni failed to keep the anger out of her voice. "Get your kids and keep them in your bedroom."

Dorothea stared at her dully.

"Now!" Loni ordered.

The woman tightened the belt to her robe and disappeared down the hall. Loni heard a shuffling and the click of a lock. She crept up to the door where Dorothea had pointed. Standing to the side, she knocked. "Billy Joe, open up!" She knocked again and shouted, "It's the police."

"What?" a surly voice snarled. The lock clicked, and the door slowly opened. "I ain't done nothin'." He was dressed in Levis and a light yellow, pearl-snapped button shirt with dried blood smeared across the front and down one sleeve. Red hair flopped in his eyes.

"Billy Joe." Loni pushed him back into the room. "You're under arrest for rape."

"Balls! Nobody can prove nothin'!"

"Turn around." She waited while he tried to stare her down. His shoulders finally slumped, and his body crumpled as he turned around. Loni handcuffed him, read him his rights, and searched him. A sneer crossed his face as she ran her hands down his body. "You want some too, bitch?"

"You're not getting out of this one." She hauled him out of his room.

Dorothea was peering through a crack in her bedroom door.

"Stay out of Billy Joe's room," Loni told her. "I need to get a search warrant." Loni wondered how many pairs of panties she would find. "You should call his father."

Dorothea shrugged. "I would if I could find him."

"Where'd you get your 'Come to Mama' plant?" Loni shoved him into the back of the SUV.

"I don't know what you're talking about."

"Sure you do. You gave it to Todd."

"Oh, that shit. Got it from the O'Neal farm last summer before you assholes closed it down." Billy Joe turned belligerent. "It's not illegal."

"Anything else besides 'Come to Mama'?"

"I got more. Tried a few." He snickered.

Loni waited. Billy Joe couldn't stop talking. "Ginseng got my juices going. And Horny Goat Weed. Want me to tell you how I used them?"

"And the meth?"

"What meth?"

"The meth you gave Todd last summer."

"No, no, no. That was coach. I don't touch that shit."

Loni let the question go. "Why Mexican girls?"

"You stupid breed." Eyes flashing, he stuck out his chin. "That's how you got here, isn't it? Mixing white in to improve the gene pool? Bet your old man raped your mother. Maybe he even killed her."

God help us, she thought. More Billy Joes were the last thing this world needed.

Billy Joe shut up for the rest of the ride to the station. She jerked him out of the truck and pushed him into the building. He shriveled with each step. "Bobby," Loni called out as she entered the building. "I'm putting Billie Joe in the holding tank until Lola gets here. Can you call her? I promised her the honor of booking him."

Shoving Billie Joe into the small, hot room, she uncuffed him and clanged the door shut behind him. She opened it and clanged it shut again. "Hear this sound, Billy Joe? You better get used to it." For the hell of it, she clanged it one more time.

"Junior won't like this," Bobby said when she came back down.

"Do I care? Don't let him out, Bobby. Junior's got no jurisdiction over this one. We got a witness and DNA on this kid for at least four rapes."

"You look beat. Want me to send James for the other two boys who helped Billy Joe rape the girl?"

"Changing the subject?"

"You need to go home soon," Bobby reached out to her. "Lola said she'd be right here." Bobby dropped his arm and went back to his stool behind the counter.

"Wait, Bobby. Can you leave an order for a search warrant on Billy Joe's room?"

"Sure. I'll get it ready for Lola to take to the judge."

At her desk, Loni laid her head down on her arms. Coco curled up at her feet and was soon snoring. They were both still there when Lola shook Loni's shoulder.

"I'm not sleeping."

"You snore awake?"

"I don't snore."

"How would you know?"

Loni lifted her head. "I've got a present for you. It's upstairs with the rest of the rat dung."

"Bobby said you picked up Billy Joe." Watching Loni, she added, "Not before he attacked another girl, I gather."

"It's Chickie."

"Oh, god, how is she?"

"She's at the clinic."

"I've got to go." Lola was already at the door when Loni hollered to her back. "What about Billy Joe?"

"You book him," she retorted. "I'd kill him."

♘

Booking Billy Joe happened fast. Loni wanted it done before she killed him. She was on her way out when two dove hunters walked into the station and cornered Loni before she could escape. Somebody had told them there was a dead body under Gimsom Bridge. They had asked some one-handed cowboy on a horse for a good place to hunt. He told them he couldn't stop because he had to report a dead man. They combed through every bush around that bridge but couldn't find any body. They wanted to make sure the police knew.

"Sounds like one of Sly's whoppers," Loni said. Bobby was laughing. "We'll take care of it," she told them. "Thanks for being good citizens."

Loni knew Sly always drank at the Last Chance Saloon. Behind the bar, she found a buckskin horse tied to a sad-looking mesquite tree. The saddle leaned against the wall. She opened the back door into the smell of stale beer and piss.

Climbing up on the bar stool beside Sly, Loni noticed he smelled more than a little horsey. She moved down one stool before she spoke to him. "Talked to some dove hunters about a dead man under a bridge. That one of your lies?"

Sly giggled, "Good one, huh?"

"They didn't think so. Said they searched a couple of hours."

"So? Maybe they won't come hunting here again."

Loni got off her stool and walked away.

"Buy me a beer?" he said to her back.

"Maybe another time." She didn't stop.

Loni's feelings raced between relief and regret as she drove home. Bobby was right. Billy Joe and his two friends would be gone a long time. If only the DNA had been back sooner, she could have saved Chickie this last horror. If only Billy Joe had been in jail and not been driving Joy's pickup, she could have saved Jimmy Barclay. If only wishes were horses . . .

> FROM: Loni Wagner
> TO: Sandi@gmailyahoo.com
> DATE: October 18
> SUBJECT: Still here
>
> I can't find Willie.
> I was finally able to arrest Billy Joe for rape. I guess that's something.
> Loni

Hoping for cheerier stories, Loni took one of her grandmother's notebooks from the boot box and crawled into bed with Coco. She rubbed Coco's nose as she began to read the story out loud.

> "My folks bought a large black milk cow. She had a white face with a large black spot over her nose. She was a character and spoiled from so much attention. I broke her to ride, as it was my job to round her up at milking time. I hated the long walk back. She let me ride her until she'd get tired of me and then she'd run under a mesquite tree and brush me off. One time an old range bull came charging at me and I lost no time climbing on old Spot. Sure surprised the bull, he stopped, stared, and strutted off. When Spot had her calf, she was so proud. When we found her, she ran to me, mooing, she licked me, and then the calf. Guess she thought we both belonged to her.

"We named the calf McGiny. He also was a pet. We had a dog named Waffles who warned us many times when rattlers were near. I had a dog named Mae. I didn't steal him. I didn't drive him back when he followed me home. Our chickens were named too. Sal's hen Penny met an untimely death when I dropped the lid of the grain bin on her head. We also had pet white-wings that were banded and they returned for years. We never caged them. They lived in a mesquite tree. We had two pet tree lizards, Maggie and Jimmy. Jim lost his tail when mama threw the poker at him for getting in the house. Every child should have the joy of ranching, fishing, hunting, working and living at peace with our neighbors."

Loni closed the notebook and replaced it in the box. "What do you think, Coco? Bet the poker in the fireplace at the ranch is the same one caused Jimmy to lose his tail." Loni pulled on Coco's wiggling stub. "Wonder what poker took your tail?"

CHAPTER TWENTY-THREE

The call came on a hot Sunday afternoon. Somebody said an Indian was sick behind the Aqua Verde Canteen. She remembered the bar and the old graveyard hidden around the back of a hill. Left over from the Vulture Mine in its glory days in the late 1800s, the tiny graveyard had about thirty wooden crosses in unreadable pieces. In one corner, a small headstone, the only one with a visible name, read "Baby Mary" and "May 2, 1877."

A thunderhead blowing in fast out of the Bradshaws billowed high overhead as dun gray and cotton white clouds fell over each other in the huge blue sky. Loni watched it while she sped the twenty miles to the tiny settlement. The one-time mining town survived mostly from big RV campgrounds. Every winter the desert filled with every kind of sleeping contraption anyone could dream up. Some days it resembled Quartzsite, homeless homes on wheels stretching for miles.

The flashing sign of the bar came into view, and Loni slowed down to pull into the parking lot. She walked up to the barkeep and asked about Willie. She knew he had been here because his favorite bolo tie hung on a hook beside the large mirror behind the bar.

"Who are you?"

"His sister."

"Out back," the barkeep said. "Smelled so bad I had to throw him out."

"Not before you took that off him." Loni pointed to the tie.

"I gave him a bottle for it," he replied belligerently.

"How much?"

"Four hundred dollars."

"Sorry?"

"Take it or leave it."

In disgust, Loni handed him a credit card and stuffed the bolo in her pocket. In back, she followed the smell of vomit to the shed. The roof was partly covered with a blue tarp, and the missing boards in the flimsy walls left spaces wide enough to walk through. The stuffing of an old couch, faded and rotted from the sun and rain, surrounded Willie. He groaned in pain. His breathing was irregular, and his lips were tinged blue. Loni had seen the same thing plenty of times on the streets of LA. She tried to help, but any time she took them to a clinic, she'd be stepping over them again the next day.

This was different. This was Willie. She tried to get him to stand, but he was a limp, dead weight. She gave up and locked her arms around his chest to drag him to her truck. A car pulled up, and a cowboy helped her wrestled him up into the seat. She belted him in.

"He's pretty much gone," the cowboy said somberly. "Better find a doctor."

"I'm on my way." She started the truck.

Loni called her uncle Herm and asked him to hurry her grandparents to the clinic. "If you get a ticket, Uncle Herm, I'll pay for it."

Chelsea moved him into the area for serious emergencies and called Doctor Benjamin. Loni sat between her grandparents, and they waited. "He has to make it," she said.

Bahb rubbed her back as Shiichoo held her hand. "Can't. Grief too deep. He ride Paint home now. Let him go."

An hour later, Willie was dead. Doctor Benjamin signed the certificate listing alcohol poisoning as the reason. Loni knew Willie died of a broken heart, but she didn't argue with Doc. Uncle Herm picked Willie up and put him in the back seat of his big pickup. Shiichoo got in beside Willie and held him to her. Loni held Bahb's crutches while he climbed into the front seat of her pickup.

Time passed in chunks, folding in upon itself, as Loni followed Uncle Herm to the ranch and climbed out of her truck. Uncle Herm took Willie into the house. Shiichoo grabbed her arm to keep Loni from following and pulled Loni toward Willie's place. "Need to get his clothes," she insisted. "Herm will help Bahb clean him up." They found clean underwear, socks, Willie's favorite shirt, and his new Levis. Shiichoo carried Willie's boots home in her lap. She gathered the clothes and left Loni to clean the boots. On her way out, she picked up his tomahawk from the table.

Night had fallen by the time she entered the house. Uncle Herm was gone, and Willie was cleaned up, dressed, and laid out on the dining room table. Shiichoo had Willie's two olla pottery jars filled with pinole and water beside him. His bolo tie was around his neck, and his hands were on his chest. Loni handed Shiichoo Willie's boots. Walking up to Willie, Loni placed his tomahawk in his hands before she leaned over and kissed his forehead. She sat down beside him.

CHAPTER TWENTY-FOUR

Time for one more chore before they buried Willie.

"Lola? It's Loni. I need a favor." Even talking hurt.

"Sure, sweetheart. Whatever I can do."

"I need you to come and cut my hair."

"Why?"

"It's tradition. Pimas cut their hair whenever they bury a loved one. It's something Willie made me promise to do."

"I'll be there in an hour. Okay?"

Loni hadn't moved from the kitchen table when Lola knocked on the door. The cup of coffee in front of her turned cold. She struggled up to let Lola in. Coco was her usual ecstatic self when she saw Lola.

"Pour yourself some coffee," Loni said. "I'll be right back." She gave her hair a quick wash in the shower before she collected scissors, comb, and towel. Back at the table, she wrapped the towel around her shoulders and sat down.

"You're serious." It wasn't a question, and Loni didn't answer. "How much do you want me to cut?"

"It's supposed to be above the shoulders. But I can't braid it that short, so cut it off my neck. It's too hot."

"I'm not sure about this."

"Didn't you say you cut everybody's hair in your neighborhood?"

"Yes, but—"

"Butts are to sit on. Just do it, please." Shiichoo came in and sat down to watch. They were both near tears.

"Shiichoo, if you're going to sit there and cry, I'm going to cut it the way I did in high school."

"No, you won't. Lola won't do that."

"I got two hands and a mirror."

Lola stared at Loni. "What'd you do?"

"Crew cut."

"You're kidding!"

Shiichoo added, "She also streaked it with godawful spray paint. Usually rainbow colors."

"You were out in high school?" Lola said in amazement.

Loni was too exhausted to give her grandmother a hard time about swearing. "I was a two-spirit and proud of it." No one said anything for several minutes. Loni heard the snicking of the scissors, and black hair fell in long batches around her feet. Shiichoo gently put it in a large plastic Ziploc bag.

"Make somebody a good wig." She sounded weepy.

"Sure," answered Lola. "There's a place that makes wigs up for cancer patients. You can send it there."

Lola snipped around her ears. "Tell me something. Why didn't any of us see how bad Chief was? I thought he was a sick old man."

"Bahb knew. He said Chief had the shiny wet eyes of pure evil."

"I'm sorry?"

"Hard shiny eyes. Did you not notice?"

"No. Why didn't you tell me?"

"Bahb says —"

"Wait a minute. Is this another one of your granddad's truisms?"

"Doesn't make them wrong!" Loni said defensively.

"I know. Just want to know what I'm hearing here. Go on."

"He says no matter what evil a person does, the only way to get somebody to believe it is to say he killed a cat."

"Works for me." Lola handed Loni a hand-mirror.

"Wow! I'm kd lang with a crooked nose."

Lola lifted Loni's chin with a finger and studied her.

"Your forehead's broader, your chin is rounder. And she doesn't have dimples." Lola shook her head. "Nah. You take after Geronimo." She laughed as she ducked away from Loni.

"Does Geronimo have dimples, Shiichoo?"

"I don't really know. Never met him since he died a good twenty years before I was born. Don't think I ever saw a picture of him smiling. Probably not."

"Were you related?"

"Could be. We were both Chiricahua Apaches from the high country although I was born on the San Carlos Reservation."

"I remember, now. Do you know how Geronimo died?"

"Fell off a horse, I think. Got pneumonia. He's buried at Fort Sill, Oklahoma." Shiichoo frowned. "Guess Usen got tired of taking care of him."

"Usen?"

"Apache High God of the Bedonkohe religion."

"I could use Usen right now." Loni fell silent and squeezed her eyes shut, fighting her tears. She felt Shiichoo take the towel from her shoulders and heard the screeching of the screen door. Shiichoo was probably shaking her hair in the yard for the birds to build soft nests. She made herself think of the small brown sparrow's push, pull, and tug as the nest grew in her mind.

Lola sat down and took Loni's hand. "I'd like to stay for the funeral. Okay?"

Loni leaned over and hugged her. "Thanks."

"People are coming," Shiichoo said as she came back in. "Time to get food ready."

"I'd like to help," Lola said.

"Of course you can," Loni answered, working on a cheerful voice. "Why'd you think I asked you over?"

Lola slapped her across the back of the head as she passed by to help Shiichoo.

The motley crew trickled into the glow of the waxing moon hanging low in the sky. Flickering candles lit the way to the old ranch graveyard. Four of Willie's friends lowered his sitting body into his final resting place and faced him south. They placed the ollas beside him. Loni and Bahb helped them shovel dirt until Willie was covered for his journey. Silently, she wished Willie and Paint a fast ride to their happy hunting grounds.

Within minutes everyone quietly disappeared into the lonely night.

CHAPTER TWENTY-FIVE

At the ranch, Loni wandered between the cemetery, hugging Roani and Stonewall, and circling Paint's grave. The sun hung directly above, burning her skin. Shiichoo grabbed her between wanderings and dabbed aloe vera on her face, neck, and hands as she made her drink large cans of warm water. "Believe in the magic, child. It will help."

Loni remembered Bahb's voice every time something bad happened. "When you walk hard road and stay true to self, it make magic to get you through."

She turned to Shiichoo. "I'm trying, but the road's too hard."

Shiichoo gave Loni a long hug and returned to the house, leaving her alone.

Overwhelmed by the loss and pain, Loni wandered through the day often stopping at Roni and Stonewall to hang onto their necks and cry.

Daniel didn't arrive until late afternoon. He got out of his pickup and walked over to her. Without a word, he held her in a long hug and rocked her until Loni stopped crying and stepped away from him.

"Don't know when I was out here last." Pointing at a small, square picket-fenced-in area, he asked, "What's that?"

"The old graveyard."

"Yeah, I remember now. Our grandparents are there."

"And great grandparents," Loni reminded Daniel. "And my mom. And now Willie. All our family history right there."

"What history?" Daniel pulled Loni back to the shade of a mesquite tree. "They were out there way before you were born. How do you know anything about them?"

"Our grandmother wrote about it." Loni pointed to the old adobe ranch house. "Our grandmother lived in that house when she was little. So did I. Grew up in the same room I did." Turning around, she pointed to the barn. "She rode her milk cow into that barn at milking time, like I did. Her cow had a calf she named McGiny that followed her around like a dog. I had a white face calf I called Whitey who lost her mama so she followed me around. I see her dog, Waffles, running right beside Jack as they chased chickens with us around that same windmill."

Loni pointed toward the mud and wood slat hut squatting by the graveyard. "I can see Grandmother Wagner dragging a blanket behind her to spend the night in the sandwich house, just like I did." She turned to face Daniel again. "Who they were, is who we are. I'm giving you all the notebooks and letters from your grandparents. Read them. Ask your folks for every story they know. And write them down for your kids before they get lost." Loni sighed. "What incredible people they were, Daniel."

"I never heard you talk like that about your dad."

Loni snorted. "Only thing he left behind was me."

"You're so full of shit."

Daniel turned back to stare at the old graveyard. "That recent dig. Isn't it too big for Willie?"

"We buried Willie with his horse and my old border collie."

"You mean old Jack?"

Loni swiped at another tear. "Bahb had to put him down last week. Said he knew Jack waited for Willie and Paint. He said a man was happiest with both his horse and a dog to travel to the happy hunting ground."

"How come Jack's not waiting for your granddad?"

"I asked him. I said we don't have any more dogs around here for him to travel with. What was he going to do?"

A small smile had appeared on Bahb's beautiful brown face as he answered her with warm brown eyes. "He said, 'Guess I take old mangy barn cat you let loose in the house.'"

"Well, guess that's not so weird. Fredric Baur, the guy who invented the Pringles potato chip can? Died in 2008 and they buried his ashes in one."

"One what?"

"Pringle can."

"Oh!" Loni was silent a minute. "I heard of someone born in a toilet. When she died, her family buried her ashes in it."

"You're shitting me!"

Loni got the giggles with James at his choice of words. "Nope."

"What'd they do then? Holler 'Don't flush the toilet.'"

"I don't know. Maybe they put the toilet in a casket and buried it with her." Loni gave Daniel a sad smile as they walked back to the barn.

Inside they stopped at Daniel's last car rebuild when he was in high school. "You ever going to finish this job?" she teased him.

"Oh, my god." Daniel walked around the old 1948 Ford pickup. The axles were on blocks, and the pickup was so beat up and rusted it had lost its color. Daniel touched it gently. "Oh, my god," he repeated. "I wondered whatever happened to this old pickup. I coulda' sold it for big bucks."

Watching him, Loni laughed. "As I recall, that's about the time you graduated and moved your loyalty to airplanes."

"I did." Daniel walked Loni out of the barn back to his pickup. "Tell Bahb I'll be back soon to get it." Daniel leaned his forehead against Loni's as he gave her one last hug. "Hang in there, cuz. I need you around." He climbed in his pickup and started the motor. Backing out he leaned out of the window. "Teasing you is my best entertainment!"

"It always was, you shit!"

"Better now, right?"

Daniel always had the last word.

CHAPTER TWENTY-SIX

The next morning, Loni got to work in time to hear Junior ranting at Bobby.

"Don't blame Bobby." Loni's anger spiked as she walked up behind them.

Junior whirled, the veins in his neck pulsing as his face flushed red. "You stupid squaw," he raged at her. "This isn't your case. I'm turning him loose!"

"You let Billy Joe out, and I'll arrest you for interference."

"You're fired!" he yelled, spittle hitting her in the face.

"Junior," Loni yelled back. "I don't work for you," She pulled a kerchief out of her pocket and wiped off the spittle.

He raised his arm, his hand in a fist. Before he could hit Loni, Bobby grabbed Junior's arm. "You don't want to do that, Junior," he said as he pulled Junior into the evidence room and shut the door. The two stayed in there for a long time, and Junior couldn't meet her eyes as he left the building.

"What did you say to him, Bobby?"

"Let it go, Loni." Patting her on the shoulder, Bobby followed Junior out the door.

The day was endless as Loni mindlessly filled in long delayed and ignored paperwork in an attempt to clean her desk. People left her alone. She was ready to go home when she got a call that made her day. "Hey Lola," Loni said hanging up. "It was Harry Beal. The Tucson detective? He said two of the Mexican mafia who escaped with Manny were arrested and returned to Tucson. Once Manny testifies, they'll send him home on the regular bus. Said it'd probably take about five more days."

"Thank you." Lola came around her counter and gave Loni a long hug. Loni was embarrassed, but she wasn't about to pull away. "Maybe it's time to have that talk? Dinner tomorrow?"

Loni vigorously nodded and dashed out the door. She hesitated at the bottom of the station steps and thought about waiting for Lola. Filling her lungs with a deep breath, she remembered she had to fix dinner at the ranch. The cool November breeze brought the smell of beignets baking across the street. Loni took another deep breath. Bahb loved beignets for breakfast, and maybe she could get a chocolate pie for Shiichoo.

A truck drove around to the back of the bakery reflecting dark green that was almost black off its side. The color was hard to see, but Loni was suddenly sure the truck was green. Damn! All this time I thought the truck was black! Is Woodland Green more black than green? She walked around the back to the loading dock where the truck was backed with its loading door open and saw Dirk load racks of bread loaves on the truck. "Hey Dirk. Where you heading with all that bread?"

"Delivering to a distributor in Phoenix. How come you want to know?" Dirk grunted as he shoved in another box. He avoided eye contact as he rolled his dolly through the large open loading dock door for another stack of bread boxes.

Loni followed him in and walked around. "They can't make their own bread in Phoenix?"

"Not like this. It's Tommy's special cactus bread. No one else has the recipe." Dirk's voice took on a menacing tone. "Would you get out of my way? I'm working here."

"Sorry." Loni stepped back and let him by. "I'm going to have to buy a loaf sometime," she said to Dirk's back. "Any left in the bakery?"

"Why don't you try the front door and find out." Dirk's ratty lank hair flew around his face as he shoved the last of the bread into the truck. He slammed the rolling door down and locked it. Without another word, he stomped by Loni and went inside, pulling down the loading dock door. Loni walked back to the front of the truck. The GMC had a dented fender below the headlight. A streak of blue paint transfer was imbedded in the dent. Loni casually scraped a bit into one of her small evidence envelopes.

Loni was disappointed Lola had already left when she dropped off the envelope with Harris Harris. The evening dispatcher could take care of it, but she really wanted to see Lola. She drove to the ranch, arriving at dusk. She completed the familiar ritual of unlatching the gate and latching it. As always, she swore she would put in a cattle guard.

Sleep didn't come easy. Loni almost got there when her phone buzzed. She swiped it and heard Lola's voice.

"You asleep?"

"Why? You want to talk now?"

"Know a better time?"

"With you anytime is good. Is everything okay?"

Loni heard a deep sigh. "I wanted you to know I told my family how I felt about you."

"And?" Loni sat up in bed, carefully listening.

Lola sounded subdued. "Two brothers aren't speaking to me, one is threatening to kill you, my dad sort of wandered off, and my mother is in the kitchen crying."

"That went well. What now?"

Lola quietly answered, "I don't know."

Loni listened to Lola's breathing before she heard a gentle hang up. Curling around her phone, Loni finally drifted into a restless sleep.

CHAPTER TWENTY-SEVEN

The paint chips were a match to the motorcycle. "Yes!" Loni shouted as she grabbed the fax from Lola and rushed into Carl's office. "Here it is, Carl. Proof this was the truck that ran the biker off the road," she crowed as she waved the paper in his face

With a big grin, Carl leaped into action. "Have Lola take this fax to the judge and get a warrant." Carl handed the fax back. I'm gonna call Tully and tell him what we got."

"Listen, Carl. Can you leave Junior out of this bust?"

"Seems he has his own case anyway. He's out doing God knows what."

"You ever gonna tell me why we ended up with Junior? It's gotta be a damn good reason."

Carl sat back and studied Loni a few seconds. "Same old same old, Loni. It's not what you know, it's who you know that gets you by in this world."

"I know. Uncle Herm preached that at us often enough."

"In Junior's case it's way too true." Carl ran a hand through his thinning sandy hair. "Seems he shot his girlfriend so he had to get out of the state or go to prison."

"Shit! Did she survive?"

"She did. Apparently Junior's self-defense plea fell through when she gained consciousness. I understand the first thing Junior said when he heard she was talking was how sorry he was he used a six-shooter on her. Said he should have known it would take a canon to kill the bitch."

"That's our Junior. But it still doesn't explain why we got him."

Carl ducked his head. "Like I said, Loni, it's who you know. Junior's dad knew a senator from Texas who knew a senator from Arizona who knew the mayor who knew me."

"Got it, Carl." Loni declared on her way out the door.

Four of them hid around the bakery, waiting for the Thursday truck to arrive. Tully hunkered down on the roof of the hotel across the alley from the back of the bakery. James ducked down in a pickup with dark tinted windows parked in front of the Western clothing store next door to the bakery. Carl and Loni huddled in the square empty trash bin beside the loading dock door. They hoped nobody would come along and dump garbage on them. Every sound made Loni jump.

Carl reached over and steadied her hand. "Careful with that gun before you shoot somebody."

"Thought that was the point, Carl," Loni teased. "How many times have you told me 'If I'm not going to use it, don't carry it'?"

"Shut up and listen."

In spite of the cool breeze, the trash bin was hot. Sweat ran into Loni's eyes. She mopped her face and handed the kerchief to Carl. The sound of a truck engine coming down the alley grew louder. Loni peeked out a hole in the trash bin. Dirk was stepping out of the truck next to the bakery's loading dock.

"Go, go, go!" Loni shouted exploding out of the bin with Carl right beside her. Dirk froze like a rabbit sensing danger. Carl cuffed him. "Looky what we got here."

Dirk spit at Carl and let out a long string of swear words. Loni watched James drag Mable and Tommy Flavio out of the bakery. At the police car Tommy slumped forward on his knees, and Mable screamed like a banshee hen whose eggs were being robbed. She kicked James where it hurt the most. Loni worked hard not to laugh as James doubled over and struggled to control his temper.

"Look at this." Carl held up a half a loaf. "After they baked the bread, they sliced it and carved a hole in the middle where they stuck the drugs."

Tommy babbled. "Dirk picked up the drugs in Alegaro in five-gallon flour cans."

Dirk snarled, "Shut up!"

Tommy said, "Too late."

Loni cringed. "Right in front of us. Wait 'til Liv hears this."

Tully strolled up to the group. "I called Jim to pick up the head of this mess. As we speak, he's arresting this big-time financier who lost big in Bush's crash."

Carl grabbed Loni in a big hug. "Hey, we did it. We finally scotched the snake."

"Feels good, huh?"

"It's what we live for. The good days."

Three hours later, the paperwork was done, and Tully had left with the prisoners. Loni gave a deep sigh as she stood up and stretched.

"Wait a minute." Lola stopped her before she could leave. "There's a report here for you." Lola handed her a fax. "What does it mean?"

"Shit! There was an explosive in my tire. The blowout was intentional."

"What's going on now?" Lola's worried voice rose with her stress.

Frowning, Loni fanned herself with the page. "I'm beginning to get paranoid."

"You know the old saying. Just because you're paranoid doesn't mean they're not out to get you."

Loni shook her head at Lola. "Damn, Lola, I feel better already."

"What was in the tire anyway?"

Loni read the fax to her. "A mixture of nickel and mercury. It explodes with heat. At sixty miles per hour, a tire doesn't take long to blow. I was lucky I had slowed down when it happened."

"Do you have any idea who did it?"

Loni tilted her head. "Who knows the most about explosives around here?"

Lola's whole body moved, setting off her bracelets in a musical off-beat tune. "No, no no! I know he can be a real asshole, but he wouldn't do this."

A buzz startled them. They headed down the hall just as Junior barreled in like a whirlwind. He crashed into Lola's counter in his hurry to get to Carl's office. Loni and Lola followed Junior in time to see him shove Carl against the wall. Junior screamed as he kicked Carl's legs apart and cuffed him. "You're under arrest, you miserable druggy. You have a right to an attorney, and I hope you get the stupid lawyer who hangs out here all the time." He dragged Carl out of his office and pushed him up to Lola's counter with Lola and Loni still following. "You have the right to stay silent, and if you try to talk, I'll shut your mouth for you. Anything you say can be used against you, but I already have all the proof I need." He slammed Carl's gun on the counter and yelled at Lola, "Book him!"

Lola and Loni stared at each other in amazement.

Carl snarled, "This ain't funny."

"Shut up, Carl!" Junior pushed Carl toward the booking room.

"Wait a minute!" Loni came out of her shock. "Wait a minute! What do you think you're doing, Junior?" Loni grabbed Junior's belt.

"What it looks like," Junior taunted Loni. "'Course you're too stupid to understand."

"I'm beginning to wonder. Seems to me like you're arresting Carl. On what charges?"

"Trafficking drugs, of course."

"On what evidence?" Loni demanded.

"On yours, Loni. It's in your notes."

"What notes?"

"The case file of your'n Carl gave me. It's all there," Junior insisted.

"No, no, no, Junior! Carl's ranch had drugs, not Carl."

"It's his ranch, ain't it?"

"Of course, but."

"But nothing." Junior pushed Carl forward. "I been poking around out there. I know there's drugs still out there, and I know Carl's involved."

"Wait a damn minute, Junior." Carl jerked out of Junior's hold. "Unlock me right now."

"Too bad, Carl." Junior grabbed his arm again. "You're going to jail."

Totally pissed, Loni caught up and took out her gun and shoved it against Junior's asshole. "Unlock Carl, or I'm going to shoot off your dick."

Junior turned his head and gawked her gun. "Loni, that ain't funny."

"See me laughing?"

"I should have arrested you, too. You knew Carl was guilty, but you let him go anyway. Makes you as guilty as him. Makes me sorry the tire blowout didn't finish you off."

Loni cocked her gun. "Now, Junior or I will shoot you. Seriously."

Carl struggled with his handcuffs. "Get me out of these so I can kill him," he told Loni."

"Wait a minute!" Lola said, "What tire blowout?"

"The one the other night. Junior really tried to kill me. He sank that low!"

"Why didn't you tell me?" Lola demanded.

Loni ducked her head and said, "You were mad at me."

Lola flipped around toward Junior. "And I defended you? How could you do something like that?" She grabbed the key out of Junior's hand and took the handcuffs off Carl.

Junior curled his lip. "Don't make no never mind. That Injin had it coming. And I've got the goods on Carl. He's going to jail for a long time. I hate a dirty cop. You'll have to slap the cuffs on him again."

Carl shouted, "You dumb sonofabitch. You get your files, get your ass in my office, and show me your evidence. It better be good."

Junior waved the files as he followed Carl back to his office. Following, Loni and Lola peered around the doorway. Junior pounded on the file.

"They used my ranch to move drugs without my knowledge," Carl bellowed.

"According to Loni's notes, you should have known something."

"I was suspicious. That's why I brought in Tully."

"Loni's notes said you were acting hinky. Said you misled her on purpose."

"She was a patrol officer, not a city cop. I tried to keep her safe."

"Don't sound that way to me. She showed you're guilty."

"Where?"

"Right there!" Junior pulled out one of Loni's reports. "See! You told Loni the travel trailer had moved, but Loni couldn't find any trailer was ever there. Same with the guard on your ranch. You knew the dead man came out of your ranch."

"This case wasn't Loni's job. If I told her the truth, she'd make it her job to protect me."

Junior pulled out another report. "How about not following up on the valve? Loni says right here the valve showed it was murder. How come you never looked for the guy whose fingerprint was in the epoxy? Or who broke in the hangar and shot at Loni?"

"We finally found the perp in some obscure private pilot database. Besides, Rebecca Roberts had nothing to do with the drugs and Loni had already arrested her."

"I don't believe you."

Carl slammed the file down on his desk. "Junior! I don't care what you believe, you pigheaded sonofabitch. You're fired. Pack up your desk and get outta my sight."

Loni and Lola followed Junior out of Carl's office and watched him slink out of the building.

Loni enjoyed watching Lola's eyebrows lift until they nearly met her hairline. Her mouth stayed a perfect oval. "Like Bahb says, the bigger you are—"

"Should've known you'd find a Bahbism for this. Why'd he do it?"

"He wanted my job." Carl hollered at them. "When you get through laughing out there, you two better get out of here before I fire you."

Lola took Loni's hand. "Good idea. Come on."

Loni helped Lola into the truck and drove them up the winding road to the top of Caliente Butte. They climbed down to one of the park benches. Loni handed Lola a pair of binoculars. The long line of the desert horizon was occasionally broken by mountain peaks. The November coolness energized Loni, and she pulled Lola to her.

Loni said, "It was a good day. We finally cleaned up the drugs. Finally got rid of Junior, and Billy Joe with his two friends will go to prison for a long time. Thanks to the results of the DNA tests that finally showed up."

Lola leaned against Loni as she studied the highway coming from Tucson. "There." Lola's excited voice jarred Loni as she stuck the binoculars into Loni's face. "Look!"

The long ribbon of the highway toward Tucson snaked over tan rugged hills and through dry sandy washes. Loni located a light speck moving in the far distance. "It's the Thursday truck."

Lola hit Loni on the arm. "Not a good time to try to be funny."

"Thought my humor was what you loved most about me."

"I said try. That's not funny."

"Okay. It's a bus."

Lola wrapped herself around Loni and kissed her. "Let's go home."

"Aren't we going to meet the bus so you can say hello to Manny?"

"Time he took care of himself."

Loni had a huge grin as she opened the door, ready to help Lola climb up. "As Bahb would say—"

Lola covered Loni's mouth with the tips of her fingers. "Get in the damn truck and drive."

About the Author

Sue Hardesty was born and raised on the Arizona desert where she was either following her prospecting mom around, watching her pick-axe rocks, or riding horses with her dad helping him trail cattle. After college she moved to the Phoenix area and taught English and Communications for many years. Retirement took her out of the desert heat as she moved to the beautiful Oregon Coast where she and her partner now run their dog on the beach every morning. And where she even takes time to write a little. You can find her website here: www.SueHardestyBooks.com.